THE REPLACEMENT

ALSO BY MATT BROLLY

Detective Liam Kilshaw series:

The Lines

Detective Louise Blackwell series:

The Crossing

The Descent

The Gorge

The Mark

The Pier

The Bridge

The Solstice

Lynch and Rose series:

The Controller

The Railroad

DCI Lambert series:

Dead Eyed

Dead Lucky

Dead Embers

Dead Time

Dead End

Dead Water

Standalone novels:

Zero

The Running Girls

The Alliance

THE REPLACEMENT

MATT BROLLY

Published by Thomas & Mercer, Seattle

www.apub.com

EU Product Safety contact:
Amazon Publishing, Amazon Media EU S.à r.l.
38, avenue John F. Kennedy, L-1855 Luxembourg
amazonpublishing-gpsr@amazon.com

ISBN-13: 9781662520440
eISBN: 9781662520433

Cover design by Tom Sanderson
Cover image: © Tim Robinson / ArcAngel Images; © Twymanphoto
© cyperc stock / Shutterstock

Printed in the United States of America

For Herbie

Prologue

The hessian bag was rough against her fingers as Janet traced its outline – the jagged, triple-stitched seam which would keep the contents within secure, safe, forever.

Her mother had made this particular bag. Janet remembered that day with perfect clarity. She could see the chipped, dry skin on her mother's hand as she asked Janet to hand over her doll, Eden.

Tears threatened as Janet pictured herself handing the doll to her mother, but she swallowed them down. Back then, she couldn't have imagined a time without Eden. Eden was a patchwork doll with fiery red hair and two piercing blue eyes. The doll's pupils seemed to move, always looking at her. Janet had no doubt Eden had a soul. It wasn't like hers, or her mother's, or her father's, but Eden was alive in some mysterious way she hadn't understood.

'This way, she'll stay the same forever,' her mother had said, as Janet caught a final look at those blue eyes – unblinking and accusing – as they disappeared inside the hessian bag.

The tears had come then, and they came back now. She could still hear the rattle of her mother's sewing machine and looked instinctively towards the corner of the room, just to be sure no one was using it.

Her mother had continued talking as she sealed Eden away. 'This way, the things we love can last forever.'

Her mother had run a final stitch across the top. 'One for luck,' she'd said, handing the doll in the bag back and wiping Janet's tears away.

Janet would catch the occasional whiff from Eden when she played with her – a sourness from the times the doll had been dipped into the river – but Eden was still there, alive within the bag.

Now, Janet traced the doll's outline through the bag, her own skin papery, chipped, and strained – a good decade older than her mother's had ever been. If she pressed hard enough, she could feel the threads of Eden's hair beneath the hessian, her perfect features and little cloth body.

Her mother had been right, and Janet was so grateful for that.

'Right, let's get you back.' Janet stood, sneaking a quick look at the ancient sewing machine – the wood darkened and stained, the mechanism rusted and worn.

She opened the wardrobe where Eden lived, placing the bag on the middle of five shelves, pride of place, a central figure among hundreds of different-sized hessian bags.

Her youngest was waiting downstairs and rose as Janet made the short journey along the corridor. 'You've fed Ernest?'

Adelaide nodded, holding out a chair for her mother before pouring tea.

Janet had gone through the same process with all her children, each with their own cupboard of perfect dolls, toys, and memories – forever safe. The children were perfect but every now and then, Janet caught the signs of ageing in their features. A faint line beneath Adelaide's eye. A strand of grey in her eldest's hair. She knew she shouldn't think about it, but it was all too easy for her to picture them safely inside one of the bags; caught forever in a state of perfection before it was too late.

They whispered thanks before eating. Janet didn't know why, but she couldn't shake the thought of Eden. The absurd desire to run upstairs, rip the bag open, and see her precious doll again gnawed at her.

But that wasn't how it worked.

If she wanted Eden to last forever, the doll had to remain inside the bag. Once the bag was opened, everything would change. Her mother had told her that. Janet had learnt the hard way when she'd dug up and opened the bag containing their cat, Mr Hobbs.

Mr Hobbs had been a beautiful creature, a bundle of fluff always curled in Janet's lap. She remembered crying when her mother placed him in the bag. Even now, if she tried hard, she could still hear the sound of his claws against the thick hessian.

She'd only wanted to see him one more time, picturing him in his little grave, curled up as though asleep. Her mother had warned her, but she'd been young and hadn't listened.

But she'd listened after that.

'See what you've done?' her mother had screamed as Janet sobbed over what remained of Mr Hobbs. 'If you hadn't interrupted, he would have stayed alive forever. Now there's nothing we can do.'

Janet had tried to put him back in the bag, but her mother had stopped her with a firm slap. 'It's too late.'

A stray tear stung Janet's cheek as she left the house with Adelaide, the fierce wind biting at her skin as they walked the short path across the land to the ravine. Time was running out. Ernest was getting sicker by the day, and his time for the bag would have to come soon, before it was too late.

'Through here, Mummy,' Adelaide said, pulling at loose vines with her gloved hands. 'Boys are so silly.'

'Show me,' Janet replied as Adelaide tugged at the chain attached to the bag.

Janet peered inside. The boy was gagged. His skin was mottled and blue. She removed the gag, feeling the cold of his flesh through her own gloves.

He tried to speak but was shivering too much to form any words. Janet studied his features, reminding herself they were distorted by injury and the chill he endured. There were similarities – the curve of his mouth, especially. But he wasn't the one.

She replaced the gag and got to her feet. 'Try again,' she said, leaving Adelaide to re-seal the bag and do whatever it was she did with those they rejected.

Chapter One

Liam Kilshaw picked up a pebble from the damp sand on Hayle Beach. He was wearing gloves but could still feel the smoothness of the stone beneath the fabric. Idly, he considered the millennia the pebble had existed, in one form or another, before launching it into the gentle waves.

'Five,' he said, as the pebble skipped the surface before sinking below.

'That was not five,' said his son, George, who had turned ten earlier that week.

It was a Sunday afternoon in late November, the sky already darkening. Purple-black clouds loomed in the distance, hovering near Godrevy Lighthouse – a place Liam didn't want to think about at that particular moment.

'See if you can beat it, then.'

George bent and plucked a similar-looking pebble from the sand.

Liam was lucky if he got to see the boy more than once a week, and every time he did see him, it was as though he was meeting a new person. His son had changed so much these last few months. It seemed he'd inherited Liam's height genes – though thankfully not the ones that Liam felt had cursed him, leaving him with alopecia from an early age.

Liam's childhood had been plagued by his hairless scalp, which he'd had since he was eight, and it had been the one thing he'd worried about when Kim was pregnant. Yet, although his limbs were elongated, George had a full head of hair and had tested negative for the genetic disorder that had led to Liam's alopecia. His movements were quick as he snapped his arm back and launched the pebble into the surf. Already something of an accomplished cricketer, George had a strong throw.

'Six,' he screamed in delight, the pebble making one extra bounce than Liam's effort.

'Recount.'

'No way. I win,' said George, as cold rain started to fall.

Dropping George back to his mum's was always tough for Liam, but today felt worse than usual. Liam had enjoyed the weekend, despite the cold ravaging the county. As he watched George leave the car and make the short walk to the front door, Liam dwelled on how much he'd messed things up when it came to his family. It was the same internal conversation that played out every week, the one where he reminded his younger self how egotistical he'd been, how misplaced his priorities were.

Kim – George's mum, and Liam's ex – answered the door and hugged her son. Behind her, Liam glimpsed the warmth of the house she shared with George's stepdad, Mark. Kim offered Liam a curt smile, and beckoned him over.

Liam sighed and walked to the front door, George already having disappeared inside. 'Kim, how are you?' he asked, wondering what he'd done wrong.

'I spoke to Millie yesterday,' Kim said, as if that was all the explanation needed.

Liam had started dating Millie during the Godrevy investigation, a major drug and murder case that Liam had been involved in several months earlier. She'd been George's schoolteacher at the time and although they were still together, things were strained. Millie was away this weekend. It had been two weeks since he'd seen her, and he'd sensed a distance growing between them. Kim had been the one to introduce them and it still felt a bit odd talking to his ex about her. 'Go on, then, tell me how I'm messing things up.'

A sly grin appeared on Kim's face. 'Why don't you tell me?'

Liam understood that she was suggesting he might be sabotaging things with Millie, like he always did with his personal relationships. Like he'd done with her.

Liam held his hands up. 'I don't know what you want me to say. I think she might be avoiding me.'

'Do you think you might be allowing her to? She's still coming to terms with what happened to her. It's OK giving her space, but you risk losing her.'

Millie had become unwittingly involved in the Godrevy case because of him. Sometimes, when he closed his eyes, Liam could still see her, chained to a pipe in a sewage tunnel, the water up to her neck. He'd saved her, and for a time the experience seemed to have brought them closer, but that had changed of late. Liam didn't know if he was purposely allowing the relationship between him and Millie to fall apart. Kim was right in the sense that he'd been giving Millie space to come to terms with recent events. But maybe subconsciously he'd been giving Millie the chance to end things with him, not because it was something he wanted but because it was easier. 'OK,' he said. 'I'll speak to her, if it will get you off my back.'

'Don't do it because of that,' said Kim, the grin turning to a frown.

'I was being flippant. I'll speak to her, I promise.'

'Good. You are allowed to be happy, Liam, you know that, don't you?'

Liam nodded and walked back to the car. He tried to shake the hollowness in his stomach as he headed back to his flat in St Ives, but the melancholy lingered. By tomorrow, it would have dissipated. His work as a detective sergeant in Devon and Cornwall's CID would see to that, but for now, the loneliness was something he'd have to endure.

Parking up, he checked his phone for messages before making the short walk to his flat. It was dark now, the wind sending an icy chill that stung his face. He upped his pace, the small seaside town feeling desolate, until he reached the steps to his front door.

He cursed, spotting a half-eaten fish supper someone had left on one of the steps, the remains smothered in ketchup. Liam bundled the package up, grateful to be wearing gloves as he dumped the litter in the bin, the congealed sauce clinging to the leather.

A cold draught greeted him as he opened the door to his flat. It felt colder inside than out. Checking the boiler, he saw the pilot flame had gone out. Wondering if the day could get any worse, he fired it back up, and was relieved to see the blue flame flicker to life.

He made some tea, then slumped on to the sofa to thaw out. At work, he often craved time to himself, but alone in the flat he felt restless. Things had been hard these past few months. The relative success of the Godrevy investigation had brought with it a string of internal investigations. The operation had exposed the illegal activities of a former Met detective working undercover, and the fallout had been a bureaucratic nightmare.

Liam had been the one to arrest the undercover officer, but that hadn't stopped the professional standards team from scrutinising him at every turn. They constantly reassured him that he wasn't under investigation, but it didn't feel that way.

He thought again about Millie, and the trauma she was still processing. He was no stranger to PTSD, having endured his own near-death experience while working for SBS – the Special Boat Service – and knew it would be a long time before Millie would fully process her kidnapping and near-death experience.

Setting the alarm on his phone, his finger hovered over Millie's name. But then, with a sigh, he put the phone down and went to bed.

◆ ◆ ◆

Last night's rain had turned to ice by the time Liam left his flat early the next morning. The sun must have risen, but it didn't feel like it had as he waited for the ice to thaw from his windscreen. Cornwall winters were never mild, but this one seemed particularly bitter.

He checked his phone as the car rumbled. What was he hoping for? A message from Millie? He was still wavering between giving her space and not wanting to mess things up.

He could already picture Kim's patronising expression if he made the wrong move – the 'I knew it' look she gave him whenever he sabotaged something good in his life.

His phone rang, snapping him out of his thoughts.

'Yep,' he said, answering the call from headquarters.

'Liam. Harry Parnell.' Parnell was one of the uniforms running the night shift. 'We've just had a call about a suspicious package on Sennen Beach. I think you live down that way, don't you?'

'Do you really need me for this? Can't you send Response?'

'Cutbacks, Liam. Anyway, it's a suspicious package. Thought you'd welcome the intrigue.'

'Thanks, Harry. Always thinking of me. Send me the location.'

Sennen wasn't exactly nearby – a good thirty-minute drive from St Ives – but Liam didn't mind. Arctic conditions or not, the idea of being out beat the strained atmosphere at headquarters.

◆ ◆ ◆

Sennen had always been one of Liam's favourite places. He'd surfed there as a teenager and loved the white sand and the sense of remoteness he felt out at sea. He drove down to the front, parked, and walked the short distance to meet the member of the public who'd reported the package.

The report said the man was with a German Shepherd, and Liam spotted him on the sand. 'Mr Bickers?' he asked, approaching.

'Police?' the man replied, brushing shoulder-length hair from his face as he loosened the dog's lead. The animal sniffed at Liam.

Liam felt the cold sting on his hairless scalp and regretted not grabbing his woollen hat. 'DS Liam Kilshaw.'

'You took your goddamn time,' said Mr Bickers, the wind still playing havoc with his hair.

Liam glanced at his watch. It was 6.45 a.m. He knew restructuring had thinned the ranks of local officers, especially in places like Sennen, but Mr Bickers didn't want to hear that. 'Apologies. Tough morning. You mentioned a suspicious package?'

Mr Bickers nodded towards the beach. 'Down there. Sammy found it, but I called him away. You never know what washes up – unexploded bombs, that sort of thing.'

'To confirm, Sammy is your dog?'

Bickers shot him a withering look. 'Of course he bloody is.'

'Right. Wait here,' said Liam, climbing down to the hardened sand.

The object was close to the shore, tangled in seaweed. From a distance, it looked like nothing more than mangled rubbish. Liam sighed, questioning his earlier preference for being outside today over the warmth of headquarters.

By the time he reached the object, his eyes were watering from the relentless breeze, tinged with salt and sand. Up close, the object appeared to be a large hessian sack, roughly two metres in size. It was sodden, seemingly washed up by the tide.

Liam pulled clumps of seaweed away, revealing the bag's rough texture. It was sealed. He had no desire to find out what might be inside. It could be anything from industrial waste to God-knows-what.

As he traced the stitching, his stomach tightened. He pushed against the sack. Beneath the layers of wet fabric, something cushioned gave way, but further down, he felt something solid.

He froze. His breath caught as he ran his hand across the shape again.

Whatever was inside the sack was human.

Chapter Two

The bag appeared to have been washed up from the sea, and the lack of movement from within suggested that whatever – *whoever* – was inside wasn't alive. But Liam couldn't take the chance. He withdrew the penknife from his inside jacket pocket and, pulling the top of the hessian bag together, began trying to prise it apart. His hand was trembling as his mind tried to remind him of his own near-death experiences at sea – the failure of equipment while working for the SBS that had resulted in him nearly losing his life, and his more recent encounter being abandoned at sea during the Godrevy investigation before the coastguard helicopter had come to his aid.

The material was tougher than he'd imagined, with no secondary membrane within, just the coarse hessian, which blunted his knife with every cut.

'Come on,' Liam said, fighting his overactive imagination, which insisted someone alive could still be inside the bag. More likely, it was just waste that had coincidentally formed into a shape his mind was interpreting as human.

As the threads came apart, his cutting became more frantic. Then he caught sight of the bag's contents.

'What have you got there?'

Liam looked up to see Mr Bickers and Sammy less than twenty metres away.

'Stay where you are,' said Liam, his breath visible in the cold air as he pulled at the bag.

What he'd seen appeared to be human hair. As he tore the bag open further, his fears were confirmed. It was a body, lying face down. Checking his protective gloves, he reached inside to touch the neck. The skin was rigid and freezing, the blood having long ceased to pump through the body.

Liam took a deep breath before pulling out his phone and calling it in. Although he wanted to turn the body over for identification, he didn't want to contaminate the scene further before the crime scene investigators arrived.

'What have you found?' Mr Bickers asked, Sammy wagging his tail as if anticipating something.

Liam stood, pulling the bag back over the remains. He walked to Mr Bickers and Sammy. 'I need to put up a cordon, and I'll need you to stay so we can get an official statement.'

Mr Bickers scratched the dog's head, Sammy emitting a low whine as if sensing something was wrong. 'It's a body?'

'Yes,' said Liam, using the heel of his walking boot to draw a large perimeter in the sand around the scene. 'Tell me again how you came across the bag.'

'As I said, I was walking Sammy, and he started barking at something. I walked over and saw . . . this. I thought it looked suspicious, so I called you lot.' Mr Bickers' earlier belligerence had faded. He stepped back from the makeshift perimeter, his shoulders slumped as he held the lead at his side.

'Did you touch the bag? It's fine if you did, but we need to know.'

Mr Bickers shook his head, taking a few seconds to answer. 'No. I saw the seaweed, and I guess my mind went into overdrive. I never thought it'd be a . . . body. What do you think happened?'

'Hard to say at this stage,' said Liam, relieved to see a patrol car pull up in the distance so he could end the conversation with the dog walker.

It was another hour before a full complement of officers were on-site. Liam's direct superior, DI Maya Trent, was the last to arrive, after CSI had formally isolated the area and erected a tent around the body. Liam considered Maya both a close friend and a colleague, and was pleased to see her, wrapped in numerous layers, including an oversized puffer jacket that stretched below her knees.

'Going skiing?' he asked.

Maya raised her eyebrows, glancing at Liam's hatless head. 'Never hurts to be prepared, DS Kilshaw. So, what have we got?'

Liam updated her on the situation, glancing at Mr Bickers and Sammy. 'We should process them now,' he said, noting the haunted look on the dog owner's face.

'OK, let me sort it. Why don't you take a twenty-minute break? Go get a coffee, you look frozen. There's a place by the car park.'

'That's very gracious of you.'

Maya smiled. 'Mine's a cappuccino. One sugar.'

By the time Liam returned with the coffees, Mr Bickers and Sammy were gone, and Maya was dressed in white CSI overalls.

'Suit up – you'll want to see this,' she said, ripping off her mask and accepting the drink.

Liam did as instructed, and together they walked under the entrance to the tent where CSI officers were taking photos and video of the scene.

'How's it going?' Liam asked Thomas Frost, one of the CSI technicians, who was crouched low, working on the body.

'This one's new on me,' Thomas said, standing.

In Liam's absence, they had turned the body over.

'White male. I'd estimate twenty-five to thirty,' said Thomas. 'Though that has yet to be confirmed.'

Liam grimaced at the remains. The flesh and musculature were intact, suggesting the body hadn't been in the bag long. But the face was almost unrecognisable as human. One eye appeared sliced in half, the other was missing, and the rest of the features were obliterated. The mouth was frozen in a horrifying rictus grin, the lips and jawline destroyed, and from what Liam could see, all the teeth were missing.

'What happened?' Liam asked.

'Here,' said Thomas, uncovering the hessian bag from beneath a plastic sheet. 'This is the side he was facing.'

The bag was stained red, riddled with hundreds of tiny slits.

'He was attacked while inside the bag?' Liam asked.

'Looks that way. I'd guess he was stabbed and struck with something like a hammer, or even a sledgehammer, judging by the injuries to his jaw and teeth which are still inside the bag.'

Liam nodded, his eyes flicking towards the sea. The tide was on its way out, and a flock of seagulls hovered above the waves, as though privy to secrets beneath the surface that the humans on shore couldn't fathom.

'Go on, ask it,' said Thomas, noticing Liam's distracted glance.

'Was he alive when this happened?' Liam asked.

Thomas pursed his lips. 'Hard to say. Dumping a porous bag with holes into the sea wreaks havoc on the evidence. But given the amount of blood staining the bag, I'd say it's likely this was done while he was still alive.'

Liam left the tent with Maya.

'Not how I was expecting my day to go,' he said, still eyeing the circling seagulls.

'Could've been worse. You could've found it while out with the lifeboat.'

Liam was a volunteer with the RNLI, based out of St Ives. Following the Godrevy case, the lifeboat station had been under investigation and had only recently reopened. Liam had yet to be on a call since the scandal involving drug smuggling and murder had rocked the county.

'True. I suppose we'll need to get an ID next,' said Liam.

Maya took a deep breath. They both knew, given the state of the remains, identification could take time.

'Start with missing males aged twenty-five to thirty,' she said.

Liam called headquarters and spoke to DC Jack Lawson. 'Check for any record of similar cases. Unlikely, I know, but worth a look.'

'Sure, boss,' said Jack, before Liam ended the call.

Despite the bitter wind, Liam was still glad to be outside rather than stuck in the office. While CSI were still processing the scene under Maya's direction, Liam walked back to the town. Sennen had a lifeboat station, like St Ives, and Liam knew several of the crew. He decided to pay them a visit, hoping they might have noticed something relevant to the case.

The streets were deserted as he walked along the front, the gale-force wind battering him from all sides. Though Sennen never drew the same summer crowds as St Ives, it was a popular destination. Today, however, it felt like a different place, with swirling grey clouds, rain-spattered windows, and an eerie silence broken only by the relentless wind.

The door to the lifeboat station was locked, so Liam knocked on the window. After a couple of minutes, Lauren Roberts, the station's coxswain, appeared and opened the door.

'Lucky I recognised your shiny head,' she said, stepping aside to let him in. 'I don't usually answer when I'm alone here. So, what brings you down?'

Liam felt the ringing in his ears fade as the wind's howl was cut off. 'Thought you might've seen us on the beach.'

'I've heard. Body washed up?'

'News travels fast,' Liam said. 'Between you and me, it's likely a suspicious death investigation.'

'Murder?'

Liam shrugged. He'd known Lauren for a couple of years. Sennen's station was the closest to St Ives, and they often worked together. She was as Cornish as they came, with a lilting accent and a wry sense of humour.

'You going to make me a tea or what?' he asked. Liam realised he was being more cautious around Lauren than he used to be. The Godrevy investigation had resulted in the arrest of Liam's former coxswain, Miles Fischer, at the St Ives lifeboat station. Miles had been something of a mentor to Liam, helping him deal with his PTSD and return to the boats. But his ultimate betrayal still stung.

Lauren pursed her lips, pretending to think it over. 'Suppose I could. As long as you promise not to arrest me.' She widened her eyes, the hint of a smile playing on her lips.

She was alluding to Fischer, and Liam understood it was her way of breaking the tension, and he gave her a nod of approval at the attempted joke. 'As long as you don't try to drown me, I think we'll be fine,' he replied, earning a hearty laugh as Lauren flicked the kettle on.

'So, what details can you give me?' she asked, handing him a steaming mug of tea.

Liam let the heat from the mug thaw his frozen hands. 'Not much yet. The body was in a bag, washed ashore.'

'Bag? What kind of bag?' Lauren's tone was sharp, her accent giving it a hint of accusation.

'Cloth. Hessian, I think.'

Lauren raised her eyebrows, as if the detail had struck a chord, but she said nothing, taking a sip of tea instead. 'Nasty tides around here, as you know.'

Sennen, being near Land's End, was notorious for its dangerous tidal patterns, which often put boats in jeopardy.

'Especially if you're in a bag.'

Lauren coughed on her drink, laughing. 'That'll be right. Very foolish behaviour.'

'Anything happen recently I should know about?' Liam asked, refraining from mentioning the injuries to the body. That wasn't public knowledge yet, and he couldn't risk it leaking.

'Boat got into trouble two nights ago, out near the Longships. Lost two containers.'

'Recovered them yet?'

'One of them. The other . . .' Lauren made a whistling sound, gesturing with her hand as though the container had sunk.

'I thought containers were supposed to float?'

'Depends on how secure they are. This one might've had holes in it.'

'What was inside?'

'I'd love to say humans in hessian bags. That'd make your job easier. But afraid not. Electricals, I believe. I can get you the inventory, if you want?'

'I'd appreciate it, thanks,' Liam said, finishing his tea.

Lauren walked him to the door, pausing as the rain smashed against the window. The wind had picked up once more, whipping debris along the street.

'What sort of bag was it again?' Lauren asked, staring at him intently.

'Hessian, I think,' Liam repeated. 'Like the old potato sacks. Only, this one was big enough to fit a person.'

'Hmm.'

'Hmm?'

Lauren's gaze didn't falter. She seemed to be weighing something up.

'It was sealed when I found it,' Liam added, deciding he was being overly cautious around Lauren and that there would be no harm in sharing the information with her.

Lauren barely reacted, her expression unreadable. 'Now that's interesting,' she said.

'How so?'

'Something my granddad used to tell me.' She paused, her eyes distant. 'You ever heard of the Bucca?'

Liam nodded. Cornwall was steeped in folklore, and the Bucca – a sea spirit said to haunt fishermen – was one he was familiar with. 'I don't think the Bucca did this, Lauren.'

'I know that, you patronising bastard,' she said. 'Bucca Dhu, the malevolent one. Unpredictable. Wild. He'd whip up a storm out of nowhere.'

Liam smiled. He knew better than to interrupt when Lauren got going. Besides, he wasn't in a hurry to step back out into the rain.

'You'd know that, as a seaman,' Lauren continued. 'What you might not know is that people used to leave him offerings – food and drink, to keep him on their side. But my granddad . . . well, he told me something different. It was Halloween, and he was trying to scare us. The storm was wailing outside, and he said that Bucca Dhu demanded more from the fishermen in the old days.'

'Let me guess – human sacrifices?'

Lauren's expression grew solemn. 'As a matter of fact, yes. But what stuck with me – what haunted me – was how my granddad said they were offered.' She leant in closer, her voice dropping to a whisper. 'He said they were placed in hessian sacks. And thrown into the sea. While they were still alive.'

Chapter Three

Liam waited for a break in the rain before leaving the lifeboat station, his mind still whirling from what Lauren had told him. Even if the tale was soaked in ancient folklore, he couldn't rule it out as a possible motive. He'd long since stopped underestimating the lengths people would go to for their beliefs, no matter how irrational. It wasn't beyond the realms of possibility that some deluded soul had sealed the victim in a hessian sack as a sacrifice to calm a storm or appease a mythical sea spirit.

Still, he was getting ahead of himself. It wasn't exactly the kind of theory he wanted to lead with when he spoke to Maya.

The walk back to the beach was punishing. The wind roared against him, and the rain returned before he'd made it fifty paces. His jacket kept his upper body relatively dry, but water streamed down on to his jeans, which clung to his legs like ice-cold shrink-wrap.

The scene at the beach was a mess. Because of the body's location, they couldn't bring an ambulance to the shore to remove it. When Liam arrived, the CSIs and uniformed officers were hauling the gurney back up to the car park, the victim hidden beneath a tarpaulin shroud.

As he watched, Liam's thoughts drifted back to Bucca Dhu. If this had been some kind of sacrifice, it had seemingly failed. The storm was still raging, as if the sea had rejected its offering.

'Where have you been?' Maya's voice broke through his daydreaming. She'd come from behind the CSIs and ducked under the shelter of a nearby overhang with him.

'I've been investigating. You know, doing my job,' Liam replied, as Maya pushed back the hood of her rain jacket. Her cheeks were flushed from the salt-laden wind, and raindrops dotted her skin. Somehow, the wild weather softened her features.

He filled her in on his meeting with Lauren, explaining the container ship's lost cargo before telling her about Bucca Dhu, and Lauren's theory of human sacrifice.

'The shipping company's worth following up on,' Maya said. 'We need to find out what was in those containers, who owned them, and a list of any staff involved.'

'And the Bucca?' said Liam, with a smile.

'Let's sit on it for now, shall we? Though it could be worth checking online groups, that sort of thing. You just never know though down here.'

'Is that a slur on my good Cornish brethren?'

'Not the good ones, no.'

Liam shifted from foot to foot to stay warm. 'OK, I'll get on with it. Any updates on the victim?'

'No ID yet,' she replied. 'But I called in a few favours. The autopsy's scheduled for this afternoon.'

'Bloody hell, someone must owe you big time,' Liam said. Autopsies were often delayed for days due to backlogs, and it took real administrative pull to adjust the schedule.

'I know where the bodies are buried – pun fully intended,' Maya said with a grin, pulling her hood back on before heading towards her car through the never-ending rain.

Liam considered heading home to change his soaked jeans, but there wasn't time. Instead, he cranked up the car's heater and angled the vents at his legs. By the time he hit the A30, steam was rising from his trousers, but they still felt just as damp as when he'd started the journey.

When he arrived at headquarters in Bodmin, the tension in CID was palpable. Though none of the team were officially under investigation, the shadow of suspicion lingered. It all revolved around Stacey Smith, the undercover officer from the Met who'd gone rogue during years of infiltration, eventually working for a Cornish organised-crime syndicate. Liam had been the one to bring her to justice during the Godrevy investigation, and judgement was still out on who did and didn't know about the UCO's involvement.

He noticed a few lingering glances thrown his way as he walked through CID to the small office where DC Jack Lawson had set up an improvised incident room. Liam's eyes scanned the photos of the body already pinned to the board, a grim reminder of the task at hand.

Liam was about to ask the DC if there had been any jurisdictional issues with the investigation when DCI Tom Hargreaves stuck his head into the office. 'Liam, a word.'

Liam turned to Lawson. 'There was a shipping incident near Sennen the other night – two containers lost, one recovered. Dig into that and see what you can find for me.'

He left the makeshift office and crossed the open-plan CID space to Hargreaves' office, shutting the door behind him at his boss's signal.

'Still no ID on the body?' Hargreaves asked, motioning for Liam to take a seat. Hargreaves headed up CID, managing Major Crimes, and Liam's more general department. Liam had no direct issues with his boss. He was a less stringent leader than the ones he'd been used to in the navy, though sometimes he thought that was to Hargreaves' detriment.

'Not yet, but Maya's managed to pull some strings and get the autopsy scheduled for this afternoon.'

Hargreaves nodded, a flicker of approval crossing his face.

'I take it that means it's staying with us?' Liam asked.

Hargreaves looked up, weighing the situation. Major Crimes could take over the case but Liam knew they were overloaded at present, so hoped to keep hold over it.

'That's not why I called you in, but I don't foresee it being a problem.'

Liam settled into the chair opposite his boss. Of everyone involved, Hargreaves had borne the brunt of the fallout from the Godrevy investigation. As the one who'd greenlit collaboration with the Met, he'd been caught in the crossfire when senior officers came under scrutiny for their knowledge – or lack thereof – about the UCO. Liam thought it was unfair, but he understood how hierarchical systems like the police operated. His years in the navy, first as a marine and later as an SBS operative, had prepared him well for the internal politics of the police.

'How can I help, sir?' Liam asked, though his mind was already restless to get back to the investigation.

'Professional Standards wants to interview you again.'

'Christ, what now? I've gone over the details of that night a hundred times.'

'Between you and me, this one's about Grace.'

Liam paused, his breath catching in his throat. DI Grace Hartley had been the Met officer assigned to the operation against the OCG in Cornwall. She also happened to be Liam's ex-girlfriend. During her time back in Cornwall, they'd come close to rekindling their relationship, which had only made Liam's situation with Millie feel even more complicated.

'From what I understand, it's procedural, but . . .'

'But?'

Hargreaves hesitated. 'This is news to me, and none of my business . . . But they're aware of your prior relationship with Grace from your training days.'

Liam's jaw tightened. 'With all due respect, that's no one's business.'

'Possibly not. But you know how they work. They'll be looking to establish if your relationship affected your judgement, or if you knew more than you've disclosed.'

Liam recalled his disappointment at the end of the Godrevy investigation when he'd found out that the OCG member they'd arrested had been a UCO. He'd questioned Grace about whether she'd known the truth. She'd denied it, as had the rest of the Met officers, but it was still hard to get past. And the fact that the incident was still directly affecting Liam and his work made it even more difficult for him to trust anyone within his own organisation.

'About the UCO?' Liam asked, struggling to keep his temper in check. 'Did Grace know?'

'Not that I am aware of.'

'It might be worth reminding them that we dismantled an OCG and put a deranged serial killer behind bars.'

'I'm on your side, Liam,' Hargreaves said. 'But they're coming to talk to you, and I wanted you to be prepared.'

Liam exhaled, containing his anger. He knew it wasn't Hargreaves' fault but that didn't make the situation any easier. 'Understood. Anything else?'

Hargreaves glanced at him, a look that carried equal parts exhaustion and caution, before saying, 'Dismissed.'

◆ ◆ ◆

Jack Lawson had an eager expression on his face when Liam returned to the incident room. Liam, however, was still distracted by the mention of Grace and the looming reality of a professional standards interview.

'I managed to get in touch with the shipping company,' Jack said. 'They're based in Holland, so it was a bit tricky, but they've got a warehouse operation in Falmouth.'

Liam glanced at his watch. 'Quick work, Jack.'

'They're emailing over an inventory for the missing container.'

Liam dropped into his chair. 'Too much to hope there were any hessian sacks in there?'

'Afraid there weren't. But I did get something. Might be a long shot, but one of the crew didn't turn up to port yesterday, and they still haven't heard from him.'

'Where was the ship heading?'

'It left Rotterdam last week and stopped in Falmouth for bunkering.'

'Bunkering?'

'Refuelling. There was also a small crew change, including the missing man.'

'Name?' Liam asked.

'Jordan Hayes. Age twenty-six.'

'When did they last hear from him?'

'They called when he didn't show up, but there was no answer. He hasn't called in sick either.'

'Do you have his number?'

'I tried it. Straight to voicemail.'

'When exactly was he supposed to report for work?'

'Two days ago, when the ship left Falmouth.'

'You've got an address?'

Jack nodded.

Liam sighed, glancing at his watch again. The autopsy with Maya was scheduled in the next couple of hours, and he wanted to be there. Delegating had never been his strength. He preferred to be directly involved. Still, finding the missing crew member could be the quickest route to identifying the victim.

'I'm giving this to you, Jack. Go see if you can track him down. Keep me updated every step of the way.'

Jack nodded, already moving back to his desk to grab his car keys.

◆ ◆ ◆

As Liam headed to the mortuary an hour later, he thought about Jack's enthusiasm. It was a stark contrast to how Liam had been feeling lately. After the Godrevy investigation, he should have been riding high on the success, but the subsequent professional standards inquiry had tarnished any sense of accomplishment. It was hard to stay motivated when the team's achievements were overshadowed by accusations of corruption.

His thoughts turned darker as he recalled just how close he'd come to losing his life during the investigation. It wasn't the first time he'd been pushed to the brink by the ocean. Years earlier, during his time with the SBS, an operation had gone catastrophically wrong when he'd been deep within the Indian Ocean. He'd survived, but some of his colleagues hadn't. The trauma of that day had left him with PTSD, and a newfound fear of open water which had ultimately forced him out of the armed forces.

The irony that Fischer had done so much to help him with his PTSD wasn't lost on him. Liam hadn't been alone that day, having helped rescue a member of the public who'd been kidnapped by Fischer's OCG. If he'd been on his own, maybe he wouldn't have made it. He'd been able to overcome his fears to help save the life of the member of the public, and although the PTSD still remained, he felt like he was perhaps getting some sort of grip on it.

However, Liam wondered if that experience explained his recent lack of enthusiasm for police work. He couldn't deny that the day-to-day grind of being a detective didn't always measure up to the adrenaline-fuelled intensity of his time with the SBS. Sometimes he feared he'd left too soon. That he should have fought harder to overcome his PTSD. Maybe all he'd really needed was for someone to throw him into the deep end – perhaps literally, as had happened with Fischer.

He chuckled at the thought, remembering an old schoolteacher who'd once pushed him into the pool during a swimming lesson. He doubted a teacher would get away with that now, and his mind drifted to Millie, who he still hadn't spoken to after his run-in with Kim. He made a mental note to call her as he pulled up outside the mortuary.

Maya was waiting for him in reception. She'd found time to change since the beach, her dry hair loose against her shoulders. The transformation was striking, especially compared to Liam, who could still feel the dampness of his own clothes clinging to him.

As they walked towards the basement, Liam updated her on Jack's discovery about the missing crewman, Jordan Hayes. Maya nodded as they descended into the mortuary to meet the pathologist.

The familiar, acrid smell of the place hit Liam, and his nose twitched in distaste.

'Thanks for doing this today,' Maya said, standing behind the Perspex glass where they would observe the autopsy.

Doug Wetzel, the examiner, stood by the examination table. He was in his fifties, with the stocky build of a former rugby prop – his white coat strained at the seams as he uncovered the body. 'Your lad's in a bad way,' he said with a wry smile, revealing the victim's obliterated features.

Even cleaned and out of the bag, the victim's face was a ruin. Liam couldn't discern any features – no eyes, no nose, just a flat, unrecognisable slab where the mouth should have been. Wetzel confirmed that the majority of the bones in the man's face had been fractured, and the numerous lacerations merged in places into gaping holes.

Wetzel's assistant recorded the procedure on video as the pathologist narrated his observations. It was some time before he arrived at any conclusions.

'First off, I can confirm the injuries occurred pre-mortem. While the external blood has been washed away by the sea, there are signs of vital reactions – tissue inflammation and clotted blood at the wound edges. All indicators point to these injuries being inflicted while he was alive.'

'Was he in the bag at the time?' Liam asked, picturing the man struggling inside the hessian sack, unable to escape as his attacker struck.

'We'll match the lacerations as best we can, but I've already found hessian fibres embedded in the wounds. We'll test them to be certain.'

Maya took a deep breath. 'Was he alive when he entered the sea?'

The question sent a chill through Liam; Fischer had toyed with his victims before drowning them. But this was something different. There had to be some significance to the hessian bag, and he thought back to Lauren's mention of Bucca Dhu.

'No,' Wetzel replied. 'This wasn't a case of drowning. His lungs are dry – no frothy fluid in the airways. Cause of death is almost certainly exsanguination from the wounds to his face and neck, or traumatic shock due to severe blunt force trauma.'

Liam let out a breath he didn't realise he had been holding. A small, detached part of him felt relieved. At least the man had been spared the agonising, drawn-out death of drowning. But then he realised he was equating what had happened to the man with his own near-death experience. This poor victim had been trapped inside a bag and tortured until he died, which would have been an equally bad – or even more hideous – way to die.

'What are the chances of identifying him, Doc?' Liam asked.

Wetzel frowned slightly at Liam's use of the word 'Doc'. 'Someone took a sledgehammer to his face, metaphorically, and possibly literally. We might get some information from the few teeth that remain, but it'll be difficult. Unless you've got his DNA or fingerprints on file, you're looking at a long process.'

By the end of the autopsy, they had an estimated time of death: between twenty-four and thirty-six hours before the body was found, which aligned with Jordan Hayes' failure to report for work. Wetzel also proposed a list of possible weapons used, including three different knives of varying blade lengths and widths. It wasn't much to go on without the actual murder weapons, though it might help refine their searches. Liam suspected the blade sizes would prove frustratingly common.

'Meet you back at the station,' Maya said, as they reached the car park. The day was racing by, but the first day of a murder investigation always did. Liam doubted he'd be home before the early hours of the morning.

'Hold on a sec,' he replied as his phone vibrated. He glanced at the screen. 'It's Lawson,' he mouthed. 'Yes, Jack?'

'Sir, I'm at Jordan Hayes' address. No one's answering the door, and from what I can see, it looks like it's been forced open.'

Chapter Four

Rain lashed at the windscreen, and the swirling wind raged outside, making Liam's progress to Falmouth through darkened streets slow and laborious. He followed the address Jack had given him, finally spotting the DC waiting under the porch of a terraced house.

The porch light cast a hazy glow around Jack, who stood aside as Liam sprinted the short distance from where he'd parked. His clothes were still sodden as he ducked under the cover of the porch. Jack motioned to the front door, which hung from broken hinges.

With the body found at Sennen and clear signs of a break-in, Jack had already secured permission to search the empty house.

'You've spoken to the neighbours?' Liam asked.

'Next door and opposite,' Jack replied. 'Mr Hayes doesn't seem to be winning any popularity contests. Next door says he's a bit of a hellraiser – comes home late, makes a lot of noise. More than one person said they're relieved he's away most of the time.'

'No one heard the door being broken down?'

Jack shook his head. 'I've got some doorbell footage to check, but no one claims to have seen or heard anything.'

The house itself wasn't particularly untidy. It was a typical two-up, two-down. The kitchen revealed an over-abundance of alcohol. A fridge full of lagers and a wine rack crammed with over twenty bottles of red. Still, Liam couldn't see any additional break-in damage.

Upstairs, one room appeared to be a home office while the other was a bedroom. The bed was unmade, but once again there was nothing obviously out of place.

'If there was a struggle here, it's not evident,' Liam said.

'Maybe they staged it to look that way?' Jack suggested.

'Maybe. But if you were staging it, why leave signs of a break-in at all?'

In the bedroom, one wall was decorated with a collage of framed photographs. Jack had received a picture of Hayes from the shipping company, and Liam recognised him in several of the photos. The images showed groups of friends partying and celebrating together. Liam tried to reconcile the smiling, handsome man in the pictures with the shattered, dehumanised face of the victim in the morgue but it was an impossible task.

'Boss, there's a laptop here,' Jack said, moving a pile of papers on a side table to reveal the device.

Liam opened the screen. The laptop stuttered to life, but as expected, it was password protected. 'Figures,' Liam said. There was no point in attempting to guess. The laptop would need to be sent for analysis to have any real chance of gaining access.

'He's in some of the photos,' Jack said, pointing to the laptop's lock screen. The image showed Jordan Hayes alongside another man. Both wore suits with matching cravats, as if dressed for a wedding. Their arms were slung around each other as they grinned at the camera.

'I can run an image search,' Jack said.

'Be my guest,' Liam said, stepping aside as Jack snapped a picture of the lock screen with his phone.

'There,' said Jack a few minutes later, holding up his phone to show Liam a Facebook profile. The man in the photo was named

Charlie Thomas. 'Lives in Cornwall. Online right now. Shall I make contact?'

'Worth a shot.'

Jack sent the man a brief message with his phone number. 'He's read it,' Jack said, watching the screen. 'Might think it's a scam,' he added, just as his phone rang.

'Put it on speaker,' Liam instructed.

Jack complied, waiting for Liam's nod before answering. 'DC Jack Lawson. Who am I speaking to?'

'This is Charlie,' said the man on the other end of the line. 'You sent me a message about Jordan?'

Jack explained the situation. Charlie listened in silence, his breathing the only indication he was still on the line.

'Mr Thomas, this is DS Liam Kilshaw,' Liam said. 'When was the last time you saw Jordan?'

'What the hell is going on?'

'We're trying to locate him. We're worried about his safety.'

'Christ,' Charlie said. 'We were out on Friday. I got married last year, and Jordan was my best man. Friday was kind of a reunion for the stag do.'

'Where did you go?'

'Just around Falmouth, hit a few pubs and then the nightclub.'

'How many of you?' Liam asked.

'Six.'

'Was Jordan with you at the club?'

There was a long pause, broken only by Charlie's faint breathing. 'He was, but, honestly, it's all a bit blurry. I don't even remember leaving.'

'Do you think Jordan left with you?'

'No, he didn't.'

'How do you know that if you can't remember leaving?' Liam asked.

'I saw a couple of the boys at brunch the next day. They said they'd seen Jordan into a taxi.'

'What kind of state was he in?' Liam asked.

'Bad,' Charlie admitted, lowering his voice. 'From what they told me, he was barely coherent. Couldn't string a sentence together. One of them gave the driver twenty quid to make sure he got home. The driver wasn't keen, but they convinced him. What's going on? Why hasn't he turned up for work?'

'That's what we're trying to find out,' Liam said.

They gathered a few more details before ending the call. Charlie gave them the names of the other men in the group, and promised to get back to them with details of the taxi firm they had used.

If not for the mutilated body, Liam might not have been giving Jordan's disappearance this level of attention. Usually, someone in Jordan's position would turn up at a friend's or lover's house after a heavy night. But the link to the shipping company, the broken front door, and the gruesome condition of the victim found on the beach were more than enough to classify Jordan as a missing person.

Closing his eyes, Liam put himself in the victim's place – trapped in the bag and attacked with knives and hammers.

His breath caught, and he blinked his eyes open. He didn't know if Jordan Hayes was the victim, or even a potential victim. All he knew was that a deranged killer had left a body on Sennen Beach, and he had to make sure something like that never occurred again. Locating Jordan was the first step in making sure that happened.

After another treacherous drive through the relentless downpour, Liam returned to headquarters. A sense of déjà vu struck him as he entered CID. The hive of activity, even at this late hour, reminded him of the Godrevy investigation. As he glanced at the crime board in the incident room, he half expected to see the faces of the victims from that period staring back at him.

Liam guessed he hadn't yet fully processed everything that had happened during the summer. He'd attended the requisite sessions with the department psychologist, mandatory after his near-death experiences, and had been cleared for duty. But he knew that, in some ways, he was still dealing with the fallout.

It wasn't new territory for him. Traumatic incidents from his time in the armed forces occasionally clawed their way back to the surface, tormenting him when he least expected it. For the most part, he was oddly grateful for those moments, believing that forgetting them entirely – or worse, dismissing them – would mean losing a vital part of himself, a part that honoured the comrades who hadn't survived.

Maybe once Professional Standards had wrapped up, he could begin to move forward. Until then, the case would linger, and with it the memories of nearly drowning at sea, and enduring the calculated, brutal murder of one of the gang members.

Back in the present, Liam updated the team on the situation at Jordan's house. Jordan was officially registered as a missing person, and the other four men from the Friday night out were contacted and questioned. Their accounts matched Charlie's. Jordan had been drunk, incoherent, and last seen getting into a taxi.

'You should head home,' Maya said to him sometime after 11 p.m. 'We're not going to get fingerprints or DNA results until tomorrow.'

'One last call. See you in the morning,' Liam replied. His energy was fading fast, but he felt too wired to stop. Jordan's friend, Charlie, had texted him the number for the taxi firm they had used over the weekend. Liam called the firm, and after some back and forth, they provided the name and number of the driver who'd taken Jordan home that evening: Paul Steinman.

Despite the late hour, Liam didn't hesitate to make the call. He was encouraged when the phone began ringing, but was less so after it rang twelve times before someone picked up. A tired voice said, 'Who the hell is this?'

'Mr Steinman, this is DS Liam Kilshaw. Your employer provided your contact details. I'm calling about a fare you picked up Friday night from Ritzy nightclub.'

There was a long pause, and Liam thought the driver might have hung up. Finally, Steinman spoke, sounding more awake. 'Oh, him. I wondered if someone might call about that.'

'Why do you say that?'

'He was causing all sorts of trouble. I was going to kick him out of the cab. Thought he was going to puke all over the place, or do something worse. Then, when I got him to his house, he refused to get out. Kept demanding I take him to the sea.'

'To the sea?' Liam asked, frowning. 'What happened next?'

'Eventually, I convinced him to leave. He stumbled out, and I waited a couple of minutes, thinking I might pick up another fare. That's when I saw him start attacking the door.'

'Attacking the door?' Liam echoed, his mind going to the neighbours' earlier claims that they hadn't heard anything unusual.

'I assume it was his front door. It was the address his mate gave me.'

'What exactly was he doing?' Liam asked.

'He ran at it a couple of times, then did this weird kick, and *bam*, the door flew open. Got to say, I was a bit impressed.' Steinman paused. 'Sorry. It was his door, so I didn't think I needed to report it.'

Sometimes Liam despaired at the lengths people would go to not to get involved with situations that made them uncomfortable. 'So you didn't check to see if he got in safely, or even if he was kicking in the right door?'

'I'm not a babysitter. Do you know how many of these pissheads I have to deal with? I step out of the cab, I put myself in more danger than I'm already in.'

'Did you see what happened after that, at least?'

'Afraid not. I left as quick as I could. Figured my job was done.'

Chapter Five

Although Liam didn't suffer from the drowning nightmares that so often disrupted his sleep, the few hours of rest he managed that night were fitful. His mind churned over the details of the investigation, until at some point during the night he fell asleep.

By 6 a.m., he'd left his flat, deciding to take advantage of a break in the weather to go for a run. As usual, he headed towards Porthmeor Beach. The narrow, winding roads behind St Ives were deserted at that hour, and he was relieved to find the beach empty. Less appealing, however, was the biting wind that whipped against him as he jogged across the frozen sand.

Thoughts of Bucca Dhu lingered – a dragon-like sea monster with shimmering blue and green scales, as he imagined it. Glancing at the tumbling surf, which roared like it was biding its time, he considered the many legends and superstitions tied to the sea. As an ex-marine and a current member of the lifeboat team, Liam was more familiar than most with these stories. During his time in the navy, the tales had been plentiful: green paint, cutting your hair or nails on board, or changing a ship's name could bring disaster. While most sailors humoured these traditions out of caution or superstition, there was always an unspoken fear that ignoring them might lead to catastrophe. Every sailor Liam had ever met had a story of a voyage gone wrong, and each was usually backed up by an unlucky portent.

One of the surviving crew members of the SBS op where Liam had almost drowned had told Liam months after that he'd seen a black seagull – a long-held bad omen – on shore before they'd set off. Despite the equipment malfunction that was to blame, his colleague insisted to this day that the event was all down to the omen.

Naturally, human sacrifice had never been part of those traditions, at least in the versions Liam had heard. And although he'd looked up the story Lauren's grandfather had told her, he'd been unable to find any tales of people being sacrificed in sacks that were thrown into the ocean.

But the idea still lingered. As he looped back along the beach, he considered that it wasn't implausible that someone in Cornwall might still believe in sea monsters, or be mad enough to think trapping a man in a hessian sack would appease one.

What didn't fit with the ritual was the savagery of the victim's injuries. That level of violence suggested a frenzied attack, driven by anger or hysteria, rather than a controlled sacrifice. It hinted at a personal connection between the killer and the victim, one steeped in rage or desperation.

Liam sprinted the last few metres across the sand, welcoming the burn in his legs and the rasp of his breath as he reached Back Road West. Instead of heading home, he decided to extend his run to the care home where his mother lived. Liam usually visited her weekly, though his consistency had slipped of late.

The care staff, familiar with Liam's early morning visits, buzzed him in without question. He climbed the stairs to the dementia ward and entered his mother's room. She was propped up in bed, watching television with her mouth slightly open. At the sound of the door, her head turned briefly to Liam before her gaze shifted back to the screen.

'Mum,' Liam said.

She didn't respond or look back.

Liam's relationship with his mother had been conflicted from an early age. His father had died when he'd been a young boy, and his mother had never recovered from the loss. Instead of being there for him, she'd turned to drugs and alcohol to numb her pain. In the past, he'd wondered if her behaviour was an act – that she was pretending not to recognise him out of shame for how she'd treated him. Though he'd never truly believed it was not dementia, the thought had sometimes made her silence easier to bear.

Now, as he stood watching her emaciated body, he tried to summon memories of who she had been before everything fell apart. But those memories felt increasingly distant. When Liam thought of his mother now, it was this frail, unrecognisable version that came to mind, rather than the vivacious woman she had once been before his father's death. In a way, he was grateful for it. It helped him forget the years of neglect, the beauty and youth she had squandered in such a short time.

His thoughts drifted absently back to the body they'd found in the hessian sack, and the horrifying injuries inflicted on the victim's face. He tried to imagine what the man might have looked like before the attack, but all he could see was the pulped, lacerated ruin that had robbed the victim of all humanity.

Not knowing what else to say, Liam left the room, feeling he'd fulfilled his duty.

◆ ◆ ◆

Before heading to work, Liam sent a text to Millie, asking if she wanted to meet up later in the week. Despite Kim's protestations that he was trying to sabotage the relationship, he was beginning to worry that maybe Millie was the one looking for a way out. He couldn't blame her. Knowing him had led to her almost dying. It felt as if she was actively avoiding him, and although he understood why, it would be much better for them both if they spoke about it.

His first stop that morning was the dockside warehouse of S&D Shipping, where Jordan Hayes worked. Liam arrived before eight and parked outside, waiting for the rain to ease. After several minutes of fruitless waiting, he gave up and dashed across the car park to the warehouse entrance.

Four men stood in the covered area between the car park and the warehouse, smoking and sipping hot drinks from novelty mugs. They all wore matching S&D embroidered overalls and watched Liam approach, ignoring him just long enough to make it clear they didn't care for interruptions.

'Help you?' one of them finally asked. He was an obese man whose overalls strained against his stomach. Uneven patches of grey hair dotted his pudgy face, which was set in a sardonic smile.

'DS Kilshaw. I'm here about Jordan Hayes.'

'What's numb-nuts done now?' said the same man.

'And you are, sir?' Liam asked.

'Terry Caines.'

'Mr Caines, Jordan failed to turn up for work yesterday,' Liam said.

'Is that so?' Caines shook his head. 'Can't say I'm surprised. Didn't think it'd be long before he messed things up.'

'How well do you know him?'

'Well enough. When he's not gallivanting around on the bloody ships, he works here for me. I could do with him now, as it happens. Where is he?'

'That's the thing. We can't locate him.'

'He's missing?'

'Yes. When did you last see him?'

Caines stuck out his lower lip in mock consideration. 'Wednesday, I guess. He had a shift then.'

'And how did he seem?'

'Like he always does.' Caines sighed. 'Look, I'm very busy. What's this all about?'

Liam decided to mention the victim, partly to gauge Caines' reaction. 'We found a body at Sennen. It may or may not be Jordan. We're trying to locate him to eliminate him from our inquiries.'

'You think it's Jordan?' Caines said, his sarcasm fading.

'We don't know yet. The body isn't easily identifiable.'

'How can I help you then?'

Liam frowned, stepping closer. 'This isn't a joke, sir. A man has been brutally murdered. And there's a chance that man might be Jordan. Does that not bother you?'

Caines took a step back, his expression unreadable. He didn't seem particularly concerned. Liam wasn't sure if he was deliberately being obtuse or if the gravity of the situation had yet to sink in.

'I'll let you know if he calls in,' Caines said.

'What exactly do you do here?' Liam asked, walking further into the warehouse.

Caines grunted and followed him, his companions dispersing without a word. 'We make last-minute adjustments to containers before they're loaded.'

'So you're aware of the two containers lost the other evening?'

'Are we bloody ever. Nobody here takes responsibility when things go wrong.'

'They blamed you?'

'We made adjustments here, yeah. But it's got nothing to do with us. Is that what this is about?'

'Do you think there's any way Jordan could have been in one of those containers?' Liam asked, avoiding any mention of a hessian bag. It was always wise to keep some details back during an investigation like this.

Caines shook his head, looking at Liam as though he'd just asked the most ridiculous question imaginable. 'Of course not. And if he had been, he wouldn't have lasted long. Those things are packed tight – air tight. And why the hell would he do that anyway? He was supposed to be on the ship, wasn't he?'

Liam continued walking across the warehouse floor, glancing at the containers being packed.

'You'll need protective gear if you go any further,' Caines said.

'Next shipment?' Liam asked, looking at the open containers.

'Unpacking the last shipment.'

'Any perishable goods?'

'Not this time.'

'This might be an odd question, but do you ever receive goods in hessian bags?'

Caines raised an eyebrow. 'What is this? Some drugs thing?'

'No,' Liam replied. 'Should it be?'

Caines chuckled, the sound forced. 'I think you've been watching too many movies.'

'Is that right? So you're saying drugs don't get smuggled into the UK?' Liam asked, his mind flashing back to the Godrevy case.

'Not through here. We're a multinational company.'

Liam bit back a retort. Much of his work in CID involved tracking the movement of drugs, both within the UK and from overseas. The involvement of a multinational company didn't exclude them from being targeted by smugglers. He changed tack. 'Hessian bags?'

Caines sighed. 'Not any more. That's old-school. Health and safety regulations have moved things on. Occasionally, you might've seen goods transported that way, but these days, they'd be vacuum-packed.'

Liam handed him his card. 'Let me know the moment Jordan turns up.'

Caines held the card aloft, his sardonic smile returning. 'You'll be the first to know, Detective.'

Chapter Six

By the time Liam reached headquarters at 10 a.m., his mood had soured further. Millie hadn't responded to his earlier text. Although he knew she'd be at school by now, her silence cemented the feeling that she was avoiding him. After all they'd both been through, it would be a shame to throw away their relationship, but he didn't know what else to do. He could hear Kim in his head, telling him to fight for Millie, but how could he do that if she wouldn't speak to him?

His spirits didn't improve at the sight of two PSD officers seated in Hargreaves' office. With the murder investigation already pressing on him, the last thing he needed was to keep revisiting the Godrevy case with Professional Standards, yet it seemed unavoidable.

Liam logged into his laptop and reviewed the case notes as he waited to be called in. His mind circled back to Jordan Hayes, wondering again if he was the victim, or just someone who had partied too hard and would eventually turn up unharmed.

Most of the day's work would be chasing leads. They were expecting lab work back, and research was ongoing to track down the manufacturer of the bag the body had been found in.

He started work, first checking in with Jordan's friend Charlie to see if there was any news. It was hard to focus, knowing that he could be summoned by PSD at any moment. Charlie had no updates, and Liam was about to call another of Jordan's friends from the stag night when Maya approached with lab results.

'No match for fingerprints or DNA in the system,' she said. 'Wetzel still thinks there's a chance of identifying the victim through dental records – one of the remaining teeth had a filling.'

Liam leant back in his chair. 'Maybe the attacker knew that and destroyed the face to make sure we couldn't identify him.'

'None of it makes sense to me,' Maya replied. 'Why put him in a bag first?'

'Maybe the killer's squeamish?'

Maya raised her eyebrows but didn't comment. 'Jack's speaking to the shipping company to see if Jordan would've had to provide DNA or fingerprints for his employment.'

'What's the ETA on dental records?' Liam asked, still trying to reconcile the image of Jordan Hayes he'd seen in photos with the mutilated corpse in the morgue.

'Could be days. You know how these things go. And with the victim's jaw in that condition, it'll be even harder.'

Liam blinked away the mental image of the victim's obliterated face as he dialled the next person on his list, Adam Knowlton, who had been at the club with Jordan on Friday night. Knowlton answered promptly, as though he'd been expecting the call.

'Has Jordan done anything like this before?' Liam asked.

'Jordan going AWOL? He's a law unto himself. I wouldn't put it past him.'

'But he's had that job with the shipping company for a while. Would he jeopardise that?'

'I doubt it's the first time he's pulled something like this. Look, I really hope he's OK, but I think he'll turn up at some point,' said Knowlton.

'I assume Charlie mentioned we've found a body in Sennen?'

There was a pause. 'That can't be him,' Knowlton said, his voice quieter.

'What makes you so sure?'

'I don't know. It just can't be.'

'Charlie told me Jordan doesn't have any tattoos. Is that correct?'

'Unless he's hiding one, yeah.'

'Any distinguishing marks you know of?'

'God knows.'

'You need to think, Mr Knowlton. This could be really important.'

'Look, I've seen the guy naked in the showers after football matches, but I can't say I paid much attention. He's pale, pasty . . . nothing stood out.'

Liam hadn't considered that Knowlton or the others might have seen Jordan naked before. 'This isn't the most pleasant thing to ask, but do you think, if you saw your friend without clothes, you'd be able to recognise him?'

Knowlton gave a nervous laugh. 'What sort of question is that?'

'I'd like to confirm whether the body we found belongs to Jordan. You say it's unlikely, but we need certainty.'

'Jesus . . . You want me to look at a corpse?'

'The face would be covered,' Liam reassured him. 'I know it's a big ask, but it would help us immensely.'

Knowlton sighed. 'I'm not sure if I can. I know what Jordan looks like . . . but naked? It's not something I dwell on, you know what I mean? I don't think I would know if it is him or not.'

'I know it's a bit left-field, but this is really important.'

'I don't know . . . Shit, where and when?'

'We'll let you know within the hour,' Liam said, thanking him and ending the call as the professional standards officers entered the incident room and invited him to one of the empty conference rooms.

The PSD officers reintroduced themselves as DCI Oliver Brooks and DI Emily Carter. Liam had dealt with the pair on several occasions since July. He noted that both looked paler than they had in the summer, as though they'd spent months locked away working on the investigation. They went through the usual preamble about his right to representation and reminded him he wasn't under caution.

Liam didn't need representation. This wasn't his mistake. He'd been the one to discover the identity of the undercover officer working for the OCG. All he wanted was for this to be over so he could focus on the current investigation.

After a brief recap of events, DI Carter finally asked, 'When were you first aware that the woman calling herself Stacey Smith was, in fact, a UCO?'

Liam leant back in his chair. Stacey Smith's defection to the OCG would have sent shockwaves through the Met. More than one officer had made catastrophic errors, and people had died because of it. They needed someone to take the fall, and Liam would be damned if it was him. 'When she told me. Seconds before she tried to kill me.'

'You had no idea who she was before then?' Carter asked.

'Of course not.'

'You first met her earlier in the investigation, at Mr Britten's house?' asked DCI Brooks, glancing down at his notes.

'I met her. She told me her name was Stacey Smith. She soon became a suspect, and we couldn't locate her. The next time I saw her, she was with a psychopath, torturing a man before drowning him. You may remember? I almost drowned too.'

The two officers exchanged glances.

'And at no point did any other officer indicate or suggest that Stacey Smith was, in fact, DS Emma Hamilton?' Brooks asked.

'Why? Did any of them know?'

Brooks offered a forced, humourless smile. 'Just answer the question, DS Kilshaw.'

Liam had been dealing with authoritarian figures since joining the navy as a teenager. Discipline had been hardwired into him, and he knew the best approach was to accept the situation and handle it methodically. Even so, he had to suppress the urge to remind the patronising DCI of everything he'd endured during the investigation – the near-death experience, the fears he'd had to overcome since leaving the navy – all in the name of public service.

Instead, he kept his response measured. 'No. No officer gave any indication of Stacey Smith's true identity before or after her apprehension.'

That seemed to satisfy them. Brooks ended the interview and thanked him for his time.

Liam waited until they had left before getting to his feet. Maya was waiting just outside.

'Everything OK?' she asked.

Liam still wasn't sure what the PSD officers were trying to get at. He couldn't really see how their investigation could impact him directly, though he wouldn't put it past them to criticise his approach. Some of his actions during the investigation had been a little off book, including taking the lifeboat to Godrevy Island. But every action he'd taken had been for the good of the case. 'Time vampires. I've no idea what their angle is, but I think we should tread carefully. Someone will be losing their job because of this.'

'Surely not one of us?'

'Not if we play the game,' Liam said, running a hand across his scalp and absently rubbing the new jagged scar.

'I'm off to meet one of the leading manufacturers of hessian bags, if you'd care to join me,' Maya said.

'Sorry, I've got a date with the mortuary,' Liam said, updating her on his earlier conversation with Adam Knowlton.

'Not much left to identify.'

'Hopefully there's enough,' Liam replied, just as his phone pinged with a message from Millie.

Sorry, can't make tonight. Maybe the weekend. x

He tried not to overthink it. They were both busy professionals and didn't always have time to meet during the week. But the *maybe* gnawed at him. In the beginning, there had been no *maybes.* He didn't want to be paranoid but it sounded like she was stalling, perhaps biding her time before ending things altogether.

Kim's voice popped up in his head again, accusing him of looking for an excuse to end the relationship. Maybe Kim was right. Maybe he was using the difficulty as a reason to leave. But as he headed towards the mortuary, one thought stuck in his mind: that ending things now might be the best thing for both of them. Millie could probably do without the complication in her life – and definitely without the risk – and Liam had so much going on with work that trying to make a relationship succeed was close to impossible. Perhaps he *was* just making excuses to make his life easier, but at least this way it could come to an amicable end with neither of them having to get hurt any more than they already were.

◆ ◆ ◆

Adam Knowlton wasn't alone when he arrived at the mortuary. He was accompanied by Charlie Thomas, whom Liam had spoken to the previous night at Jordan's house.

Both men were in their mid-twenties, with rough stubble across their faces and dark bags under their eyes. Liam wasn't sure if their appearance was due to concern for their missing friend or if the effects of Friday night's binge still lingered in their system.

He led them down the stairs to the mortuary, where he'd witnessed the autopsy. 'I think it's best if you go in one at a time to view the body,' Liam said, as they reached the door. 'It'll eliminate the risk of groupthink. The face will be covered, so you won't see the injuries. Still, it won't be easy. If you need to leave at any point, let me know. Who's first?'

The two men exchanged uncomfortable looks. The blood drained from Adam's face, and Charlie placed a hand on his friend's shoulder. 'I'll go,' he said, stepping forward.

Liam handed Charlie a face mask as they entered the mortuary, where Wetzel's assistant was already waiting.

'This is weird,' Charlie said, glancing at the covered body on the gurney.

Liam nodded. He couldn't recall ever asking someone to identify a body without the face being visible. 'Are you ready?'

Charlie took a deep breath and nodded. At Liam's signal, Wetzel's assistant stepped forward and uncovered the victim's body from the neck down.

The room was silent as Charlie stared at the body. He closed his eyes momentarily before turning away.

'Take your time,' Liam said calmly.

Charlie nodded again, opening his eyes and giving the corpse another look. He turned to Liam. 'There's absolutely no way that's Jordan,' he said, moving to the door.

Chapter Seven

When she'd first approached him, Alex had been so scared he'd almost walked away. He'd seen her before, of course. But then their paths had started to cross with uncanny regularity – so much so that Alex had altered his morning routine, choosing to walk the same woodland trail each day in the hope of seeing her with her dog.

Alex had always been shy around women, though he'd attracted more than his fair share of attention. He blamed his awkwardness on the boys' school he'd attended since he was eleven, though that didn't explain how his friends spoke so easily with the local girls, or the summer tourists, whose fleeting presence made them all the more tantalising.

Yet, despite his usual discomfort, something about her had stirred an inner confidence he hadn't known he possessed when she'd finally walked over to him.

'My name is Adelaide,' she'd said. 'This is Lyla.'

Lyla, the mongrel trailing after Adelaide with doleful eyes, seemed mismatched with someone so striking. Alex should have noticed it then, the incongruity of such an unremarkable dog belonging to someone so extraordinary.

‘I’m Alex. This is Bailey,’ he replied, nodding at his Great Dane, who trotted over to greet them.

‘I see you every day,’ Adelaide said, falling into step beside him as though it were the most natural thing in the world.

Her voice made him breathless, but he managed to speak. ‘I might have noticed you too,’ he said, grinning despite himself, his cheeks flushing as Adelaide mirrored his smile.

When she’d taken Alex, and he’d awakened in the cave, his first thought had been for Bailey. He’d imagined the dog roaming the woodlands in search of him or making his way home to alert someone of his disappearance.

But now, all Alex could imagine were the terrible fates that might have befallen his clumsy, lovable companion. He wanted to remember Bailey as he had been, comically large but soft as anything, wagging his tail and bounding through the woods without a care. But when he pictured him now, he was either alone or worse.

Alex shivered as he heard the gate creak. The cold didn’t bother him any more – it never got that cold in the cave – but seeing Adelaide always provoked the same visceral reaction. Maybe it was the juxtaposition of her attractiveness and erratic behaviour, or perhaps her moments of kindness and cruelty, but seeing her brought out conflicting emotions in Alex: a twisted mixture of dread and need.

‘I brought you some soup and lovely homemade bread from Mummy,’ she said, smiling at him the same way she had that day in the woods. An innocent smile, so full of beauty and promise.

Alex tugged at his chain and rushed towards her, grabbing the tray of food from her hands. Ignoring the burning heat on his tongue, he slurped at the soup, barely pausing to breathe.

Adelaide sat down just out of reach of his chain, her movements delicate and deliberate. ‘Be careful, Alex,’ she said.

For the briefest moment, he believed she was genuinely concerned. He wiped soup from his mouth with the back of his hand and tore into the bread. Between bites, he glanced at the bag by her side. 'What's that?' he asked, spitting crumbs as he spoke.

Adelaide tilted her head, her expression placid. 'Your hair is getting a bit messy. I need to tidy you up in case Mummy sees you.'

Alex's stomach twisted at the mention of her mother. But now he knew better than to comment. Early on, he'd made that mistake. They had been sitting by a fire and he'd said something about her mother. Without speaking, she'd produced a small knife from her pocket and had held the blade over the flames before searing it onto the sole of his foot. He'd never dared speak about her mother again, and Adelaide had never alluded to the incident.

He finished the bread and sat motionless, watching her in the soft light of the gas lamps that lit his section of the underground prison. Despite everything – his captivity, the horrors she'd inflicted on him and almost definitely others – Alex couldn't help but marvel at her beauty. He had no words to describe her. There was something unworldly about her, an ethereal glow that made her almost painful to look at.

'Are you going to let me, Alex?' she asked.

Instantly, his will evaporated. Her confidence was absolute, leaving no room for resistance. He didn't bother struggling. What was the point? He had so little strength left, and even if by some miracle he managed to overpower her, what then? There were others here, or had been. He heard them sometimes, faint echoes in the darkness. And even if he were alone, the chain binding him to the rock made escape impossible.

'That's it, turn around,' she said, her voice carrying an intimate breathlessness that sent a shiver down his spine.

Alex obeyed, turning and sitting up straight. The futility of his situation was apparent as Adelaide reached into her bag and produced a pair of scissors.

He stared ahead, frozen, as she stepped closer. The metallic snip of the scissors filled the silence, sharp and deliberate, as she began to cut his hair.

Chapter Eight

Adam Knowlton corroborated Charlie Thomas's assertion: the victim found in the hessian bag at Sennen was not Jordan Hayes. Both men, speaking to Liam independently, noted that Jordan wasn't in the kind of physical shape the victim appeared to have been in before his death. Jordan was a heavy drinker. Both also commented that he had something of a beer belly and lacked the musculature of the victim.

Without matching Jordan's DNA or fingerprints to the corpse, the identification wasn't legally conclusive, which meant that Jordan Hayes was still being treated as a missing person separate from the unnamed victim found on Sennen Beach.

On Thursday morning, Liam was on his way to visit the parents of Jamie Brady, a twenty-seven-year-old who had gone missing six months ago. Much of Liam's work involved vulnerable individuals who were often targeted by drug gangs establishing county lines to sell drugs into local communities. These people frequently disappeared, and Jamie's case had been no exception. Liam recalled speaking to Jamie's parents when they'd first reported him missing. It was now officially a cold case, but Jamie was on the missing persons register and Liam looked in on the casefile once a month for updates.

It was a familiar story. Unemployed and drifting, Jamie had fallen in with the wrong crowd. He started using drugs, staying out late, and one night didn't return.

Only Jamie's mother was home this morning, his father away at work. Mrs Brady led Liam into the living room of their terraced house in Redruth. The room was tidy and meticulously organised. Liam wondered if this was how they always lived or if a special effort had been made for his visit. He took a seat on a white leather sofa as Mrs Brady went to the kitchen, returning with a mug of tea. She placed it on a glass coaster decorated with the Cornish flag.

'Thank you for taking the time to see me,' Liam said. He recalled how distraught and exhausted Mrs Brady had looked when he first interviewed her. Life with Jamie's drug use and late nights had taken its toll. Though Liam doubted she'd want to hear it, she seemed much better now, less tired, a hint of life behind her eyes. The smile she gave him as he sipped his tea even seemed genuine.

Liam started with the usual questions, confirming that she hadn't heard from Jamie or anyone connected to him, before shifting to the real reason for his visit. 'I have a photo I'd like to show you. It's of a man we believe to be a similar age to Jamie,' he said. He'd repeated those words four times that week already, as his team worked across the county to identify the hessian bag victim by cross-referencing missing persons files.

Mrs Brady's mug began to tremble in her hands, and Liam leant forward, taking it from her and setting it on a coaster. He wasn't sure how effective this approach was, even though it had been his idea. Both Charlie Thomas and Adam Knowlton had appeared so certain the body wasn't their friend's that Liam believed others might similarly recognise, or be able to eliminate, their missing loved ones.

But Liam knew that most missing people didn't have anyone actively waiting for them. And in cases like Jamie's, even a devoted loved one like his mother might struggle to identify a body from photographs alone.

Still, with the hessian bag victim unidentified, Liam felt he had no choice. He handed Mrs Brady the photos, watching as she stared at them, her face ashen. After a long silence, she handed them back. 'I'm really sorry,' she said, her voice trembling. 'I don't know.'

◆ ◆ ◆

The raw November wind stung Liam's face as he walked back to his car. Though it hadn't rained in the past few days, the forecast hinted at snow over the weekend. The chill seemed sharper, more cutting. He upped his pace to a jog, the cold air burning his lungs, then broke into a sprint as he reached his car, opening it with numb fingers.

He'd only been walking for two minutes, but it was still enough for the cold to seep through him. Sliding into the car, Liam switched on the engine and waited for the heat from the vents to bring some colour back to his skin.

Investigations could often be frustrating, but the impossibility of identifying the hessian bag man was testing his patience in a way he wasn't accustomed to. Tracking down a murder suspect was difficult enough, but doing so without knowing the victim's identity made the task exponentially harder.

In addition to combing through reports on male missing persons aged twenty to thirty, Liam and his colleagues had been leaning on the local drug-dealing community for leads. Following the recent collapse of an OCG, a power vacuum had opened in the area. New gangs and smaller operators were vying to fill the void, and it was feasible that the hessian bag man was the work of one of those.

But Liam didn't think the death was gang related. Miles Fischer may have drowned his victims with a psychopath's relish, but OCG deaths often went under the radar, or were simple affairs – stabbings or occasionally shootings.

The Sennen murder was different. It still felt to Liam ritualistic in nature, and he couldn't shake the idea of someone out there living in fear of Bucca Dhu, and it worried him that another sacrifice might soon be at hand.

One faint glimmer of progress came from Maya's meeting with the hessian bag manufacturer. They had determined that the bag's dimensions didn't match anything currently on the UK market. Tests were still pending, but the manufacturer had concluded that the bag was almost certainly homemade. The stitching was uneven, the material varied, and there was no manufacturing stamp. While it wasn't much to go on, lab analysts believed they might be able to match the stitching to a specific sewing machine, if one were ever found.

Liam headed into St Ives to meet a colleague from the lifeboat house who had called him earlier that morning. Parking by the railway station, he took the short coastal path to the wharf. St Ives was his hometown, and he'd lived there on and off for most of his life. With his large frame and distinctive look, he'd been well known in town even before the Godrevy investigation. Now, thanks to that case's national attention, he was something of a local celebrity. As he approached the lifeboat station, he caught more than one curious glance directed his way.

His colleague, Philip Skewes, was working on the larger of the two lifeboats – the Annie Wilkinson – when Liam arrived. Phil was the new operations director, a seasoned volunteer who had transferred from the team at Looe.

'Hey, Liam,' Phil said, without looking up from the boat.

Liam glanced at the vessel, a familiar tightness gripping his chest as memories of taking the boat out alone to Godrevy Island resurfaced. 'You wanted to see me?'

'Typical police, straight to the point. I heard about the body on the shore at Sennen. Very strange.'

'You don't know the half of it,' Liam said, blinking away the haunting vision of the victim's obliterated features, the full extent of which hadn't been released to the public.

'Lauren told me you were talking about the Bucca?'

'*She* was. If I could blame all the deaths in this county on a mythical sea monster, I'd be laughing.'

'Just because it isn't real doesn't mean folk don't believe in it,' said Phil, walking over to the kitchen area and switching on the kettle.

Liam grabbed two mugs and dropped in teabags, adding a splash of milk to each. 'Not you as well.'

'Stranger things happen at sea, and all that,' Phil said with a shrug. 'No, what I mean is, the Bucca might not exist – might just be a metaphor for the sea's destructive power – but that doesn't mean some people won't try to appease it.'

'You think someone would really sacrifice a human for that? What would they gain?' Liam asked, frowning.

Phil poured the boiling water into the mugs. Steam billowed through the chill air of the lifeboat house. 'You'd be surprised what folk believe in, the old ways and that.'

'Well, whatever they were trying hasn't worked,' Liam said, nodding at the windows as rain began to batter the glass.

Phil sipped his tea. 'Maybe the body was never supposed to reach the shore. Maybe you finding it broke the spell.'

Liam raised an eyebrow, sipping his own drink. 'And here I was thinking the navy had the highest concentration of superstitious nut-jobs.'

'We're everywhere, Liam, my lad,' Phil said with a grin. 'However, that's not why I wanted to speak to you. Could be nothing, but hearing about all this reminded me of something from back in the day.'

'When exactly was *back in the day*?' Liam asked. Phil was twenty-five years his senior.

Phil raised his eyebrows, mock offended. 'Back in the nineties. I imagine your mum was still wiping your arse back then?'

Liam laughed. 'Sorry, old man. Continue.'

'Anyway,' Phil said, affecting the voice of an old man, 'back in *my* day, we helped your lot, the police, with a drug-smuggling operation. What brought it to mind was what we found aboard one of the boats we intercepted once.'

'Dead people in bags?' Liam asked dryly.

'Not quite. But we did find a large number of hessian sacks on board. They were supposed to be filled with coffee beans but were actually stuffed with something much naughtier.'

◆ ◆ ◆

Liam was still thinking about his conversation with Phil as he waited in the school playground later that day to pick up George. The hessian bags, which were meant to carry coffee beans, had instead concealed cocaine. After some digging, Liam discovered the incident had taken place in 1998 off the south coast near Mevagissey.

The coastguard, assisted by the RNLI, had intercepted a boat carrying the drugs, which had a street value exceeding £50 million at the time. Although the use of hessian bags seemed coincidental, Liam had arranged to speak with one of the police officers involved in that case the next day.

Liam pulled his coat tighter as the first class was let out. There was no respite from the cold, and he was thankful that George's cricket practice was an indoor session. He scanned the group of waiting parents and carers, noting more than one curious look sent his way. Towards the police officer who was having a relationship with one of the teachers.

Millie wasn't George's teacher this year, but Liam knew which class she taught. He couldn't help but feel disappointed when he saw her teaching assistant lead a snaking line of children out of the building instead of her.

Liam turned his attention back to George's classroom, his thoughts still lingering on the other thing he'd discussed with Phil – the idea that Liam's discovery of the body might have broken the offering spell on Bucca Dhu.

'Dad!' George's voice snapped him out of his thoughts as his son came running to him, arms outstretched.

Liam had been so wrapped up in his thoughts that he hadn't noticed George's class being dismissed. He knelt for a quick hug before looking up to wave at George's teacher.

As they walked back to the car, Liam kept an eye out for Millie, though she was wisely staying indoors. 'I thought cricket was a summer sport,' he said, as they climbed into the car, starting the engine and cranking the heat to full.

'Dad, you say that every week. You *know* it's indoors,' George replied with a laugh.

Liam smiled, but his mind remained clouded. He relished his time with his son and hated how distracted he felt as he drove them to the leisure centre in Penzance for George's nets session. Liam knew the time would come when George wouldn't be so eager to share every detail of his day, so he tried to focus on his stories about school. Yet no matter how much he wanted to listen, his thoughts kept drifting to the victim in the hessian bag, to the man's mutilated face, to the questions that still had no answers.

At the centre, George skipped off with his oversized cricket bag, leaving Liam to retreat to the café. The investigation was all encompassing, even interrupting his dad-time, it seemed. He was about to call Maya for an update when her name flashed on his phone.

'Sorry to bother you, I know you're with George, but I thought you'd want to know,' Maya said as he answered.

'Go on.'

'It looks like we can eliminate someone from the hessian bag investigation.'

Chapter Nine

Was it possible that no one knew he was missing?

During the cold, lonely nights – or days, for all he knew; time made little sense here – Alex grew more and more concerned that no one was looking for him.

He was only twenty-five, for God's sake, but he'd led a solitary life. He was a self-employed data analyst, and without any current projects, no client would miss him, though a few had probably written him off for not responding to emails. As for family, there was only his dad, who lived in Leeds. Like Alex, he wasn't a great communicator, and it wasn't unusual for a couple of months to pass without them speaking.

The same went for his friends. Even if they had been messaging him, none of them would be overly concerned that he wasn't responding. It wasn't because they didn't care – they were good guys; in fact, the opposite was true. They accepted Alex for who he was, which often included stretches of solitude when he went silent in the WhatsApp group or skipped out on impromptu gatherings.

The disappointing truth was that the people most likely to notice his absence were his neighbours. He lived in a crumbling house on the outskirts of Penzance, and although he only recognised most of the other residents by sight and not by name, they might have noticed he'd gone. Then again, maybe not. It wasn't as though deliveries would be piling up outside his door. He often locked himself away for days at a time anyway – so who would really realise?

He had given a key to one of the neighbours a few doors down called Joan, but weeks would often past before they spoke to one another. He guessed the only one who would truly be missing him would be Bailey, and Alex continued living in the hope that his beautiful big dog was alive.

Scraping his hands across the rough stone floor, Alex pushed himself up on to his haunches and then to a full standing position. Although time didn't exist properly in the caves, an internal sense told him that Adelaide would return soon, and, God help him, he was looking forward to seeing her.

It was clear that one day she would do him harm. Occasionally, he heard screams in the night, abruptly cut off as if swallowed by the cave itself. Yet, he was so starved of company – ironic, given how much he avoided it in his usual life – that even the threat of her plans didn't diminish his longing for her presence.

As if she'd been listening to his thoughts, Adelaide appeared in the cave's opening, carrying her torch. She looked different, her ethereal beauty unchanged but overshadowed by a dour expression on her face.

'Here you go, sweet Alex,' she said, handing him a bag of supplies.

'What's the matter?' Alex asked, surprised by the concern in his voice, which he wasn't sure was for her, or for his own self-preservation.

Adelaide sat down, crossing her long legs with a dancer's elegance. 'It's my brother. I don't think it will be long now.'

Alex's heartbeat intensified, some deep, primordial instinct warning him that those words should terrify him. 'Is he ill?'

'He's been ill for a long time, Alex. And we still haven't . . .'

Alex's heart continued to pound in his chest. He both wanted to know – and feared to know – what Adelaide would say next, but she remained silent. 'I'm sorry to hear that,' he said eventually, though his voice barely registered over the drumbeat in his ears.

Adelaide's flawless brow furrowed. 'We might have to trim that hair a little more. Otherwise, Mummy will say "no" again.'

Alex's pulse raced so fast he thought his heart might burst. What the hell did 'no' mean? Was she talking about letting him go? Perversely, sitting so close to his captor was somehow comforting. Her talk of her family was confusing, and it struck him that the most plausible explanation was that this was all the young woman's fantasy. What if there was no 'Mummy' or a sick brother? Somehow the thought that it was just the two of them was more frightening. 'What do you mean, Adelaide?' he managed to ask, though he wasn't sure if he'd spoken aloud or merely thought the words.

Adelaide stood in a single, fluid motion. 'Oh, look,' she said, bending down so her face was close to his, close enough that he could smell her skin, which carried a faint scent of the sea. Reaching behind him, she plucked something from the cave floor.

'It's a little mouse,' she said, holding the creature in her palm.

The mouse didn't move, either from shock or injury. Its tiny eyes peered at Adelaide, and for a moment, Alex thought it was possible for such a small creature to experience awe.

'I don't think he's well,' Alex said.

Adelaide rummaged in her pocket and produced a small cloth bag. 'Don't worry about that. This little thing will be beautiful forever,' she said, opening the bag and gently placing the mouse inside.

Chapter Ten

Maya had told Liam that a body matching Jordan Hayes' description had been found on Maenporth Beach in Falmouth. At this stage, Liam didn't know if Jordan's death was linked to the hessian bag victim, but he needed to see the body for himself to confirm that it was Jordan. After visiting Jordan's house and asking his friends to endure the harrowing task of identifying the faceless corpse from Sennen, he felt he owed them that much.

He waited in the sports centre café for George to finish cricket practice. They had planned to have dinner together, and as he waited he played through what he was going to tell his son. As George returned, all smiles and red faced, Liam told him the situation before dropping him off at his mother's house.

Every time work disrupted plans like this, Liam couldn't help but dwell on what George would think of him as he grew older. He already felt like an on-and-off parent – too much like his own parents had been – and worried that these small disappointments would accumulate in George's mind until they overshadowed everything else. Would all George remember of him one day be a collection of let-downs, days ruined by Liam's work?

Liam had promised to make it up to George that weekend, but the disappointment had been clear on the boy's face as they drove to

Kim's. His ex's knowing look at the door hadn't helped, and George had said a curt goodbye before heading inside.

Floodlights illuminated the rocky shoreline near Maenporth as he arrived forty minutes later. CSIs were busy documenting the site, but one look at the body was enough for Liam to know that the man was Jordan Hayes.

'Cause of death?' he asked Maya, who was shivering despite her layers of clothing.

'Too early to say for sure,' she replied, her voice muffled by her scarf. 'But his neck is broken, and there are multiple fractures. It's possible he was washed in from Pendennis Headland.'

'You think he was a jumper?'

'That was my first thought. And it would be my only thought if we weren't dealing with this other thing.'

Liam crouched for another look at the body. He didn't know much about Jordan Hayes beyond what his friends had told him. None of them had mentioned that Jordan might have been at such a low point that he would consider taking his own life. But Liam understood how some people, and especially men, often kept such struggles to themselves. Perhaps Friday night had been a mask, or worse, a secret farewell.

Jordan's death may not have been as horrific as the Sennen victim's, but it unsettled him. Liam had seen far too many dead bodies in his life, yet this one struck him differently. It was difficult to imagine that this mangled figure had ever been full of life. In the harsh glow of the floodlights, the body seemed almost artificial – a grotesque replica of Jordan Hayes; something incapable of ever having been alive.

'I'll notify his friends,' Liam said at last. 'There's a laptop at his place we'll need to collect.'

Returning to his car, he made the short drive to Charlie Thomas's apartment near the wharf to deliver the news. Charlie answered the door with the same haunted look he'd worn at the mortuary, though after Liam spoke this time his eyes brimmed with tears. He stepped aside to let Liam in, his voice cracking as he introduced him to his wife, Charlotte. She was cross-legged in an armchair, but pushed herself upright when she saw her husband crying.

'What's happened?' Charlotte asked.

Charlie, through tears, explained Jordan's death.

'I can't believe it,' she said, turning to Liam for confirmation.

It was a few minutes before Charlie had composed himself enough to speak. He sat beside his wife, their hands intertwined, while Liam took a seat opposite them. Behind him, rain battered against a floor-to-ceiling window, adding a rhythmic undertone to the conversation.

'What happened to him?' Charlotte asked.

'That's what we're trying to uncover. For now, we're treating it as a suspicious death,' Liam replied, his mind flickering to the hessian bag victim. 'Can you think of anyone who might have wanted to hurt Jordan?'

'You think someone killed him?' Charlotte asked, her eyes wide with shock.

'We don't know yet. But we are investigating a murder at the moment. The victim was a similar age to Jordan, but the circumstances appear to be quite different.'

'He could certainly piss people off, but not enough for anyone to want him dead,' Charlie said.

'Piss people off how?'

'As I said, he enjoyed a drink. It was like he had two personalities. Sober Jordan was quiet, even shy. Drunk Jordan . . . well, he could be a handful. Not much of a filter, if you know what I mean. That said, I don't remember him ever getting into a serious altercation. Not since we were younger, anyway. He had a bit of a silver tongue, didn't he, Char?'

Charlotte nodded, though she seemed more shaken than her husband.

'This is going to be difficult to hear,' Liam said, 'but do you think there's any chance Jordan might have taken his own life?'

Charlie slumped back in his chair at the question, pulling Charlotte with him. Liam was used to this reaction. People rarely welcomed such a question, as it often brought with it a sense of misplaced responsibility.

'Not that he said . . . I can't imagine,' Charlie said.

'I think he was lonely,' Charlotte said.

Charlie turned to look at his wife, surprised. 'Yeah, maybe. We never really talked about those things, you know?'

'None of you do,' Charlotte said. 'Charlie's the only one married, the only one in a stable relationship. The rest of them . . . well, they just piss their lives away. You should've seen the state of this one on Saturday,' she added, glancing at her sheepish-looking husband.

'Did Jordan ever say anything to you, then?' Liam asked.

Charlotte shook her head. 'I hardly see those lads any more. When I do, they aren't exactly the conversational type. They play football together, but sometimes I think that's just an excuse for the drinks afterwards. I don't know if he was suicidal or not, but I always got the impression he was lonely. I think they all are.'

Later that evening, Liam was still thinking about Charlotte's words as he arrived back at his flat. He was a bit older than Jordan and his friends, but the gap didn't feel that wide. The thought nagged at him. Suicide was one of the leading causes of death for men under thirty in the country. He'd heard too many stories like Jordan's before.

As he sat down, Liam thought about his own friends and colleagues – those in the force, the lifeboat crew, others from his navy days, even old school friends he sometimes bumped into while working. He resolved to check in on a few of them, making a mental note to reach out in the coming days.

Sleep that night was a battle. He lay in bed, staring at the ceiling, his thoughts cycling between the hessian bag victim, Jordan Hayes, and his own current predicament. Although he lived alone, Liam didn't feel truly lonely. His life was full of work, and when he wasn't on duty, he spent much of his free time with George. Yet, there were moments, fleeting but undeniable, when returning to his empty flat gave him a jolt of something he couldn't quite define. As he finally drifted off to sleep, he couldn't help but wonder if Jordan Hayes had felt the same way.

When the dreams did arrive, they came with an unsettling new dimension. Liam was back under the water, struggling for breath but this time he was trapped within a hessian bag. It shouldn't have made any difference – either way he was destined to drown – but the inclusion of the bag intensified his panic. His dream self knew that even if he did reach the surface, he would still be trapped. In his panic he began clawing, trying to get purchase to rip open the bag. But his struggles were made redundant by the pressure of the water surrounding the sack.

He woke covered in sweat. What sleep he'd managed had done little to lift his mood. Despite the freezing temperatures, Liam decided to go for a run before work to shift his mindset. St Ives was desolate at that hour, the streets and sands claimed only by the few hardy souls willing to brave the icy weather.

The ground was slick with patches of frost, forcing Liam to tread carefully as he made his way down the backstreets to the beach. Though the hessian bag victim had been found in Sennen, that case was all he could think about as he sprinted across the frozen sand.

The cold air burnt his lungs, but he welcomed it. Turning sharply, he sprinted back the way he came, repeating the cycle ten more times before heading home to shower and change. The workout, punishing as it was, left him sharper and ready for the day ahead.

◆ ◆ ◆

At headquarters, a small photo of Jordan Hayes had been added to the incident board. Until they had confirmation of how and why Jordan had died, his death couldn't be ruled out as unrelated to the hessian bag remains.

Liam knew better than to jump to conclusions. Jordan's laptop was with the tech team, and another sweep of his house was planned for later in the day. They were looking for anything that could confirm their suspicion that Jordan had been responsible for his own death.

The PSD officers were still lingering in the building. Liam had seen them on the ground floor that morning, deep in conversation with the assistant chief constable. Their continued presence was a mystery. If negligence had occurred during the Godrevy investigation, it was the Met's UCO who had jeopardised everything. Yet, as long as the PSD officers remained in Bodmin, a shadow hung over the department as dark and oppressive as the clouds outside.

After the morning briefing, Liam accompanied Maya to a meeting in Truro town centre with the retired CID officer DI Kevin Scott, who had left the force twelve years ago. The ex-officer stood to greet them as they entered the chain coffee shop. Liam handled the orders, opting for a black Americano, before returning to their table.

'I was just telling your guv'nor how I spotted you both as soon as you walked in,' Kevin said, nodding his thanks as he accepted his latte.

'Good detective never loses it,' Liam replied, humouring him.

Kevin smiled, wiping a line of froth from his upper lip after taking a sip. 'Heard about the body in Sennen. Nasty business, from what I gather. I suppose that's why I'm here?'

'A colleague from the lifeboat told me about the drug bust you led in the nineties,' Liam said, noting the self-satisfied grin still plastered across Kevin's face.

'Ah, yes, the coffee bean smugglers,' Kevin said with a chuckle. 'Thought it might be that. You mentioned your body was found in a bag? Similar to the ones those gangs used to smuggle drugs back in the day. Makes sense.'

Kevin, now in his late sixties, clearly enjoyed being the centre of attention. Liam couldn't help but think the man was probably as lonely as Jordan Hayes had been. He wondered what he himself would be like at Kevin's age. It was a sobering thought, made more poignant by the rapid decline he'd witnessed in his own mother. Ageing crept up too fast; it was an inevitability that Liam couldn't ignore.

'What can you tell us about that time?' Maya asked, bringing the conversation back on track.

Kevin recounted the investigation in meticulous detail, as if he'd been rehearsing his account for weeks. Despite his enthusiasm, nothing he said wasn't already in the file Liam and Maya had reviewed that morning. Kevin looked slightly taken aback when Liam interrupted him.

'What about the bags they smuggled the drugs in? Did you ever trace where they came from?'

The ex-DI sipped his cooling latte. 'The bags were the same kind used by the coffee company. Most of them were still filled with coffee beans, though all of it had to be destroyed.'

Liam showed him a picture of the hessian bag from Sennen, with and without the body still inside. 'I know it's a long time ago, but does this ring any bells?'

Kevin retrieved a pair of spectacles from his pocket and placed them on before taking the phone from Liam. He murmured to himself, squinting as he studied the image. 'How big is that bag?'

'About two metres in length,' said Maya.

'I don't think the coffee bags were that big, but I can't say for sure. Is there nothing in the file?'

'No specifics on measurements.'

Kevin shook his head. 'Sorry I can't help you more.' He paused, frowning. 'Funny thing, though. I saw one of those guys the other day.'

Liam exchanged a glance with Maya. 'What guys?'

'One of the smugglers. An old codger now, like me. He was put away for ten years. I saw him over at Heartlands. His granddaughter was playing with mine, would you believe!'

◆ ◆ ◆

The one-time smuggler, Michael Hughes, now lived in Hayle, a seaside town across the bay from St Ives. Liam knew the area well, both from his childhood and his time investigating the Godrevy case.

Maya turned left at the Copperhouse pub, driving uphill before turning into a street lined with terraced houses. They parked outside the address they had for Hughes, Maya knocking on the chipped paint of the front door.

Hughes was in his seventies, short and stocky, with an easy smile that only faltered slightly when they displayed their warrant cards. Liam imagined Kevin hadn't thought of Hughes as a threat any more. It was funny how appearances changed perceptions, how an ageing figure could inspire sympathy even when their past deeds warranted no such leniency.

Liam wasn't in the business of judging appearances, but he also knew better than to underestimate anyone.

'How can I help you, officers?' Hughes asked.

'May we come in, sir?' Maya asked.

Hughes' demeanour shifted. His smile faded as he folded his arms in front of him. 'Can I ask what this is about? My wife's inside, and . . .'

'We know of your past, Mr Hughes, and we don't want to upset anyone,' Maya said. 'But this is important.' She glanced at the darkening sky, her breath visible in the chill air.

'I'm afraid not,' Hughes said. 'I don't mean to annoy you, but my wife would freak if I let you in. I'm lucky she's stayed with me as it is.'

Liam explained about the body found in Sennen, detailing the corpse discovered inside a bag. Hughes squirmed at the mention of the bag, his eyes darting down the hallway behind him. 'What does this have to do with me?'

'When the boat you were on was seized,' Liam said, 'the drugs were being stored in hessian bags, labelled as coffee beans. We believe the bags are similar.'

Hughes laughed. 'I knew that bastard spotted me,' he said. 'Scott, right? God, I've never met a man who loved himself more.'

'What can you tell us about the bags you used?' Maya pressed.

'Oh, come on,' Hughes said, exasperated. 'That was over twenty-five years ago. Those bags were genuine. A shipment of coffee. We didn't buy them from Woolworths, for Christ's sake.'

It had always been a long shot, but Kevin Scott spotting Hughes was a coincidence that needed to be explored. Liam shifted the questioning to Hughes' recent movements, asking where he'd been in the days before the body washed ashore. But even as he spoke, the questions felt hollow.

Liam was about to ask if Hughes had known Jordan Hayes when Maya's phone buzzed. She checked the screen and glanced at Liam.

Liam handed Hughes a card with his details. 'If anything comes to mind, it's an active murder investigation,' he said.

Hughes took the card without a word and closed the door.

Maya's phone pinged as they returned to the car.

Liam stamped his feet against the cold. 'What is it?' he asked.

Maya smiled. 'Despite this waste of time, it looks like we might finally have an identification for hessian bag man.'

Chapter Eleven

Alex was surprised when Adelaide returned so soon. He rationed his supplies, spacing out the food between her visits, and there was still some left when she appeared as she always did: a glowing vision in the entrance to his section of the cave.

He rubbed his eyes, wondering if he was creating a vision of her that wasn't true. He hadn't even processed his internal reaction to her presence when the reason for her arrival became apparent.

She had a man with her, cuffed. 'It's raining,' she said, as if that explained everything.

The man grunted, stumbling, his eyes tiny slits, as Adelaide eased him to the ground.

'Who's this?' asked Alex.

'You don't need to concern yourself with that,' Adelaide said. 'What you can do is stay quiet while I get him ready.'

Alex watched silently as Adelaide clipped the stranger's hair, then pulled a brown jumper over the man's head. 'Can you help me, sweet Alex?'

Alex stepped forward, his chain rattling behind him. The slack in the metal gave him a momentary thought. He could pull her close, loop the chain around her neck, and end this. But the strength to act wasn't there. Nor, if he were being honest with himself, was the true desire.

'You should be thanking me, sweet Alex,' Adelaide said as he helped guide the man's limp arms through the pullover's sleeves. 'There, what do you think?'

She held the man upright in a sitting position. Despite his lolling head and glazed eyes, there was something familiar about him. 'Was he out walking his dog too?' Alex asked, instantly regretting it.

Adelaide let go of the man, and he slumped on to the rocky ground. 'Now, that isn't nice, Alex,' she said. 'I told you, you should be thanking me.'

'Thanking you for what?'

'I found him for you,' she said, pulling the man back upright. She played with his hair, cradling his face in her hands, before securing him to one of the chains bolted into the cave wall. 'I'll be back when he wakes up,' she said, disappearing before Alex could respond.

What did she mean, *found him for you*? Would this man, who looked so familiar, be a permanent addition to Alex's prison? The thought churned in his stomach. It wasn't that he didn't want company – he was desperate for it during the long, quiet hours spent contemplating his existence – but the man's arrival felt like a message. This was permanent. Adelaide, and the 'Mummy' he had yet to meet, intended to keep him here forever.

Alex tried to sleep but couldn't. He kept waiting for the man to wake, wanting answers. How had he got here? Why was he here? But the stranger remained unconscious. At one point, Alex crept closer and pressed two fingers to the man's neck to check for a pulse. The skin was cold and clammy, but the pulse was steady and strong.

'You shouldn't touch him, Alex,' came Adelaide's voice.

How long had she been standing there, watching? Now that he thought about it, Alex wasn't even sure she'd left. This place played tricks like that.

She placed her fingers over his and removed his hand from the man's neck. A shiver ran through Alex. He wasn't sure if it was an unpleasant sensation or not.

'We don't want your scent on him, do we? It might change Mummy's mind,' Adelaide said.

She lifted the stranger effortlessly, her strength startling. From her pocket, she pulled a small vial. Popping it open, she held it under the man's nose. Even from several metres away, Alex recoiled at the sharp sting of ammonia in the air.

The man convulsed as if jolted by electricity. His bleary eyes flickered open, and he took in the cave and its occupants without a word.

'What do you think, Alex?' Adelaide asked, her hand still gripping the man's hair. 'Do you think he's ready?'

'Ready for what?'

Adelaide tousled the man's hair, her fingers lingering. 'For Mummy, silly.'

Alex shrugged, and the smile on her face warped into a sudden, hideous grimace. Her beauty twisted into something grotesque, her eyes darkening, her mouth pulling into an inhuman snarl. Then, just as quickly, the vision vanished, leaving her glowing and ethereal once more.

'We need this to work, Alex,' Adelaide said. 'Time is running out, and I really don't want you to meet Mummy. I *really* don't.'

She led the stranger out of the cave. Alex watched them go, leaving him alone and bereft once more.

Chapter Twelve

By the time Liam and Maya returned to headquarters, a photo of the hessian bag victim had been pinned to the crime board in the incident room. Liam stopped short at the sight of the handsome, smiling man staring back at him.

'Frank Oakley,' said Jack Lawson, his gaze fixed on the photo, not making eye contact with either of them. 'We sent out the dental records as far locally as we could. Got lucky. One of the dentists is part of a UK-wide chain, and they had Mr Oakley's X-rays on file.'

Mr Oakley.

The name felt jarring to Liam. He was half-relieved that they could now treat the victim with the respect he deserved rather than using the hessian bag moniker, but it also made the crime feel more immediate, more personal. The name transformed the body into a person. Liam fought back the surge of anger and dismay at the thought of what had been done to him, trapped in a hessian bag as knives and mallets rained down.

'What do we know?' Maya asked, taking a seat.

'We've got an address for him in Bedfordshire, near Luton. He was reported missing two months ago. Apparently, he visited Cornwall – Wadebridge, specifically – during that time, but his family doesn't know if he ever made it home. Parents are still in Bedfordshire. Mum, dad, two sisters.'

'He lived alone?' Liam asked, thinking of Jordan Hayes, who had been a similar age to Oakley.

'Yeah. He was doing temp work, so no one really noticed when he didn't show up for work. Luton nick reckons he could've been missing for a week or more before the parents reported it. Doesn't sound like he was much of a communicator.'

Identifying the victim was a breakthrough, but there was no sense of relief in the room. Liam spent the afternoon on the phone with the officer who had overseen the initial investigation into Oakley's disappearance. The work had been thorough, and Liam recognised the familiar patterns of a well-documented but frustratingly fruitless missing persons case.

The parents had been informed of their son's death. With no need for a formal identification, Frank's body would be released to the family for burial. The parents had agreed to meet with Maya and Liam the following day.

Maya suggested they travel to Bedfordshire that evening to speak to the family first thing in the morning. Liam, who always kept spare clothes in his locker for such occasions, agreed. Before heading upcountry, they planned to stop in Wadebridge, at the last-known location they had for Frank.

The drive from Bodmin to Wadebridge took just under an hour. Liam drove as Maya sat quietly in the passenger seat, her gaze fixed on the passing scenery, the hedgerows blurring into the misty countryside beyond.

As they approached Wadebridge, the town began to take shape, a cluster of slate-roofed buildings nestled along the winding River Camel. Liam turned off the A39, the road narrowing as it curved into the heart of the town with its quaint shops and small cafés.

The old stone bridge that gave Wadebridge its name came into view, arching over the river. Mist curled along the water's surface, shrouding the scene with an almost serene beauty. For a fleeting moment, the picturesque setting felt at odds with the grim reality of their investigation. It was hard to imagine that anything so monstrous as the events leading to Frank Oakley's death could have taken place here.

Liam dismissed his musings as they drove further inland, his focus shifting to the practicalities of what may have happened. Sennen was about sixty miles from Wadebridge by road and it would have been all but impossible for a body to have made its way from the River Camel to the coast of Sennen naturally. 'If he was killed here, it's a long way for a body to have travelled,' he said.

Maya, appearing preoccupied as she gazed out of the window, murmured her agreement as Liam pulled into the caravan park where Frank Oakley had stayed. The site resembled a building project more than a holiday destination. A prefab hut served as reception, and was surrounded by bags of cement and piles of bricks. As Liam stepped out of the car, shivering against the cold, he found it hard to imagine anyone willingly staying here. He wondered how much effort it would take for the owners to turn the place into somewhere appealing by summer.

Maya knocked on the door of the hut before opening it. The temperature inside wasn't much better; a man in a bulky puffer jacket looked up from behind his desk.

'You the police who called?' he asked.

Maya nodded, and both officers displayed their warrant cards. 'Mr Jebbison?' she asked.

'Adam,' he said, gesturing to the chairs opposite him. 'You wanted to talk about someone who stayed here recently? Take a seat. Sorry about the cold. I'd rather work through it than waste money on heating.'

Liam sat, still shivering, and glanced around at the sparse, unwelcoming office. 'Do you have people staying on-site now?'

'A few. This place doesn't usually look so up in the air. We use the winter months to catch up on maintenance when we can.'

Maya showed him a picture on her phone. 'We're here about this man, Frank Oakley.'

Recognition flickered across Jebbison's face. He handed Maya two sheets of A4 paper. 'I remember him. After your colleague called, I put together the details we have on file. Not much, I'm afraid. He booked ahead, though, so we have his home address.'

Maya handed the papers to Liam. 'He was here the first week of October?'

'That's right.'

'How does the check-in process work?' Liam asked.

'Most of it's online. When he arrived, he would've given us his reference code, and we'd hand over his keys.'

'Did you personally check him in?' Liam asked.

Jebbison nodded. 'Yes, that's my initials next to the check-in status.'

'What was he like?'

'I'll be honest, I barely remember. He was polite, but once they've checked in, we don't see much of them unless they visit the bar or there's an issue with the caravan. The bar was shut that week, and he didn't contact us once.'

'And what about when he left?' Maya asked.

'He dropped his keys in the deposit box.'

'You saw him do that?'

'No, but the keys were there in the box.'

'On the day he was supposed to leave?' asked Liam.

Jebbison hesitated, frowning. 'Probably. Could've been the day before. I check the box every day around 3 p.m. Sometimes people leave early.'

'So, you didn't actually see him leave?'

'No, sorry.'

'And he had a car?' Maya asked.

'Yes, a red Outlander,' Jebbison said, glancing at his computer screen for confirmation.

They were already aware of the vehicle and had issued a nationwide alert on the number plate. 'You don't remember seeing the car leave the site?' Liam said.

'Not on either of the days. We don't record comings and goings. It's not time-efficient, and we can't afford any high-tech equipment. We're a budget park.' Jebbison paused, his expression shifting slightly. 'There was one thing, though, I thought about after speaking to your colleague.'

Maya tilted her head, prompting him to continue.

'I was working late one night and noticed Mr Oakley returning. It was about 11.30 p.m. I'm always a little concerned when I see people driving back at that time of night. You know, it's just after the pubs kick out, and we've had issues with drunk drivers before, especially in the summer.'

'You think Mr Oakley had been drinking?' Maya asked.

'No. At least, I don't think so. But I did notice something.' Jebbison hesitated. 'He wasn't alone.'

Chapter Thirteen

The description of the second person seen in Frank Oakley's car on the possible night of his disappearance was vague, but it still felt like a small breakthrough in the investigation. The caravan park manager had described a woman wearing a baseball cap. He hadn't been able to see much of her face but claimed he'd seen enough to consider her attractive, noting her large eyes.

As descriptions went, it wasn't much, but it was enough for Maya to order a CSI team from headquarters to search the caravan Frank Oakley had stayed in. Despite two other sets of guests having stayed in it since, it was a lead they couldn't ignore.

As they drove through the night towards Bedfordshire, Maya broke the silence. 'How's that teacher friend of yours?'

Maya had been involved in the Godrevy investigation and knew first-hand what Millie had endured. She was the only person from headquarters Liam could speak to about such things, but tonight he didn't feel much like talking.

'I'm not too sure. We haven't seen much of each other lately.'

'I know you don't need me to tell you, but it must have been so hard on her. I imagine she just needs time.'

Liam's thoughts briefly drifted to the Indian Ocean, where his breathing equipment had failed during an SBS operation. Even years later, the memory always caused a tightness in his body. Today was no different. His hand unconsciously moved to his chest as he took a deep breath. He couldn't deny Maya's point. Though he'd regained some of his old confidence with open water, the incident would always be with him.

He wanted to tell Maya he understood, that he wished Millie would open up to him so he could help her. But the words failed him. In his mind, he heard Kim accusing him of using Millie's anxiety as an excuse to avoid commitment. He pushed the thought aside and turned up the car's heating.

'You're probably right,' he said, signalling he didn't want to discuss it further.

'It was hard on you as well. I think you forget that,' said Maya, clearly not ready to let it go.

Liam blinked away images of a man being dangled into the sea, pulled in and out of the water until he was drowned. Liam had suffered the same torture before being left for dead as well, and he shivered recalling those minutes spent in the water waiting for rescue. 'I don't know what to say, Maya. It was hard on everyone. I guess it comes with the territory for us, but Millie isn't used to this life.'

Maya looked at him. 'Give her some time, but don't leave it too long.'

'OK.'

'OK?' said Maya, a lilt to her voice as she checked he wasn't being flippant.

Liam held his hands up, smiling. 'I appreciate your advice, thank you.'

'Don't get too schmaltzy now,' said Maya, with a grin, as she switched on the radio.

◆ ◆ ◆

The following morning, Liam went for a run before meeting Maya for breakfast at a chain hotel on the outskirts of Luton. Running on unfamiliar roads through a desolate industrial estate had felt strange. Less than twenty-four hours away from home, and he already missed the proximity of the sea.

At 10 a.m., they arrived at the Oakley family's home. Liam was surprised by the relative opulence of the detached house, nestled in a leafy suburban area. It reminded him never to jump to conclusions about anyone or anything.

The door was answered by Frank's sister, Megan, a poised twenty-nine-year-old, who led them into the living room where their parents waited. The family was particularly good-looking; not only was Megan striking, but the parents were well dressed and athletic. Both rose to shake hands with the detectives, their movements deliberate but polite.

As Megan made tea, Maya confirmed the reason for their visit. Liam watched as the parents listened, their grief restrained. People processed loss in different ways, and though the Oakleys were upset, Liam saw a quiet acceptance in them. It felt as though they'd been bracing themselves for this moment for weeks, perhaps months. Hearing the news didn't seem to bring relief, only confirmation of something they already knew deep down.

'How was your relationship with your son?' Maya asked, as Megan returned from the kitchen carrying the drinks.

Liam noted the quick exchange of glances between mother and daughter as he accepted his cup of tea.

'Things were a little strained,' said Mr Oakley, seated beside his wife. Their bodies were close enough to touch, but there was no embrace, no hand-holding.

'In what way?' Liam asked.

'Frank is . . . was always a bit wild,' Mrs Oakley said. 'He started drinking with his friends at an early age, and that soon turned into drug use.'

'We tried to help him. We did everything we could,' Mr Oakley added. 'We gave him a little money. Paid for him to see a counsellor, but he rarely went.'

'When did you last see him?' Maya asked.

All three family members glanced at one another. Liam caught the shared regret in their expressions – downcast eyes, heavy sighs – but there was no hint of accusation. The regret was mutual, something Mrs Oakley put into words.

'Christmas last year,' she said.

'You haven't seen your son in eleven months?' Maya asked.

'It wasn't our choice,' Mr Oakley replied. 'He showed up last Christmas completely out of it. We had a blazing row, and he left. We've tried reaching out to him since, but . . . he didn't want anything to do with us.'

They looked like a close-knit family, but Liam wondered if Frank had felt like an outcast, and whether that sense of exclusion had exacerbated his behaviour and addictions – or perhaps was a result of it.

'You knew he'd gone to Cornwall?' Liam asked.

Mrs Oakley glanced briefly at her daughter again, as if they shared a secret unknown to Mr Oakley. 'I happened to call him as he was driving down there. For once, he answered.'

'Did he say why he was going?' Maya asked.

'He was never very talkative,' Mrs Oakley replied. 'He just said he was going down for a few days and I . . .' She hesitated, shooting a look at her husband. 'I invited him for Christmas.'

Liam watched Mr Oakley's reaction closely. He masked it well, but the slight widening of his eyes betrayed him. This was news to him.

'What did he say?' Liam asked.

'He said he would think about it,' Mrs Oakley said. Mr Oakley shifted uncomfortably, moving his leg so it no longer touched his wife's.

'Was he travelling alone?' Liam asked.

'As far as I'm aware.'

'Was he planning to meet anyone?' Maya added.

'He wouldn't tell me things like that.'

Maya described the woman the caravan park manager had seen in Frank's car the night before he left the site. Mrs Oakley shook her head.

'I wouldn't know anything about that.'

'He was never short of female attention,' Mr Oakley said, with a faint edge Liam couldn't ignore. Was it resentment? Jealousy? He couldn't tell for sure.

They revisited the questions the family had already been asked. Did Frank have enemies? Could they think of any other areas he might have visited? Had there been any sightings of his car?

The answers offered little that could immediately help, but Liam was glad they'd made the journey. Something felt off about the family, and knowing what might prove useful as the investigation unfolded.

Both parents stood as Liam and Maya prepared to leave, but Mr Oakley told his wife he would walk them to the front door.

'If you can think of anything else,' Maya said, handing Mr Oakley her card as they stepped into the cold.

'There is one thing,' Mr Oakley said, hesitating. 'It's not a secret, but you might not be aware . . . and I guess you should probably know. I'm not Frank's biological father.'

Mr Oakley explained that although his name was on Frank's birth certificate, the boy's biological father had died in a road traffic accident before Frank was born. Liam's gaze lingered on a family photograph hanging near the front door, showing Frank and Grace as toddlers. He wondered if not being Frank's biological father had shaped Mr Oakley's relationship with his son and if, back when that photo was taken, he could have imagined how strained things would become by the time Frank reached adulthood.

After asking a few questions about Frank's biological father, Liam and Maya left for the local police station to pick up the keys to Frank's house.

'That was all a bit strange,' Liam said as they drove. He couldn't shake the image of the photograph, the smiling little boy who had somehow become a murder victim.

'He sort of blurted that out, didn't he?' Maya replied. 'It's unlikely we'd have found out otherwise.'

Liam had been wondering the same thing. If Frank's biological father were still alive, it might have been relevant, but as it stood, the revelation only cast an odd shadow over Mr Oakley. 'Assuaging his guilt?'

'You think he followed his son to Cornwall, killed him, wrapped him in a bag, and sent him out to sea?' Maya asked.

'Stranger things have happened,' Liam replied, with a laugh.

'I think he was trying to separate himself from the rest of the family,' Maya said. 'Did you notice how the parents sat next to each other?'

Liam nodded. 'I did. Neither of them, or the daughter, for that matter, looked to be in mourning.'

'Happens,' Maya said. 'People play at happy families, but sometimes it means someone gets excluded.'

Liam thought about Megan's comments regarding Frank's addictions. He wondered how much of Frank's exile from the family had been self-inflicted and how much had been imposed by his parents. The parallels to his own upbringing – his father's premature death, his mother's addictions – were unavoidable. It made him think of George, and how Liam had been forced to cut short their time together after cricket the other day. Sometimes things like that were unavoidable, but the thought that he would ever be so estranged from his son was terrifying. He promised himself to work harder on spending time with George, vowing that whatever happened in their relationship, they would never end up the same way as Frank Oakley and his family.

After retrieving keys from the letting agents, they stopped at a garage for a quick lunch of pre-made sandwiches and coffee before heading to Frank Oakley's house where they met the CSI team who had been called to search the house.

Frank had lived in a run-down terraced house in a less salubrious area than his parents, reminiscent of Jordan Hayes' home in Falmouth. Dressed in protective uniform, Liam knocked on the door before entering, only to be greeted by a mound of post blocking the entrance.

'I thought the days of junk mail were over,' he said, lifting the pile and carrying it into the open-plan living room, where he dumped it on the sofa.

The house was in disarray and showed signs of long-term neglect. The kitchen sink was piled with dirty dishes, presumably left by Frank before heading to Cornwall.

They began their search. Despite the mess, it became clear that Frank had lived a minimalist lifestyle. His belongings were sparse, a few clothes in the wardrobe and an old laptop, which was bagged for analysis.

Returning to the living room, Liam sighed, reflecting on the scene. He wondered what someone would think if they searched his own flat after his death. Though he lived a more disciplined life and owned more possessions, was there really that much of a difference?

A CSI had been working on a pile of junk mail from the sofa, and handed a small package to Maya. 'Handwritten,' he said, holding up an A5 padded envelope. 'Postmarked Penzance.'

'Open it,' Maya said, handing it to Liam.

Liam nodded and tore open the envelope. Inside, the contents were wrapped in red crêpe paper. Something about the vivid colour put him on edge. Peeling back the tissue, he revealed a miniature hessian bag, coated in red dye.

Liam's brow furrowed as he pressed a finger against the bag's surface, feeling something soft inside.

Chapter Fourteen

It wasn't until late afternoon that the hessian bag was opened. Given the potential significance of what they might find inside, the decision was made to transport the small replica bag back to Bodmin for analysis by the forensic lab team.

Despite it being a Saturday, Maya once more called in some favours and managed to have the bag examined the same day. Dr Sarah Penrose, a trace evidence analyst, took swabs for DNA and used chemical fuming to search for fingerprints before unstitching the bag.

Liam watched, unsure of what to expect. With steady hands and the use of tweezers, Sarah removed what appeared to be a hand-stitched doll from inside.

'Intricate work,' she remarked, placing the doll on the table under the lab lights.

'It's him, isn't it?' Maya said.

Liam stared at the doll, its crude features unmistakably resembling Frank Oakley's photograph, the version of him before the horrific injuries. The doll even wore miniature versions of the same jeans and jumper Frank had been wearing when he was found.

'It could be. Same clothes. Only this time, they didn't stab the face eighty-seven times,' said Liam, frowning.

The doll was left with Sarah for further testing as Liam and Maya returned to CID, where they updated the team in the incident room.

'Anyone ever come across something like this before?' Maya asked, scanning the room.

'Are we assuming the killer sent the doll to the victim's house?' Jack asked, leaning forward.

Liam uploaded an image of the envelope to the whiteboard. It was covered in a neat array of postage stamps that added up to the correct postage.

'As you can see,' Liam said, 'the envelope is postmarked Penzance. However, due to its size, it was likely posted in a regular postbox before being processed at the main sorting office. It could have come from anywhere in the local region. The date stamp is the Monday after Mr Oakley's body was found. For now, we're working with the theory that the killer – or someone connected to them – sent this replica to Mr Oakley's house after his death.'

Photos of both Frank Oakley and the doll were added to the whiteboard. The resemblance was unsettling.

'The detail is remarkable,' said DCI Hargreaves, who had decided to sit in on the briefing.

'I wonder if they made it before they killed him,' Jack mused.

'They could have worked from photographs,' Maya said.

'Or from memory,' Liam added, his mind flashing back to Frank's featureless corpse.

'I guess it's a type of preservation, isn't it?'

'What do you mean, Jack?' Liam asked.

'Like an Egyptian mummy in their tomb, preserved forever.'

'I imagine it's feasible that we used to bury the dead in bags before coffins became a thing. Could be some kind of link there.'

The room fell silent before Liam recalled his conversation with Lauren from the Sennen lifeboat crew. 'There's a legend that in some areas they sealed offerings in hessian bags to appease the sea gods.'

'You mean the Bucca?' Jack asked.

Liam raised an eyebrow. 'I didn't realise it was that well known.'

Jack looked away, his expression thoughtful. 'I come from a fishing family,' he said. 'Never heard of human sacrifice, though.'

'Animal sacrifice?' asked Liam.

'Nothing like that. From what I understand, offerings were things like bread – wine, maybe. I think they could have offered fish as well, but no idea if they were alive or dead. My dad used to drop pieces of bread before setting off.'

'OK, I think it's worth doing a bit more research into that,' Maya said. 'We should also contact local arts and crafts places, especially around Penzance and Sennen. Let's find out how someone might go about making a doll like that. There could be templates or workshops.'

'I'll do a deeper dive into Frank's family and friends,' Liam added. 'See if anyone has a history of making these types of things. And I'll take another look at Jordan Hayes' place, just in case we missed anything there.'

Liam sent a quick text to Millie before heading back to Jordan's house. He still hadn't heard from her since her last non-committal message, and he assumed they wouldn't be seeing each other that weekend. But after his conversation with Maya, he wanted to talk to Millie more than ever, if only to tell her he understood what she was going through. He suggested meeting for a drink either that evening or the following afternoon before setting off for Falmouth.

By the time he reached Jordan's house, the message remained unread. Letting himself in with the key they'd been given after

Jordan's death, Liam took another look around. This time, he focused on searching for any sign of a cloth doll. He started with the post, but this time it was nothing but flyers. He worked through the house in methodical fashion, but came up empty-handed.

Although Jordan and Frank were of a similar age, Liam couldn't find any other meaningful connection between their cases. He wasn't sure if he was trying to will a link into existence to make sense of the chaos, but there was nothing in Jordan's house to suggest his death was anything other than suicide.

After locking up, Liam drove home to St Ives. The night was still and clear, the deserted back roads taking on an eerie, almost unwelcoming quality. Against his better judgement, his mind wandered to the Bucca Dhu legend, picturing bodies wrapped in hessian bags, preserved as offerings. He thought about the replica doll sent to Frank Oakley's house, intact within its hessian prison, and couldn't help but picture the victim inside the actual bag, still alive and not knowing what was about to happen to him.

If the killer had sent the doll – as seemed likely – there had to be some significance to the gesture. Was it an apology? A twisted reminder of who Frank had been before his horrific death? Was the killer cruelly toying with Frank's family in the aftermath of his murder? Or was it somehow linked to Bucca Dhu – the doll a keepsake, a twisted memento of the man who had been used as a sacrifice?

The Oakleys hadn't been shown the doll yet. Liam could only imagine the torment it would cause them.

At home, Liam checked his phone for a reply from Millie. Still nothing. With little else to distract him, he decided to have an early night. It wasn't how he'd pictured his Saturday evening, but he welcomed the prospect of extra sleep. Cocooning himself in the warmth of his duvet, he drifted off within seconds.

◆ ◆ ◆

He woke at six to an unfamiliar glow filtering through his curtains. Opening them, he stared out in disbelief at the sight of St Ives blanketed in snow.

Pouring a coffee, Liam sat by the window and marvelled at the scene. It looked like something out of a Christmas movie – the charming Cornish town dusted in pristine white. He checked his phone to confirm it was still November. Snow was rare in Cornwall, especially along the coast, and he couldn't recall a time it had fallen this early; he guessed the recent cold snap had made it possible.

Liam wished he could see George today, to share the novelty of the snow with him, but it wasn't his weekend. He considered calling Millie, knowing they needed to at least talk about what was happening between them, but it was too early, so he showered and dressed before heading into town.

The snow was still falling – light, fluffy flakes adding to the few inches already settled. As he walked downhill, making fresh footprints in the untouched white, he felt a flicker of childlike joy. But the feeling was tinged with something else. The gnawing sense that the moment would be so much better if he could share it with someone.

He found a café open along the wharf and ordered a coffee. Outside, the beach was a carpet of snow, the stark white contrasting with the deep blue of the ocean waiting in the background. Soon, the tide would reclaim the shore, washing the snow away. Liam decided he would wait until nine to call Millie. He couldn't remember ever seeing such a sight in St Ives, having lived here, on and off, all his life. He didn't want to waste the opportunity to share it with her.

After breakfast, he walked along the beach, savouring the crunch of snow underfoot, then made his way to the back roads leading to Porthmeor Beach. By the time his phone read 9.20 a.m., his earlier resolve about Millie had faded. He decided that maybe it was for the best that things had slowed down between them, and told himself he would wait for her to reach out to him instead.

Even so, when his phone rang twenty minutes later, as he was climbing Alexandra Road, he couldn't deny the flicker of anticipation. That feeling turned to disappointment when the screen displayed 'Unknown Caller'.

He took in a deep breath, debating whether or not to answer. It was supposed to be his day off, but in reality there was no such thing in an active murder investigation. 'Kilshaw,' he answered.

'Sir, PC Peter Thorne from headquarters. We just received a call you might want to follow up on.'

'Alright. What's the situation?'

'A couple from Penzance called in a few minutes ago. They say they've only just learnt about the body found in Sennen last week. Thing is, they believe they saw something suspicious the night before the body was discovered.'

'Suspicious how?'

'That's the thing, sir. They claim to have been on the beach late that night, early morning. From a distance, they think they saw someone carrying what could have been a body to the shore.'

Liam stopped walking. 'How certain are they about what they saw?'

'Not very. It was dark, and they weren't close. But they seemed shaken enough to report it now.'

'Got it. Where are they?'

'They're at home. I've got the address if you want to follow up.'

'Send it to me. I'll head over shortly.'

Liam hung up, a familiar weight settling on his shoulders. He hadn't expected his day off to last, but the prospect of a new lead reignited his focus. If the couple's story held any truth, it might be the type of opening they'd been looking for.

By the time he returned home, retrieved his car, and set off, the snow was thawing. Soon, it would have melted away, becoming nothing more than a fleeting memory.

The main roads were clear, the day's traffic having rid the surface of any settled snow. Yet, as he approached Sennen, he was pleased to see a light dusting of white still clinging to the buildings and pavements.

He parked near the town's front and made his way towards the café where he'd arranged to meet the couple who had called in that morning. On the way, he stopped by the lifeboat house, peering through the frost-tinted windows, but Lauren and the rest of the team were nowhere to be seen. Continuing along the promenade, he passed excited children bundled up in scarves and coats, playing in the remnants of the snow with their families.

The café was bustling, but Liam spotted a couple in their twenties sitting near the entrance. They weren't speaking to each other. The man was absorbed in his phone, while the woman sat stiffly, her discomfort suggesting they were waiting for someone.

'Ella and Jacob?' Liam asked, as he approached the table.

The man looked up, startled, dropping his phone on to the table.

'Yes, I'm Ella Howard, and this is my boyfriend, Jacob Perry,' the woman replied, her eyes briefly flicking to Liam's perfectly hairless scalp, and then to his eyes with a shy grin, as he displayed his warrant card.

Liam sat down, ordered hot drinks for the three of them, and encouraged the pair to recount what they'd told headquarters.

'We've been away for the past week, an arts festival up north,' Ella said, as their drinks arrived. She took a sip of her hot chocolate and winced at the heat. 'We only found out about the body when we got back yesterday.'

Liam wasn't sure if Frank Oakley's death had made the national news, but their explanation seemed plausible for now. Ella explained how they'd been sitting on the rocks near the shore late that night when they noticed someone arrive. It was dark, but they thought they'd seen the person carrying something heavy.

'And what time was this?' Liam asked, directing his question to Jacob, who had yet to say much.

Jacob bit his lower lip and exchanged a glance with Ella before replying. 'About 3 a.m.'

Liam leant back and took a sip of his coffee, trying to remain neutral. He recalled how bitterly cold it had been on the beach last week. The fierce wind biting at his face and stinging his eyes. He suppressed a look of disbelief. 'You were both on the beach at 3 a.m.?'

The pair lowered their gazes, looking guilty, and Liam thought he understood why. 'You'd taken something? Look, you can tell me, you're not going to get in trouble.'

Ella glanced nervously at Jacob, then admitted, 'We'd taken some shrooms. We like to go to the beach when we do it. You know, for the sounds and the water.'

'But it must have been freezing.'

'We have these coats,' Jacob said. 'Thermal ones, full-body things.'

'You take your pastime seriously,' Liam said, earning a nervous laugh from Ella, who had been watching him intently since he sat down.

Jacob fidgeted, glancing between Liam and Ella. 'Look, man, we're here to do you a favour.'

'Alright,' Liam said, gesturing for Jacob to continue. 'Tell me exactly what you think you saw.'

'We're not sure. We were . . . you know, tripping, but I remember saying to Ella that there was someone carrying something. Something big. You remember that?' Jacob asked Ella.

'I do. It was a bit freaky. We wondered why anyone would be on the beach at that time of night.'

Liam frowned at the irony. 'Seriously?'

'We don't usually see anyone. That's why we like it.'

'So, you saw them carrying something?'

Ella shifted her gaze from Liam to Jacob and back again. 'We read in the paper about the body being found in some kind of bag. Is that true?'

'What do you think they were carrying?' Liam pressed.

'It could have been that,' Ella replied. 'Whatever they were carrying, it was on their shoulders.'

'And then what?' Liam asked, suppressing his doubts about the report.

Ella clenched her teeth. 'I'm afraid I lost it a bit.'

'Lost it?' Liam repeated.

'She started tripping her arse off,' Jacob said, with a grin.

'Jacob,' Ella said, with a hint of humour.

Jacob shrugged. 'She panicked. Desperate to leave. So we headed back. When I last looked over, I couldn't see them any more, but by that point, I wasn't paying much attention. I was focused on calming Ella down.'

'Was it a man or woman who was carrying the object?'

'It was impossible to tell.'

'Did you see anything else that might help?' Liam asked.

Ella avoided his gaze, her eyes fixed on the ground, clearly embarrassed.

'There was a Land Rover,' Jacob said. 'It was parked next to our car, but I don't remember it being there earlier.'

'A Land Rover? Did you get a number plate?'

Jacob shook his head. 'I think it was a Land Rover. An older model, proper off-road type with the spare wheel on the back.'

'Colour?'

'It was dark, man. Sorry. But it was two-tone, you know? The roof was a different colour. Real old model.'

Liam thanked the pair and left for his car. The tide was coming in, already dissolving what remained of the snow along the shore. As he walked, he called Maya to relay the meeting.

'Do you believe them?' Maya asked.

'I wouldn't use them as court witnesses, but I think they saw something.'

'We'd need to check with the doc again. According to him, the body had been in the sea for at least twenty-four hours.'

Liam thought back to the Godrevy investigation and how the killer had tormented victims by repeatedly dumping them in the sea and recovering them before they drowned, a process that continued until their eventual death. 'Maybe they were moving the body,' he suggested, picturing a boat dragging the hessian bag along the water.

'Let's say, for argument's sake, someone did leave the body on the beach. Why would they do that?' Maya asked.

'Could be they dumped it in the water and hoped the tide would take it out.'

'That would be foolhardy, and why submerge it in the water in the first place?'

'Maybe they wanted the body to be found.'

'I don't like the sound of someone making a statement like that,' Maya said.

'Especially now we know they sent the doll to the victim.'

The line went quiet, both of them lost in thought.

'I wonder what Frank Oakley did to piss them off so much,' Maya said.

'Yes, and what happens when someone else does the same thing?'

◆ ◆ ◆

Millie texted just as Liam was climbing back into his car.

I can meet tomorrow night. 8 p.m. at the Lifeboat?

Liam tried not to read too much into the curtness of the message, but it was clear something was bothering her. If nothing else, he supposed, it would be clarified tomorrow.

See you then, he replied, feeling like a teenager as he debated whether to add an *x* to the message. He decided against it.

With no pressing plans until his meeting with Millie, Liam headed to the Sloop pub in St Ives to meet some of the lifeboat crew in the afternoon. By then, the snow was a distant memory, its only remnants the occasional frozen patch hidden from the day's sun.

The pub had an old-world charm, the smell of beer greeting him as he ducked beneath the low ceilings.

A handful of the crew were drinking, though most were on call. Liam had taken himself off the roster since Frank Oakley's body had been found, though the lifeboat hadn't had a callout since. It was strange sitting with so many new faces. Just a year ago, the team had included three of the culprits involved in the Godrevy Island deaths.

Phil Skewes, the new coxswain, handed him a cider. 'Glad you could make it. How's the case going?'

Liam noted the pause as the rest of the team fell quiet. They all knew what he'd endured during the Godrevy investigation and likely thought he was eyeing them as potential suspects. 'Same old.

Long process,' he said, careful not to mention the doll sent to Frank Oakley's house.

'When will you be back on rotation?' asked Janice Selby, the lifeboat's office manager. 'Always good to have experienced hands on board.'

The team smiled at him, and Liam was thankful to still feel accepted. Looking around, he realised how much younger they seemed, making him feel like an elder statesman despite Phil being twenty years his senior. 'Once we've wrapped up this investigation,' he said, wincing slightly as he sipped the cider.

He stayed for a couple of hours, enjoying the company, though his thoughts remained on the Frank Oakley case. Before leaving, he bought a round of drinks. 'Stay safe,' he said, feeling the eyes of his team, and perhaps the entire pub, on him as he stepped outside. A near gale-force gust of wind greeted him, mercifully at his back as he made the climb home.

Shutting the door behind him, Liam made some pasta while the wind rattled against the flat. He thought of the young couple he'd met that morning, how they'd braved similar conditions last weekend while high on magic mushrooms. He wondered if, in their hallucinatory state, they'd conjured an image of Bucca Dhu in their minds, and if the storm had been mild compared to what might have come had Frank Oakley not died.

The thought brought a wave of irritation. It was absurd to entertain such superstitions, though he couldn't deny that a belief in Bucca Dhu, or any such myth, might eventually help lead them to the killer.

Exhaustion overtook him, and he was asleep by 10 p.m. The week had been relentless, and he knew his workload wouldn't ease anytime soon. Sleep was his best option.

His dreams were storm-haunted. As so often happened, he found himself beneath the sea's surface, lungs burning, clawing for breath, with the latest cruel twist of being trapped inside a hessian bag.

He woke drenched in sweat, gasping as though he'd just breached the ocean's surface. It wasn't usual for his active investigations to weigh so heavily on his subconscious, but he shrugged it off, guessing that being encased in a bag wasn't so different to being trapped beneath the surface of the water.

He was about to fall back to sleep when his phone buzzed. He glanced at the clock. 2.45 a.m.

'What?' he said, answering, his mouth dry.

'DS Kilshaw. Sorry to wake you. This is Sergeant Peterson from headquarters. We just received a call about something suspicious found on the beach at Porth Nanven. Sounds like the same MO as your hessian bag investigation. Thought you'd want the heads up.'

Chapter Fifteen

Any trace of yesterday's snowfall had been erased by the freezing rain, which lashed against Liam as he sprinted to his car. His small umbrella offered little protection as he navigated the darkened streets of St Ives, his car parked four streets down.

Thank God for bored teenagers, he thought, punching in the coordinates sent by headquarters. The hessian bag had been discovered around 11.45 p.m. on Sunday night, but a garbled report delayed the police's arrival by over an hour. When they finally reached the stony beach of Porth Nanven, a secluded cove near St Just on the south-west coast, it became clear they were dealing with more than a suspicious package. CSI was already on scene, confirming the bag contained a body.

That was all Liam knew so far. As he wound his way through the back roads, his mind raced with questions. Could this victim be identified? Had they suffered the same horrifying fate as Frank Oakley?

Porth Nanven wasn't a place Liam knew well. It wasn't a prime surfing spot, so it had held little interest for him growing up. From what he remembered, it was picturesque but rugged, its beach scattered with large, smooth boulders unique to the area, that had given the beach the nickname Dinosaur Egg Beach.

When he pulled into the car park forty minutes later, the scene had an eerie, otherworldly quality. The tide was high, the sea licking halfway up the shore, and spotlights illuminated the crashing waves. Mist curled and danced in the beams above the giant egg-like stones. A group of teenagers sat huddled on the car park wall, wrapped in foil blankets.

'DS Kilshaw,' Liam said, nodding to the uniformed officer standing with them. 'They found the body?' he asked, under his breath, as he looked at the teenagers.

'Yes, sir.'

'What were they doing down here so late?'

'The usual. Lots of empty bottles. They haven't admitted it, but I'd bet they've been on something stronger too.'

'In this weather?'

'Fair play to them. They wrapped up well.'

'I'll speak to them in a minute. Tide coming in or going out?'

'Out, sir. High tide was about thirty minutes ago.'

Liam clicked on his flashlight and stepped on to the shifting stones, heading to the tent where the CSI team was working. He kept his distance, watching them photograph and film the scene until Thomas Frost, the same CSI who had worked on the scene in Sennen, approached.

'Love these early morning callouts, don't you?' Frost said, pulling down his mask.

'Absolutely. What are we looking at?'

'Same set-up as Sennen so far. We've taped everything, but the bag was sealed, and the victim was face down. What was left of the face. Completely unrecognisable. Multiple lacerations, blunt force trauma. Same story.'

'Was it washed up or left here?'

'That's the strange part. The placement is above the current high-tide mark, which you'll see more clearly in daylight. But there are definite signs the body spent time in the water, just like before.'

'We're not even sure the last victim washed ashore any more,' Liam said.

'I heard. I'll need more time, but my guess is the same here. The body was placed after spending time in the sea, probably elsewhere.'

Liam donned a CSI suit and followed Frost to the body. The other team members stepped aside as he approached. The victim had been turned on to their back, and Liam tried to steel himself against the sight under the glaring spotlights, but it was impossible. His mind flashed to Jordan Hayes' friends, enduring the grim task of identification at the mortuary. Another family would likely face that same nightmare now. As before, all traces of humanity had been eradicated. What had once been a face was now a mess of pulp, utterly unrecognisable as human. Liam leant closer, noticing a loose strand of seaweed clinging to the victim's chest. 'The bag was sealed, as before?' he asked.

'Yes, we cut it open. Everything's been recorded,' Frost confirmed.

'Any sense of age?'

'From the skin and musculature, I'd estimate mid- to late-twenties.'

'And time of death?'

'Rough estimate, but I'd say within the last twenty-four hours.'

Liam's brow furrowed. 'Twenty-four hours?'

'No sign of rigor yet,' Frost replied.

It was early Monday morning, which suggested the killing had occurred late Saturday night or early Sunday. 'So we think he could have been in the sea already, then moved here, all within twenty-four hours?'

'The doc will give you a clearer timeline, but the body is relatively fresh.'

Liam stepped back from the scene and made his way up the rocks towards the teenagers, trying to make sense of everything. Both victims had been mutilated beyond recognition, yet their bodies had been deliberately left to be found. In Frank Oakley's case, the killer had even sent him a replica of the bag and body. It was contradictory. An act of horrific violence paired with an almost theatrical desire for the crime to be discovered.

Was it a display of pride, taunting the families and police? Or could the replicas and placements be a form of remorse, an attempt to atone for actions spiralling out of control?

Whatever the motive, another killing suggested the perpetrator was growing more confident. While that confidence could lead to mistakes, Liam feared further deaths might come before the killer slipped up.

The teenagers huddled under foil blankets near the car park wall. Two of the four smoked nervously, extinguishing their cigarettes when Liam approached. The uniformed officer handed him a list of names. Two boys and two girls, all seventeen or eighteen, each looking fragile and terrified under their metallic coverings.

Liam introduced himself. 'I know this must be difficult. Your parents have been contacted and are on their way. Who found the bag?'

The group exchanged uneasy glances until one girl, wide-eyed and leaning against one of the boys, raised her hand.

'Sarah?' Liam asked.

She nodded.

'Can you tell me what happened?'

Sarah looked to her friends for support before beginning. 'We were running across the beach, and I tripped over it. When I looked to see what it was, I realised it was a bag, and I thought about what happened over in Sennen . . .' Her voice broke, tears spilling down her cheeks. The boy beside her put an arm around her shoulders.

'Did anyone else touch the body?' Liam asked.

'No,' the boy answered. 'We got out of there as soon as we could and called you.'

'What time did you get to the beach?'

'Just before midnight, I guess,' Sarah said.

'Did you see anything suspicious?' Liam asked, aware the uniformed officer had likely asked the same question.

All four shook their heads. 'We were in the pub until about eleven,' one of the boys offered.

'Anyone there seem out of place?'

'No one was in except us,' the second boy replied.

'And a couple of old guys at the bar,' added the other girl.

'Did you notice any vehicles on your way down?'

The teenagers glanced at each other before Sarah spoke. 'There was a car. We saw it as we walked down the road.'

'Yeah, the Jeep,' one of the boys said.

'No, it was an old Land Rover,' the other boy said. 'Like an old-school Defender.'

'You sure it was a Defender?' asked Liam, recalling the vehicle spotted in Sennen by the couple on magic mushrooms.

'I think so. It was like one of those you see on a farm.'

'Colour?'

The boy grimaced. 'Light blue, maybe. It had a different colour roof. White, I think.'

'You didn't catch the number plate, did you?'

'Sorry, no,' Sarah said. 'But I did notice the driver. She saw me.'

'She?' Liam asked.

'I think so. She was wearing a baseball cap. When she saw me, she kind of pulled it down over her face. It all happened so fast, but it felt like she didn't want me to see her.'

Within the hour, the teenagers' parents arrived to collect their children. Each offered Liam an apology, as though it were their fault the kids had stumbled upon the body. Cornwall, with its vast, sparsely populated expanse, offered little for teenagers to do. Even in the more built-up areas, the coast remained an irresistible draw.

Liam recalled many nights spent on the beach himself, drinking, smoking, and watching the sunrise. Granted, those nights had been in the warmer months. He watched the teenagers being driven away, grateful that, beyond the shock of discovering the bag, they hadn't seen what he had.

Maya arrived as the sun rose, wearing sweatpants under a three-quarter raincoat, her hair pulled back. 'Don't,' she said, before Liam could tease her about her get-up.

The CSI team was packing up. The body lay on a gurney, ready to be taken to the morgue, while the bloodstained hessian bag was preserved for testing.

'No ID yet?' Maya asked, her breath misting in the cold morning air.

Liam shook his head. They stood in silence, watching as the CSIs carried the body across the stones to the waiting ambulance. The sea shimmered with fiery hues as the sun broke the horizon, the mist still lingering over the rocks. Soon, the body would be gone and nature would reclaim the scene as though nothing had happened. Liam doubted the teenagers would return to this spot anytime soon.

He updated Maya on the sighting of the Land Rover Defender. 'Matches the vehicle spotted in Sennen. Woman in a baseball cap. Could be the one seen with Frank Oakley in Wadebridge?' Without a number plate, it wasn't much to go on, but two sightings of a similar vehicle was a start of sorts.

'Let's map out the nearest ANPR locations,' Maya said. 'It's a common vehicle, but with the lack of traffic at that time of night, we might get lucky.'

They both knew the odds. In a city, finding the vehicle would have been far more likely, with the help of CCTV cameras too. Here, with miles of winding roads and sparse surveillance, the Land Rover Defender could have travelled undetected.

The rest of CID and a contingent of uniformed officers were called in to canvass local residents. Liam wasn't optimistic, but sometimes all it took was one sharp-eyed witness spotting a number plate to crack a case. He'd seen investigations turn on smaller details. No matter how meticulous a perpetrator thought they were, it was often the simplest oversight that undid them.

But that was assuming the woman in the Land Rover was the killer, which was at least two leaps too far at this stage.

While Maya supervised the house-to-house questioning, Liam took a sweep of the local area, driving towards St Just, the nearest town to Porth Nanven. He didn't expect to find anything – the area was too remote, and the killer had managed to dump two bodies without detection, but reacquainting himself with the surroundings felt necessary.

He parked by the harbour in St Just and bought a pasty for breakfast from a local bakery. The sky was overcast, and the harbour had a desolate feel. Walking along the harbour wall, he watched seagulls spiral in the wind and couldn't shake the sensation that someone, perhaps the killer, was watching him.

As he finished his pasty, he pulled up the maps app on his phone. The distance from St Just to Porth Nanven was less than two miles, the space between them a patchwork of fields and moorland. He zoomed in, tracing the narrow lane that meandered out of St Just. The satellite view showed wide expanses of green punctuated by clusters of trees and occasional solitary farmhouses, their roofs tiny specks in the landscape.

The previous week had been spent questioning locals in Sennen, where Frank Oakley's body was found. This included visits to farms and remote properties. As Liam scrolled through the map, he noted Sennen was six miles from Porth Nanven. It suggested the killer could be local, but that didn't explain the anomaly of Frank Oakley last being seen in Wadebridge.

Feeling the weight of his sleepless night in his muscles, Liam bought a coffee and called headquarters to request ANPR footage. As expected, official coverage was sparse. The closest active road camera was on the A3071 to Penzance. On the off chance, he requested footage from four hours either side of midnight, hoping for a glimpse of a Land Rover Defender.

There were private cameras scattered across the area – at farms, homes and garages – but it would be a colossal task to chase the sighting down.

Making a public appeal was an option, but in a rural area where such SUV vehicles were common, it could backfire. The flood of potential leads might overwhelm the investigation and prove counterproductive.

Liam returned to Porth Nanven, the beach now transformed under the sunlight breaking through the clouds. With the tide further out, the oppressive claustrophobia and dread he'd felt earlier had dissipated. Only the two remaining CSIs, combing the rocks and surrounding area for any useful material, hinted that something sinister had occurred here. By tomorrow, even that evidence would be gone, leaving the cove as serene and unspoilt as ever.

'No other sightings of a Land Rover Defender last night,' Maya said, joining him in the small car park. 'And no one saw anyone dumping a giant hessian bag on the beach, either.'

'When will we get the autopsy?' Liam asked.

Maya let out a breath. 'Could be a couple of days if we're lucky.'

'Even for a second murder?'

'We're short-handed. There's a backlog. And I already used my favour getting Frank Oakley's autopsy bumped up the line.'

'Only one favour in the bank?'

'I'll speak to DCI Hargreaves, see if he can push this one forward.'

'If the body was dumped before midnight, that's two Sundays in a row,' Liam pointed out. 'It'd be nice to avoid a third.'

'You're preaching to the choir, Liam. See you back at headquarters.'

Liam sighed as he climbed into his car. 'I guess so,' he said, starting the engine and heading towards Bodmin.

Chapter Sixteen

Two victims now adorned the crime board in the incident room. Frank Oakley and an as-yet unidentified man. In the absence of a photograph for the second victim, an image of the hessian bag in which he'd been found took its place.

Liam stared at the blood-soaked bag with its multiple lacerations, searching for answers, as if the interwoven threads of the fabric might reveal some hidden pattern, some clue to what the hell was going on.

Next to the board, a white screen played out images from the investigation. Liam tried not to dwell on the extreme violence inflicted on both victims, instead forcing himself to think logically.

Considering the victims first, he thought back to his uneasy meeting with Frank Oakley's family. Beneath their sadness, Liam had sensed an undeniable sense of estrangement. If he were being unkind, he'd describe their grief as tinged with something else. It hadn't quite been relief, but there had been a weary acceptance, and it seemed as though Frank had been absent from their lives long before his death.

The family had spoken of Frank's addictions and tendency to isolate himself. Would the same be true of victim number two? The team was already combing the missing persons register. Many mispers were addicts or individuals in the midst of personal crises, which added little to the profile but was worth considering as a starting point.

Liam doubted the second victim would remain unidentified for long. While initially it had been possible to view Frank's placement in Sennen as accidental, the second body's deliberate placement in Porth Nanven made it clear that the killer wanted these victims to be found. The replica hessian bag and doll sent to Frank's house also suggested the killer wanted the victims to be identified.

His thoughts were interrupted by the arrival of the two professional standards officers from London, stepping into the main CID area. Liam watched them head towards DCI Hargreaves' office. Why it was taking so long to wrap up the Met's mistakes was beyond him, but PSD weren't known for their speed.

This present investigation had clear parallels to the Godrevy Island case, where Miles Fischer had drowned victims and sometimes left them to be discovered. Those murders had been drug-related, and considering Frank's known addictions, Liam made a call to Luton CID to speak with one of their vice officers.

Unfortunately, Frank wasn't known to them. Luton had ongoing investigations into several drug gangs, but Frank hadn't appeared on their radar. The scale of their operations meant pinpointing any connection would take time. Liam knew Maya was already coordinating with the station, ensuring a CID officer was assigned to dig deeper into Frank's life, but for now that line of enquiry was going to have to wait.

Liam stopped what he was doing as the PSD officers left Hargreaves' office, expecting to be summoned, but they left without a word. Liam shook his head, exasperated at the distraction, and turned his thoughts to the one suspect they had in the current case. An unidentified woman in a baseball cap driving an old Land Rover Defender. The vehicle had been potentially sighted leaving Porth Nanven and at Sennen Beach, at the times the bodies had been left. A female wearing a baseball cap had also been spotted at the Wadebridge campsite with Frank Oakley.

It was a tenuous connection for now, and Liam wasn't about to get carried away. Until they located the vehicle or identified its driver, the sightings were little more than a frustrating loose thread, but it was, at the very least, something.

Liam was about to speak to Jack about tracking the vehicle when his phone buzzed. He'd been summoned to DCI Hargreaves' office, after all. He didn't know what Professional Standards had concluded, but all he wanted was to leave the Godrevy investigation behind him. Hopefully, this meeting would make that possible.

'Come in,' Hargreaves said, after Liam knocked on the office door.

'Is this ever going to end, guv?' Liam asked as he sat down opposite his boss.

'We'll come to that. But first, I understand we've yet to identify this second body?' Hargreaves replied, steering the conversation elsewhere.

'Yes, sir. But I think it's only a matter of time.'

Hargreaves looked distracted. The last thing anyone wanted was a potential serial killer loose in Cornwall, especially so soon after the Godrevy killings, and he imagined his boss was feeling pressure from various directions.

'There's been a dismissal and two suspensions,' Hargreaves said, at last. 'Effectively, at least.'

Liam needed a moment to process, his mind returning to the summer and the confrontation on Godrevy Island with the UCO, Stacey Smith.

'Stacey Smith's handler, DCI Simon Turner, has retired,' Hargreaves said, raising an eyebrow.

'Convenient. Who else?'

'Another officer from the Met's team, DS Maurice Charlton, has been suspended. And . . . DI Hartley.'

'Grace?' Liam's voice tightened.

'I'm afraid so.'

Liam recalled how he'd grown suspicious of his ex-girlfriend after the investigation. She'd promised him she hadn't known the identity of the UCO, and while he'd believed her, he'd worried there had been something she'd been hiding from him. 'But she didn't even know who Stacey was, did she?'

'That's not the point. The Met views the operation as a shambles, and someone needs to take the fall.'

Liam's mind flashed back to Grace's arrival at headquarters earlier that summer. Seeing her again had been a surprise – a pleasant and confusing one. If Millie hadn't been in his life, there was every chance he and Grace might have rekindled their relationship. Now, just a few months later, she was facing suspension.

'How serious is it for her?' he asked.

'I'm not sure. I get the feeling that it is just a precaution at this stage. However, she was one of the most senior officers involved, so there is a chance she could lose her job.'

Liam was torn by the information. He had to concede that he'd had his own doubts about Grace towards the end of the investigation, but she wasn't to blame for Stacey Smith's behaviour. 'That hardly seems fair.'

'Maybe not, but you'll be relieved to know we're in the clear.'

Liam frowned. 'That's cold comfort, considering we dismantled a burgeoning drug operation and brought down a sadistic serial killer.'

'I thought you'd want to know,' Hargreaves said, already turning his attention to his computer, a clear sign the meeting was over.

Back at his desk, Liam tried to focus on the current investigation, but his thoughts kept circling back to Grace. Someone had to be held responsible for Stacey Smith's actions. In a hierarchical system like the police, accountability was enforced with strict codes and consequences. Smith had gone rogue, becoming complicit in the deaths of multiple people. Someone had to answer for how it had been allowed to happen.

But did it have to be Grace? One of her superiors had taken the decision to retire, so there didn't seem a need for an extra scapegoat.

Grace might have known that somewhere in the system a UCO was active, but Liam had identified Stacey Smith as a suspect early in the investigation. It made no sense that Grace, knowing a UCO was involved, would withhold that information. She wouldn't have allowed them to proceed without informing the team.

Not that it had to make sense. In cases like this, accountability often meant heads rolled. Stacey Smith's handler losing his job was inevitable, but given the scale of Smith's crimes, it was unsurprising, if unjust, that others were seeing their careers put on hold as well. He hoped Hargreaves was right, and this was all a precaution until Grace was officially in the clear.

Liam scrolled to Grace's name in his contacts, his thumb hovering over the call button. He remembered the mix of disdain and embarrassment on her face when he'd turned down her offer for a drink. Things with Millie had been going so well that he hadn't wanted to risk complicating them. Breaking up with Grace after their training days had been tough, and back then it had all felt too messy. Would it be any different now?

He set the phone down, pushing the thought aside, and logged back into his laptop. He couldn't afford distractions – not Millie, not Grace. His focus needed to stay on the investigation. They had to figure out why these men were being killed and stop the killer before it happened again.

A few minutes later, Jack walked over, laptop in hand, his fingers tapping against the casing. 'Boss, you're going to want to see this,' he said, setting it down on Liam's desk. 'We had some hits on searching for Defenders on one of the traffic cams on the A3071 southbound.'

Liam leant in as Jack pulled up a series of video highlights.

'Three Land Rover Defenders were recorded during that period,' Jack said, practically buzzing as he did so. 'Which is surprising, given how little traffic there was at that time.'

Liam watched the footage: two Defenders speeding past a bend in the road. The camera had caught brief glimpses of the drivers and, more importantly, their number plates. Jack moved to Liam's side, his excitement growing.

'The best is saved for last,' he said, advancing to the final clip.

A third vehicle appeared on the screen. Behind the wheel was a woman in a baseball cap.

'We're checking all three drivers, but this one stands out,' Jack said, pointing at the screen, and the old-style two-tone Defender. 'Notice anything about the plates?'

Liam paused the video, studying the grainy footage. 'Unreadable.'

Jack nodded. 'I've been through it frame by frame. Never visible. I've sent the footage for further analysis, but from what I can tell, they've been deliberately obscured.'

Liam moved the video forward, scrutinising the image. The plates were indistinct, blurred by what could have been dirt or some kind of cover. 'It's subtle, but it's something. Good catch.'

'I'll track the route from that point,' Jack said. 'See if we can find another camera that caught this vehicle.'

'That's great work, Jack. Before you do that, print an image of the driver and get it on the crime board. We might just have ourselves a suspect.'

◆ ◆ ◆

Liam left the office at six that evening, guilt gnawing at him despite knowing he'd more than earnt the break after working through most of the weekend.

The image of the lone woman in the Defender lingered in his mind. With her baseball cap, she matched the descriptions given by the teenagers and the campsite owner where Frank Oakley had stayed.

With the other two drivers spotted on camera being eliminated from their investigations, Jack had spent the day combing through potential sightings of the vehicle but had come up empty. Without a number plate, the image of a woman driving a Land Rover didn't add up to much. The grainy, pixelated footage was useless for a public appeal. Their best hope lay in footage from other cameras they were still waiting on.

The image remained with him as he walked into the bar on the wharf in St Ives where he was meeting Millie. Ignoring a few familiar looks thrown his way, he climbed the stairs to the restaurant with its sweeping view of the harbour. He was ten minutes early and was surprised to see Millie already waiting.

'Just got a stab of déjà vu,' he said, as he approached her table, recalling their first date. He'd been embarrassingly late that night and had to leave early for a lifeboat shout. It felt like another lifetime, though it had only been in the summer.

'One thing's different,' Millie said, running a hand through her shortened hair.

Liam had noticed the haircut as soon as he'd arrived. Her once long, flowing locks had been replaced by a sharp, fashionable bob. It suited her, accentuating her already striking features, making them look sharper, more defined. 'It looks great,' he said, trying to muster genuine enthusiasm.

'Thanks. I got you a drink,' she said, gesturing to the pint on the table.

Liam sat down, already sensing where this was going. 'Why do I feel like a condemned man?'

'You're not condemned, Liam,' Millie said, with a wry smile. 'But I think you know we need to talk.'

'I think maybe I need to listen,' Liam replied, taking a long sip of lager, then another before setting the glass down.

'It's not you. God, that sounds so cliché,' Millie said, shaking her head. 'You're wonderful, Liam. Things were going so well between us.'

'Were?' Liam said.

Millie sighed, looking into her glass. 'I thought I could get past it, but I can't. Even now, when you walked in, I was happy to see you . . .'

'But,' Liam said.

'But I can't stop thinking about what happened. How that man took me. How I almost drowned in that horrible place.'

Liam's chest tightened as the memory hit him. He'd rescued Millie from a sewer tunnel, pulling her out just as the rising water reached her neck. His hand moved to his chest involuntarily as his breathing became laboured. He may have been able to face the open water better than before, but it was all too easy for his PTSD to be triggered.

'I don't know what to say,' he said after a beat, his breathing returning to normal. 'Except that I understand. I wish it wasn't this way, but maybe you're right. Maybe you can't move forward with me around as a reminder.'

He wanted to say more but didn't know how to articulate what he was feeling. Kim raged in his head, telling him he was blowing it. But what could he do? Millie was probably right. She was better off without him. Trying to convince her otherwise at the moment didn't feel right. It didn't matter how he felt, this was about her.

'Maybe not now,' Millie said, running a hand through her new haircut, a gesture that struck him as both nervous and resolute.

Liam managed a faint smile. He didn't want to leave immediately, but it was awkward staying. 'I think it's time I made my exit,' he said, standing. 'You look after yourself.'

'You too,' said Millie, kissing him goodbye on the cheek.

Chapter Seventeen

Liam quickened his already considerable pace as he ran on to Porthmeor Beach, towards the sea. At six-foot-two, with broad shoulders and a hairless head, the sight of him sprinting across the firm sand, large feet pounding into the surface, might have alarmed anyone watching, if the beach hadn't been deserted.

He ran until his lungs burnt and his heart hammered in his chest. He didn't need a psychologist to tell him why. He was still processing what had happened the night before. Millie's new haircut, her new direction, her decision to step away from their relationship. He'd been outwardly composed when he'd returned to his flat. They'd only been dating for a few months, and he understood why she didn't want to continue, knowing she'd suffered indirectly because of him.

He couldn't blame her, but as he collapsed on to the sand, breathless and aching, he welcomed the simplicity of focusing only on his immediate discomfort. For a few fleeting moments, his sole concern was catching his breath and stretching his tight muscles. Once done, his thoughts returned to the mess he was making of his life.

By the time he arrived at headquarters later that morning, his self-pity had eased. He'd treated himself to an impromptu fry-up after his run, and the food had tempered his gloom. Still, his mood must have shown on his face because Maya intercepted him by the lifts.

'Everything OK?' she asked.

Maya was five years younger than him, though sometimes it felt like the reverse. Maybe it was because she was his boss, but she had an uncanny ability to sense his shifts in mood. Either that, or he was simply easy to read.

The lift doors opened, and they stepped inside, the air stale with hints of body odour. 'Just tired,' he said.

'You don't need to come in so early. You worked all weekend. Take some extra time off if you need it. I'd rather have you rested and alert.'

Liam told Maya a truncated version of last night's meeting with Millie. She was the only person at the station he could talk to about personal matters, but he didn't want to dwell on it as they had more pressing concerns. 'I guess it's nothing a cup of coffee won't fix,' he said, signalling his desire not to talk any further.

Maya held his gaze, as if willing him to talk some more. Sighing, she said, 'In that case, black, one sugar,' as the lift opened.

Liam smiled and walked to the kitchen, where he found a fresh pot of coffee already brewed. A small but welcome omen for the day ahead.

'The autopsy's booked for this afternoon,' Maya said, as he placed a steaming mug on her desk.

They were the first to arrive in the incident room. The heating was cranked too high, and Liam wiped a bead of sweat from his forehead as he glanced at the crime board, the image of the hessian bag still a stand-in for the unidentified victim. He wondered what the autopsy would reveal beyond what they already suspected. That the second victim, like Frank Oakley, had been placed in the bag before being savagely attacked and killed. 'Can't wait,' he said, sipping his lukewarm coffee.

The morning was spent tracing the two-tone Land Rover Defender they hoped would bring everything together. Jack was trying to map its route before and after it had been caught on the ANPR camera. The team were still scouring the area for other cameras that might have captured a clearer image of the vehicle, and, ideally, its number plates.

For Liam, it was another exercise in patience. Every step forward was slow, but he knew that even a small breakthrough could make all the difference.

As he reviewed the video footage they'd recovered, his mind occasionally drifted to thoughts of Millie. Despite everything she'd endured, he'd naively believed they'd weathered the worst of it. Looking back, he couldn't fathom why he'd thought that way. If anyone understood the delayed grip of trauma, it was him.

Though he'd made progress in dealing with his PTSD and his fear of open water, there were still moments when it consumed him. He would wake from nightmares drenched in sweat or would feel panic near the water. Millie's ordeal was much more recent, and no less traumatic. Of course she hadn't fully processed it. And it was now obvious that his presence in her life only served as a reminder of her ordeal. As selfish as it felt, he couldn't afford to think about his own needs. If stepping away from her was what she needed, he was prepared to do that.

His phone rang, jolting him from his thoughts. For a moment, he half expected it to be Kim, ready to give him an earful. She'd introduced him to Millie and would likely be one of the first to hear about the break-up.

'Kilshaw.'

'Liam, it's Jo on the front desk. There's someone here to see you. A Mrs Judi Wakefield. Says she saw your name in the paper.'

'Regarding?' Liam asked. Headquarters wasn't exactly a place where people casually dropped by, and it had been a long time since he'd been summoned directly by a member of the public.

'I think it's about the hessian bag killings. She says she's received something in the post, but she'll only show you.'

Liam hung up and flagged Maya as he left the incident room. 'Judi Wakefield,' he said. 'Claims she's received something in the post.'

'Don't recognise the name,' Maya replied, as they descended the stairs to the ground floor.

Downstairs, Jo gestured at a distraught woman in a bright red winter coat seated in reception.

Liam approached alone. 'Mrs Wakefield? I'm DS Liam Kilshaw. I believe you wanted to see me?'

The woman looked up, her tear-streaked face pale. 'My son, Robin,' she said, staring at Liam as though he were an apparition.

Liam sat beside her. 'Has something happened to Robin?'

'He didn't come home on Saturday. Sometimes he doesn't.' Her voice faltered as she rummaged through her handbag, eventually pulling out a plastic carrier bag. 'Here,' she said.

Liam took the bag and peered inside, spotting a white manila envelope. He signalled Jo for gloves, which she brought over. 'May I?' he asked, donning the gloves and removing the envelope.

Mrs Wakefield nodded, her red-rimmed eyes fixed on his hands as he opened it.

Liam's stomach sank as he saw the miniature hessian sack. 'Jo, please take Mrs Wakefield to an interview room,' he instructed, before sealing the hessian sack in an evidence bag and heading with Maya to the forensic lab in the building.

Given the urgency of the case and Mrs Wakefield's presence, a technician was assigned to examine the sack right away. Liam wasn't interested in DNA or fingerprint results just yet. All he wanted to know was what was inside. But the technician insisted on running initial tests on the exterior before opening it, adhering to protocol.

Liam tried to suppress his impatience, but he already knew what they'd find. The thought of it only deepened the knot in his stomach, the pain stretching around to his lower back.

'I'd best speak to Mrs Wakefield,' said Liam.

Maya nodded. 'I'll let you know as soon as we confirm what's inside.'

Liam entered the interview room a few minutes later to find Mrs Wakefield blowing her nose, her eyes red and puffy. An untouched cup of tea sat in front of her, the steam swirling in the air-conditioned room.

'Thank you for your patience, Mrs Wakefield,' said Liam, sitting opposite her.

'Judi,' she said, her voice trembling. 'His phone is dead.'

'Robin's been missing since Saturday?' Liam asked.

'That's the last time we saw him. He spends a lot of time at his mates' places, or with his girlfriend.'

'Girlfriend?'

'Jules. Julie Patterson. I called her this morning, after I opened the . . . thing. She hasn't seen him since Friday.'

'And his mates?'

Judi shook her head, sniffling. 'I called one of them – Hugo. He's the most sensible one. He hasn't got back to me yet.'

'Do you have their details?' Liam asked, his mind preoccupied with the replica hessian bag and the grim likelihood of what it contained, and why it had been sent.

Judi handed over her phone, and Liam noted the details, forwarding them to the rest of the team. 'Do you have a picture of Robin?' he asked.

Her hand trembled as she navigated her phone before handing it back. 'I didn't understand what this all meant until I looked it up online. That's how I found out about you.'

Liam glanced at the photo, his stomach tightening as he registered the striking resemblance between Robin Wakefield and Frank Oakley. 'He's a good-looking boy,' Liam said, memories of the mutilated body on the beach at Porth Nanven surging to the forefront of his mind.

'It's him, isn't it?' Judi said, her voice accusatory, her tear-filled eyes locking on to his. 'That body you found?'

'It's far too early to say, Judi,' Liam said.

Judi shook her head, her gaze unwavering. 'It's him. I know it is. I felt . . . something. On Sunday. Something weird. Here.' She pressed a hand to her chest. 'I should've known it was him. I should've checked on him.'

Liam's phone buzzed, breaking the tense moment. Maya had sent a photo. A rag doll retrieved from the hessian bag, its features bearing a chilling resemblance to the photo of Robin Wakefield he'd just seen.

'How old is Robin?' he asked, glancing back at Judi.

'Twenty-five.'

'What does he do for a living?'

'He works for a shipping company based out of Falmouth. He's been saving up to get a place of his own. That's why he still lives with us.'

'Do you know the name of the company?' Liam asked.

'S&D Falmouth,' she said.

Liam masked his surprise at her mention of the same shipping company Jordan Hayes had worked for. 'And do you know what Robin had planned on Saturday?'

'From what I can tell, him and the boys were doing what they always do on Saturdays. They were out on the town, drinking.'

Liam asked a few more questions, gathering as much detail as he could before broaching the question he was half-avoiding. 'Judi, this is going to be hard to answer, but I need to ask. You know we've found a body, and I want to eliminate Robin as a possibility. Is there anything distinguishing about him that could help us? Tattoos, scars, anything like that?'

Judi's breathing grew laboured, her eyes reddening further. 'He broke his leg,' she said. 'He has a scar on his ankle. His left ankle. I'm sure of it. Does the body you found have that?'

'I don't know yet,' Liam said. 'What sort of scar?'

'He did it playing football. He had a plate put in his ankle. Yes, definitely his left leg. I remember it now. I can still see him on crutches. Does the body have that?' she asked, incessant, close to desperate.

'I'll check,' Liam said, feeling a wave of relief as the door opened and a family liaison officer entered the room.

He introduced the officer to Judi and stepped out, grabbing his phone as he left the building. Once out of earshot, he called the mortuary.

The confirmation came immediately. The body found at Porth Nanven had a small metal plate in the left ankle.

Chapter Eighteen

By late Tuesday afternoon, the body found at Porth Nanven had been confirmed as Robin Wakefield. The autopsy results showed the patterns they were expecting. Like Frank Oakley, Robin had been alive when sealed inside the hessian bag. Although the bag was found on land, evidence suggested Robin's body had been submerged in seawater before being placed on the shore.

Liam sat in the incident room with the rest of the team, the atmosphere tense as they analysed the latest findings. The hessian bag sent to Robin's mother had been opened, revealing a miniature replica of the victim, complete with a cheerful, smiling face.

The mug of coffee in Liam's hands had gone tepid as he stared at the rolling images on the whiteboard. What struck him most was the uncanny physical resemblance between the two victims. They were of similar height, both having thick black hair and piercing blue eyes.

'Maybe some guy is jealous that these two were getting women when they weren't?' Jack said.

'Getting?' Maya said.

'Sorry, ma'am, you know what I mean. From all accounts, neither Frank nor Robin were short of female admirers.'

Maya waved off the comment, her expression tightening. 'Why the bag though? Why not disfigure them out in the open?'

'Could be squeamish,' Liam said. 'Maybe it was easier to do what they did when they didn't have to look at the results directly.' His eyes flicked to the screen as an image of Frank Oakley's mutilated face appeared, the destruction almost incomprehensible.

Maya folded her arms, grimacing as she studied the photo, her eyes narrowing as if the answer were hidden in the carnage. 'There's more to it than that. Placing the bodies in the bag has to mean something.'

'Why send the replica to the family?' Jack asked.

'Could be a twisted peace offering. A way of making amends, or they could simply be taunting them,' Liam replied, setting his mug down.

'A killer with delusions of a conscience. Not sure I like that idea,' Maya said. 'What about that sacrifice theory you mentioned before, Liam? The Bucca . . . whatever it was?'

'Bucca Dhu,' Liam said. 'I've looked through online groups, but if anyone's clinging to those old ways, they're not advertising it.'

'Dig deeper,' Maya said. 'With this second body left on the shore, there could be some symbolic significance we're missing.'

The team divided up tasks. The immediate priority now was tracking Robin's movements over the weekend leading up to his death. The shipping company he worked for would need to be contacted, as would Jordan Hayes' friends to discover if any connection existed between Jordan and Robin beyond their shared workplace.

With Maya heading out to speak to Robin's girlfriend, Julie Patterson, Liam focused on the list provided by Robin's mother. He managed to reach one of Robin's friends, Jacob Sutton, who worked in Truro, and arranged to meet him within the hour.

As Liam drove, he realised he hadn't thought about Millie since Mrs Wakefield's arrival at the station that morning. Thinking about it now was like opening a fresh wound. He replayed the conversation from Monday night, wondering if he should have said more. Maybe all she'd wanted was some reassurance, but then again the new haircut suggested a reinvention. Change. It had been a long time since he'd felt seriously about anyone, not really since Grace, and it was as if he'd forgotten how to act.

Pulling into the car park of the insurance building where Jacob worked, Liam forced himself to blank out all extraneous thoughts and focus solely on the case.

Jacob Sutton was waiting in reception, his cheap suit doing little to mask his youth. Despite being in his mid-twenties, he looked like a boy lost in disbelief. His face was ashen as Liam approached, displaying his warrant card.

'Is there somewhere quiet we can go to talk?' Liam asked.

'Is he really dead?' Jacob's voice cracked, and his wide, unblinking eyes betrayed his shock.

'I'm really sorry, Jacob. We've formally identified Robin's body.'

Jacob's shoulders slumped, his expression blank. A colleague stepped forward, guiding them to a vacant interview room. 'I'll get some water,' the colleague said before leaving. Liam sat next to Jacob, who stared ahead, his mouth slightly open, his eyes unfocused.

'I know this is tough, Jacob,' Liam said, 'but I need your help to find out who did this to your friend.'

Jacob blinked, his gaze shifting to Liam. 'It's such a shock. I can't believe it.'

'When did you last see Robin?'

Jacob tilted his head, looking upward as though the answer might be written on the ceiling. 'Saturday. We were out all day. Rugby was on. We spent the afternoon in some pubs, grabbed some food, then hit a few more.'

Liam handed him a pen and some paper. 'Can you write down the names of the pubs you went to, with approximate times?'

Jacob took the pen, a slight tremble to his hand. 'I'll try, but we were drinking pretty heavily.'

'Was Robin with you all night?'

Jacob nodded. 'Yeah. We ended up at Jesters. You know it?'

Liam knew the late-night club in Truro, open until 2 a.m. on weekends. It was a regular Saturday night trouble spot for the younger crowd. 'Did you leave with him?'

Jacob's laugh was hollow. 'No. As soon as we got in there, Robin was on the pull. I don't think I saw him again after we arrived.'

'What time did you get there?'

'Just before eleven. We always get there early. Avoids the queue after the pubs close. They don't like groups of lads at that time.'

Liam hesitated, considering his next question. 'You know what happened to Robin, don't you? Specifically, I mean.'

Jacob nodded. 'He was in a bag, wasn't he?' Jacob said, squirming in his seat.

'Can you think of anyone who would want to do this to him?'

Liam was surprised by Jacob's hesitation. 'Robin was a good-looking guy,' Jacob said, eventually. 'I loved him, but . . . he wasn't always the most considerate. He liked women, a lot. He didn't stick around long, though. That pissed some of them off. And sometimes . . . they had boyfriends. But this?'

'One thing doesn't add up. Robin's mum said he had a girlfriend.'

'Julie?' Jacob's expression darkened, caught between confusion and disdain. 'I'm afraid that girl's a bit deluded. He hooks up with her now and again, but they weren't going out. I think his mum wants him to settle down. Wanted him to,' Jacob said, swiping a tear from his eye.

After gathering a list of pubs and the names of others who'd been out with Robin on Saturday, Liam drove the short distance to Jesters nightclub. The sky had darkened, the temperature dropping a few degrees, close to zero. Though Liam usually enjoyed the autumn months, it felt as if the season had been skipped, winter already laying its icy grip on the county.

The club section of Jesters was closed, but the adjoining restaurant remained open. The place was all but deserted, save for a couple scrolling through their phones in a nearby booth. The quiet made Liam's footsteps feel louder as he entered the building, his breath visible in the chilly air.

A young waitress approached Liam with a half-smile. She had a stud in her nose and looked unimpressed as he displayed his warrant card.

'Is the owner in?'

'Owner?'

'Manager. Someone in charge.'

'You can speak to my manager. Wait here,' she said, disappearing into the back. A few minutes later, she returned with a man in an apron who clearly didn't appreciate the interruption.

'Andy Minter,' the man said, folding his arms. 'Help you?'

Liam explained the purpose of his visit. 'I need access to your security footage from Saturday night.'

'The club's closed until Thursday,' Minter replied, as if that was the end of the matter.

Liam leant forward, his patience wearing thin. 'Maybe you didn't hear me. This is a murder investigation. If I don't get access to your cameras in the next few minutes, there won't *be* a club to open on Thursday. Do you understand?'

Minter looked him up and down, lingering on Liam's hairless scalp, his expression a mix of indignation and resignation. 'I'll make some calls,' he said, shaking his head as he walked away.

'Get you a drink?' the waitress asked, lighter now, her smile more sincere.

'Coffee would be great,' Liam said, grateful for the small kindness.

He took a seat by the window. Outside, the town was at a standstill, as if no one wanted to brave the bitter cold. The waitress soon returned with the coffee and, to his surprise, sat down opposite him.

'It's on the news,' she said.

'What is?'

'Robin. He's the one who died, right?'

Liam was startled that Robin's name had already reached the press but guessed it was inevitable. 'You knew him?'

'We all knew Robin,' she said, with a smile.

'What's your name?'

'Sally.'

'How well did you know him, Sally?'

'I didn't. Not in *that* sense. But he had a reputation.'

'I've heard he was a popular lad.'

'A little *too* popular.'

'That bother you?'

'Me? I don't care. I'm not into boys. But he upset a few people. I've seen my share of emotional breakdowns because of him.'

'So, you didn't like him?'

Sally shrugged. 'That was the thing. He was a nice guy. Really nice, actually. Always smiley, polite. He knew everyone's name and always asked how I was doing. That's probably how he got away with it. He was charming. It's just a shame he couldn't keep his cock in his pants.'

Before Liam could respond, Minter reappeared and dropped a set of keys on to the table. 'You two seem to be getting along. Why don't you show DS Kilshaw here the office? You probably know how to access the cameras better than me anyway.'

Liam grabbed his coffee and followed Sally through a narrow corridor to a metal door leading into the adjacent club.

'How long have you worked here, Sally?' he asked, as they walked.

'Too long,' she replied with a wry grin, leading him upstairs to a small office. She unlocked the door and gestured inside. 'Take a seat. You want the footage from Saturday night, right?'

Liam brushed some papers off a maroon faux-leather armchair and sat down. The office overlooked the empty nightclub through mirrored windows. A battered lawyer's desk was cluttered with wires, papers, and an array of four screens, which flickered to life as Sally plugged in the system.

'Everything's on hard drive now, or in the Cloud,' she said. 'I think they do it to protect themselves if something happens. I'll load Saturday's feed. As you can see, we've got four cameras. One outside, one on the staircase, and two inside the club.'

The feeds began running simultaneously on the screens, timestamped at 7 p.m.

'Can you skip to ten-thirty?' Liam asked. Unless he got lucky, there wouldn't be much to see at this point. The footage would have to be thoroughly analysed by the tech team at headquarters, with each feed reviewed from beginning to end. But Jacob Sutton had mentioned that Robin and his friends had arrived just before eleven, and sure enough, the outside camera caught the group of five men at 10.59 p.m.

The doorman let the group through, and the second screen showed them ascending the staircase to the club entrance. Robin Wakefield was all smiles as he climbed the steps with his friends, waving and laughing as if he didn't have a care in the world.

'It's so weird seeing him, knowing what happened,' Sally murmured.

If Robin had any inkling of danger, he didn't show it as he stepped into the club. Liam shifted his attention to the third screen, which covered the club's interior. The camera quality was grainy, and at times blurred the moving figures. The club was busy, with a few people dancing and others gathered at the bar.

'There,' Sally said, pointing at the screen. Robin appeared, weaving through the crowd, nodding and waving at acquaintances as he made his way to the bar.

Sally was right. It was unsettling to watch Robin like this. According to the autopsy, he would be dead by early Sunday morning. Yet on-screen, he was utterly carefree.

'Can you increase the speed? Let's track where he goes,' Liam said.

Sally sped up the footage. They watched as Robin moved in and out of sight, Sally occasionally pausing the feed when he reappeared. Several blind spots in the camera coverage complicated things, and at one point, Robin was off-screen for a full thirty minutes.

'There's a smoking area out back, and no cameras near the toilets,' Sally explained.

Liam kept his eyes on all four screens. 'There,' he said, spotting Robin on the fourth feed, walking arm-in-arm with a long-haired woman.

'I know I shouldn't say it, but this is exciting,' Sally said, with a grin. 'Any jobs going?'

'Slow the footage,' Liam said, ignoring her comment. He watched Robin and the woman navigate the edge of the dance floor. 'He looks unsteady.'

'Most of them are at that time of night.'

Liam leant closer. 'Can you zoom in?'

Sally shook her head. 'Sorry, this is as close as it gets.'

Robin seemed to cling to the woman for stability. 'Do you know her?'

'No, but I'd like to.'

'Have you seen her before?'

'We get loads of people here. I'm usually behind the bar, so unless they're regulars, they all blur together.'

The pair left the screen, reappearing on the second and then the first feed as they exited the club. They walked arm-in-arm down the street before vanishing from view.

'Heading towards Fairmantle Street,' Liam murmured. 'Thanks, Sally. I'll need a copy of this footage.'

'I've got a USB drive somewhere,' Sally said, rummaging through a desk drawer.

Liam rewound the feed, freezing the frame on an image of the woman Robin had left with. The picture from the exterior camera was even worse than those inside the club. Hopefully, the team at headquarters could enhance it.

Because it was more than possible that this mysterious woman was Robin's killer.

Chapter Nineteen

Alex had lost all sense of time since Adelaide had last visited him. She'd returned only once since taking the second man with her, depositing another bag of groceries just within his reach before leaving in silence.

Reality had become a slippery concept since she'd left him in this place, but as she'd walked away, Alex was sure he'd glimpsed blood on her clothes. For a fleeting moment, she'd seemed draped in it from head to toe. He blinked, and the vision was gone, leaving only a gnawing unease.

He couldn't stop thinking about the stranger, as he nibbled on stale bread, washing it down with careful gulps of water. His mind tried to protect himself, blocking out the worst of his thoughts, but cracks formed. He'd find himself wondering what Adelaide, and her mother, had done to the man. Occasionally, the mental wall crumbled, and his imagination ran wild with gruesome possibilities.

He forced those thoughts away. His sanity was fraying, and if he let himself linger too long on what might have happened, or what could happen to him, he'd lose what was left of it.

He needed a plan. That was what people in peril always did in films. Play the long game, biding their time until it was the right moment to escape. But as he tugged at the chain bolted securely to the cave wall, he couldn't imagine such a moment presenting itself.

His best chance was Adelaide. She'd said more than once how much she liked him. If he could get her to talk, to open up, maybe he could figure out why she was keeping him here, and what she'd done to the stranger.

She wasn't a remorseless killer, he was sure of that. Troubled and confused, yes, but he'd seen kindness in her too. And while he feared the influence her mother might have on her, he thought it was possible he could reach her.

His thoughts turned to his own mother, gone too soon, and the quiet, withdrawn boy her death had left behind. He pictured his father slumped in his armchair, always surrounded by beer cans. Parents could mess you up, and Alex knew that as well as anyone. Whatever Adelaide was suffering, it had roots that went deep.

He was sleeping the next time she came to the cave. Her cool hand on his forehead roused him from a dreamless void.

'Hello, beautiful Alex,' she said.

Despite himself, he didn't move at first. He should have recoiled, but her touch was the first human contact he'd had in what felt like an eternity. For a few seconds, he didn't want it to stop.

When she pulled her hand away, he pretended to stir, sitting up against the cold wall. His chain rattled against the stone as he spoke. 'I miss my friends.'

Adelaide's hair was tied back, her cheekbones more prominent than before. There was something enigmatic in her gaze, as if she carried the weight of some unknowable burden. 'Don't fret about such things now, Alex,' she said, her Cornish lilt both soothing and unsettling.

'What are you going to do to me, Adelaide?' he asked, his voice trembling.

Her smile was unreadable. Compassion, ridicule, and something else he couldn't define seemed to flicker across her face. 'I think you might be our only chance, Alex,' she said, pressing her hand to his cheek. 'You look so much like him now. You're ready, Alex.'

She stepped aside, revealing an old-fashioned metal bath perched on clawed feet. Steam curled up from the water, filling the air with warmth. Alex stared, dumbfounded. He hadn't heard her bring it in.

Adelaide dipped her elbow into the water, testing its temperature. 'It's ready, sweet Alex,' she said.

'I want to go home,' Alex said, his throat tight.

'You will soon,' she replied. 'But first, let's get these clothes off you.'

It was only then he noticed the fresh set of clothes folded neatly beside the bath. They were the same colour and style the stranger had been wearing before he'd been led out of the cave.

Alex wanted to fight, to scream at her that all of this was wrong. But he didn't. His clothes clung to him, filthy and damp, and he meekly allowed her to use scissors to cut them away. The chain made it difficult to remove his jumper, but she worked around it, her movements methodical and precise.

When he finally stood naked before her, he felt no shame. He stepped into the steaming bath, lowering himself into the water as she guided him. She washed him with tenderness, like a mother bathing a child.

For a few moments, he almost felt human again.

When it was over, she removed the metal band from his wrist and wrapped a towel around him, her hands firm but careful. He was free, technically. But he didn't run. Instead, he let her dress him in the new clothes and make small adjustments to his damp hair before locking him back in place.

Stepping back, Adelaide looked at him as if in awe. 'You're ready now,' she said softly. 'I think you're going to save him, Alex. I think you're going to save us all.'

Alex nodded, his stomach churning as Adelaide turned her back on him, leaving the scissors she'd cut his hair with on the stone ground.

Chapter Twenty

The wind picked up as Liam drove back to headquarters, its whistling sound reverberating against the car. Absently, he wondered if Bucca Dhu was already demanding new blood, and if so, would it get its wish?

Back in the incident room, he met with Maya to review the nightclub footage. They printed a grainy image of the woman Robin had last been seen with and pinned it on the board before assigning a team to work overtime, combing through the footage for more images.

Liam discussed his meeting with Sally and her suggestion that Robin was something of a womaniser. 'What did the girlfriend have to say for herself?' he asked.

Maya shook her head. 'Poor thing. I think she knew what Robin was up to behind her back. She gave me the impression she was waiting for him to grow up, to be ready to settle down with her.'

'Leopard, spots,' Liam said.

'Exactly. She was out with her parents on Saturday, and hadn't planned to see Robin on Sunday. She tried calling him in the afternoon, but it went straight to voicemail. She assumed he was sleeping off the night before.'

Neither Frank Oakley's nor Robin Wakefield's phones had been found. The last location pinged for Robin's phone was on the street outside the club.

'From what I've seen of the footage,' said Liam, 'Robin was either blind drunk or on something.'

'Maybe he'd been spiked?'

'They'd been on the piss all day, but you could be right.'

The video analysis would take all night, but Liam had no intention of going home. The cold, miserable weather outside was deterrent enough, and staying at headquarters felt more productive than moping in his flat. It was already after 8 p.m. when he started making calls, trying to source additional camera footage from the surrounding area near the nightclub on Saturday night. An initial shot of adrenaline coursed through him, but experience soon tempered his optimism. It was possible they were on the brink of a breakthrough, but it equally could be true that they were chasing another dead end.

It was too late to expect immediate answers, but Liam still succumbed to the frustration of it all. He distracted himself by conducting more research on Bucca Dhu mythology but found nothing much new. Aside from an annual village ceremony where children offered homemade gifts to nature, there was no evidence of anyone actively practising ancient rituals to appease mythical sea gods.

At 11.30 p.m., Liam checked in with the team reviewing video footage. They assured him they would call if anything significant turned up, so he finally decided to head home. On his way out of the incident room, he switched off his computer and was about to grab his coat when a shout startled him. 'Boss, before you go.'

'Jesus, Jack, I forgot you were here,' Liam said, as he turned to see DC Lawson at a corner desk.

'You're going to want to see this,' Jack replied, his face lit by the glow of his monitor. 'CCTV from a garage in Ludgvan.'

Liam was too drained to summon much enthusiasm for yet another video clip. 'Just tell me.'

'We've got her. The woman and the Defender. Running the plates now,' Jack said, typing rapidly.

Liam walked over, trying not to get too excited.

'Here we go. Woman's name is Daniella White. I have an address for her in Hendra.'

◆ ◆ ◆

Liam wasted no time calling Maya, who had left the station twenty minutes earlier. The connection between Daniella White and the crime was tenuous, and he wanted her opinion before proceeding to contact the woman. They had the one potential sighting of a woman driving a Land Rover Defender leaving Porth Nanven on the night Robin Wakefield's body was found, and another for a vehicle matching the same description being parked in Sennen on the night Frank Oakley's body was found. In addition, there was the visual of the woman accompanying Frank Oakley at a campsite in Wadebridge, and the sighting of an unconfirmed figure carrying a body in Sennen. If any of the witnesses had been able to identify a number plate, or give a description of the woman, their case would be stronger. As it stood, the evidence was circumstantial at best, and Liam needed to confirm whether it was enough to justify visiting a member of the public at midnight.

'Does this Daniella have a record?' Maya asked.

'Not even a parking ticket,' Liam replied. 'She's a solicitor.'

'OK, let's weigh this up. Witnesses saw a woman leaving the Porth Nanven scene in a Land Rover Defender, and a vehicle matching that description appeared on CCTV six miles away on a major road. It's far from conclusive.'

'It's an older model, and it's two-tone. Not many like it around any more.'

The line went quiet as Maya considered the situation. 'We don't know how far this is escalating. If we can match Daniella White to the woman in the nightclub . . . Where's she based?'

'A place called Hendra, near Stithians.'

'OK, send me the details. I'll meet you there.'

Liam grabbed his coat and ran down the station stairs. He usually avoided getting carried away when visiting potential suspects, but the gruesome images of the victims and the lack of solid leads had taken a toll. The chance of upsetting a member of the public seemed a small price to pay for progress.

Outside, the wind had picked up, nearly knocking him off balance as he sprinted to his car. His windscreen was frozen, and he tapped impatiently on the glass as he waited for it to defrost before setting off.

The back roads to Hendra were narrow and pitch-dark, the landscape quiet and foreboding. Cornwall sometimes had a way of making you feel like the last person alive, and as Liam checked his satnav to ensure he was on the right track, the isolation pressed down on him. He eventually reached a gated lane, parking his car and shining a torch down the pathway. In the dim light, he could just make out a small, detached house, and the silhouette of two cars outside, one of which was an old Land Rover Defender.

Maya arrived minutes later. They decided to park up and walk the lane. 'Isn't this how all horror movies begin?' she asked, pushing open the gate, their boots crunching on the frozen gravel.

Naval superstitions aside, Liam didn't go in much for rituals and wasn't easily spooked. But Maya was right about the eerie atmosphere in the remote area. He drew in a deep breath, recalling his recent nightmares where he'd been trapped within a hessian bag like the victims. And as they walked down the darkened alley, he fought away the thoughts of Bucca Dhu that his imagination threw his way, including its latest creation of a frost-speckled serpent floating in the night sky. 'I think it's how they end,' he replied, double-checking his coat for his extendable baton and pepper spray.

'Looks like we'll be waking her up,' Maya said, as they passed through a second gate to the property.

Liam shone his torch on the Defender, which was next to a Jaguar sports car with the most recent set of plates. 'It's the same vehicle.'

'Since I have reservations about this, you can do the honours,' Maya said, jumping slightly as the front door swung open.

A woman in a dressing gown stood in the doorway, her expression one of mild annoyance. 'Can I help you?' she asked.

Liam displayed his warrant card. 'DS Kilshaw and DI Trent. Are you Daniella White?'

'May I?' the woman asked, stepping forward to scrutinise the cards. She seemed unfazed by the appearance of two strangers on her doorstep after midnight. 'I am she. Do you know what time it is?'

'We apologise for calling so late, but we need to speak with you about matters relating to a major investigation.'

Daniella hadn't switched on any lights, making it difficult for Liam to fully assess her resemblance to the woman from the nightclub footage. What he could see, however, was that she was strikingly attractive. Long red hair framed her face, and her large, expressive eyes conveyed a mix of incredulity and irritation.

'You can't be serious,' she said. 'What could possibly be so important that it can't wait until morning?'

'Your car has been identified at, or leaving, multiple scenes of crime,' Maya said.

'What?' Daniella's expression shifted to one of exasperation, though there was a trace of amusement, as if she couldn't quite believe the situation.

'May we come in to discuss it?' Liam asked, bracing himself against the biting wind swirling around them.

'No, you may not.'

'I think it would be beneficial for you to let us discuss this with you,' Maya said.

'Oh, really? Well, perhaps before turning up at someone's house in the middle of the night, you should consider forewarning them. I have absolutely no idea why you're here, and frankly, I'm baffled by what you're suggesting. Do you have a warrant to enter my house? If not, and you don't wish to arrest me, I bid you goodnight.'

Her voice carried a faint Cornish lilt. She was every bit the composed professional, and Liam imagined she could be a formidable solicitor.

'Where were you on Monday morning between midnight and 2 a.m.?' Liam asked.

'I shouldn't have to do this,' Daniella said, her sigh audible. 'But I will, to save us all time. I work as a solicitor for a national firm in Truro. I'm not a criminal solicitor, but as you'd expect, I know my legal rights. I'm genuinely astounded you'd show up at my house at this hour without any prior notice. Normally, I'd be more than willing to help you, but in this circumstance, I am politely declining. If you'd like to speak with me tomorrow, please call my office to arrange an appointment.'

She handed Liam a business card before firmly closing the door, leaving them standing in the darkness.

'Any more bright ideas, DS Kilshaw?' Maya asked.

'We could arrest her,' Liam suggested, raising an eyebrow.

Maya chuckled. 'Next time we speak to that woman, we'd better come prepared.'

Liam ran his torch over the Land Rover Defender before leaving. In the dim light, it appeared as though the vehicle had been recently cleaned, though he couldn't say for certain.

Back at the car, he said goodnight to Maya before pulling up the nightclub image on his phone. He studied the grainy photo, trying to convince himself it matched Daniella White, but until they obtained clearer footage, it was impossible to be sure.

He reached St Ives just after two. As he parked, he cursed under his breath, slipping on a patch of black ice and overextending his hamstring. Limping slightly, he climbed the stairs to his flat, ready to put the long day behind him.

Unlocking the door, he almost missed the folded piece of paper on his doormat. Groaning at his aching leg, he bent down to pick it up. His eyes widened as he unfolded the note, and recognised Grace's handwriting.

Chapter Twenty-One

Adelaide returned before Alex had time to process what he'd done. As soon as she entered, her presence filled the cave with an unsettling mix of warmth and dread. She instructed him to stand up.

Alex obeyed, trembling as he rose to his feet. He feared she'd noticed he'd taken the scissors, but if she had, it seemed she'd forgiven him. She tussled his hair and kissed him on the cheek.

'You're so beautiful, Alex,' she said, her voice trembling with emotion. 'You've become exactly what I wanted. She won't be able to refuse you. Here, I got these for you.'

Before he could ask what she meant, Adelaide bent down and slipped a pair of leather shoes on to his bare feet. The fit was tight, the material hot against his brittle skin. She then placed a zip tie around his wrists and unchained him from the wall.

'It's for your own safety,' she said, taking his arm and leading him out of the cave.

Alex had spent countless nights imagining the layout of the cave system where he had been held captive. During that time, he'd often thought he heard distant screams, faint echoes suggesting other prisoners somewhere within the stone labyrinth. But as Adelaide guided him down a narrow passageway, he was shocked to learn that he'd been closer to the outside world than he had ever realised.

'Take it slowly,' Adelaide said, pausing halfway, as Alex's eyes started to water. The daylight ahead was blinding, spilling through the cave's opening just twenty metres away. He looked down, shielding his gaze until his vision adjusted.

Adelaide placed a pair of sunglasses over his eyes. Now that they were in the relative brightness of the passageway, Alex could see her more clearly. She wore a long white dress that clung to her frame, her red hair falling to her shoulders in soft waves. Even through his fear, Alex felt his breath catch at her otherworldly beauty.

'Ready?' she asked.

Alex nodded. His throat was too parched to speak.

Step by step, she led him to the cave's mouth, the air growing colder with every movement, the damp chill of the cave replaced by the sharp wind of the outside world. When they crossed the threshold, Alex felt the full weight of the fresh air in his lungs.

He was somewhere near the coast. The roar of the sea filled his ears, and the salty air stung his skin. They walked across frozen grasslands, the brittle blades crunching beneath their feet. Alex's gaze darted around the landscape, desperate for a clue to his location. It reminded him of Cornwall but nothing looked familiar. The sun was hidden behind a thick veil of clouds, the dim light suggesting it was late afternoon.

Adelaide guided him over a small hill and up a steeper incline until they reached the edge of a gulley. In the centre of the depression stood another woman, dressed in white like Adelaide.

A surge of desperation filled Alex. He wanted to scream, to call for help, but the sound caught in his throat. Fear, or perhaps resignation, smothered his instincts.

'Be respectful, Alex,' Adelaide said, her grip tightening on his arm. 'Only look her in the eye if she asks you to.'

They descended into the gulley together, Adelaide's arm looped through his as if they were a happy couple strolling through a garden. Alex had to remind himself of his mortal danger. It was as if Adelaide was playing with his mind and memory. She was the enemy, but at times he felt as if she was everything to him. He began to wonder if she'd been drugging him all along. His memory felt tainted, and as he struggled to maintain his balance, his hands still bound by the zip tie, he thought he no longer knew what was real.

'Here he is, Mummy,' Adelaide said. 'Didn't I tell you he was beautiful?'

Alex tried to keep his gaze fixed on the ground, but curiosity got the better of him. He glanced at the woman Adelaide had called Mummy. In his captivity, he had imagined a frail, hunched figure – an elderly crone straight out of a dark fairy tale. But the reality was far more unsettling.

Though older, the woman was a striking reflection of Adelaide. Her once-red hair had faded to a silvery grey, but her high cheekbones and almond-shaped eyes mirrored her daughter's. Despite the deep wrinkles criss-crossing her skin, her beauty was undeniable. She exuded an air of authority that made Alex's skin crawl.

'Look at me, child,' she said, as Adelaide removed his sunglasses.

Alex obeyed, his heart pounding as he met her gaze. Her eyes were wide and penetrating, their warmth undercut by a profound darkness lurking within them. When she reached out to cup his face, her touch was smooth but unnervingly cold.

'It's him, isn't it, Mummy?' Adelaide said, stepping closer.

The older woman began to cry, tears streaking down her lined face. 'Yes, child,' she said. 'You've done well. He's come back to us.'

Adelaide wrapped her arms around her mother, the two women locked in an embrace. Alex stood frozen, his mind racing. Their intimacy unsettled him, not because it was affectionate but because it felt so alien. The love between them seemed steeped in something far darker than familial bonds.

The older woman broke the embrace and turned back to Alex. 'You've brought him back,' she said. 'He will be the one to set things right.'

Alex's stomach twisted, his heart hammering in his chest. He didn't know what they meant. But deep down, he knew one thing for certain: whatever 'setting things right' entailed, it wasn't going to end well for him.

Chapter Twenty-Two

Bleary-eyed, Liam took the note into his bedroom and unfolded it. The handwritten words read:

> *Hi Liam, I'm sorry for the subterfuge. I am staying at the Blue Jay Bed and Breakfast. I am using an unregistered phone so they can't see who I have been talking to. It would be great to see you. Grace x*

Grace's new number was written beneath her signature, but Liam knew better than to call from his own phone. With the demands of the hessian bag investigation, he hadn't spared much thought for Grace's suspension. While there would be no crime in contacting her, if it was on record that she'd reached out to him – or worse, that they'd actually spoken – it could lead to trouble for him down the line. Her precautions suggested she knew that too.

It was an unwelcome complication, but there must have been a reason for her reaching out to him, especially as she'd travelled all the way down to Cornwall.

As he lay in bed, thoughts of Grace distracted him from sleep. He'd always expected her to excel in the police, and her rapid rise and poise during her time in Cornwall had impressed him.

He couldn't deny his continued attraction to her. They'd been young when they'd dated, their first jobs taking them to opposite ends of the country, her to London, him to Cornwall. When she'd worked in Cornwall during the Godrevy investigation, he'd thought he'd seen hints of lingering feelings on her part, though he wasn't sure how he felt about it himself. At the time, he'd dismissed the notion, largely because of Millie. But had there been something there, something he'd purposely ignored – through self-preservation, or perhaps the fear of commitment Kim accused him of having.

Eventually, sleep must have come. He woke groggy at 6.30 a.m., the grey dawn breaking as rain lashed the windows. Pouring himself a strong coffee, he contemplated going for a run but abandoned the idea after a glance at the swirling wind outside blowing loose litter through the streets. Instead, he opted for a shower, dressed, and set off for Bodmin, slipping Grace's note into his inside pocket for safekeeping.

At nine, he was called into a meeting with DCI Hargreaves and Maya. For a moment, as Hargreaves began to speak, Liam braced himself for a mention of Grace and some bizarre turn of events, perhaps her on the run. But the focus was on Daniella White.

'Maya has briefed me on last night. While I think it was probably acceptable for you to visit her, I'd urge caution going forward,' said Hargreaves.

Liam had spent the early morning researching Daniella. As she'd claimed, she worked at the Truro branch of a large London-based firm, specialising in commercial law. She'd studied at Exeter and qualified five years ago.

'We need to interview her, boss,' Liam said. 'We have enough to at least talk to her.'

Hargreaves held up a hand. 'Of course we'll interview her, but her firm has a criminal division. They won't make it easy. Let's tread carefully and play the game. Arrange a time for her to come in.'

'And the car? We need to search it,' Liam said.

'Then we ask nicely,' Hargreaves replied, a small smile tugging at the corners of his mouth.

Sometimes, Liam thought his superior could be overly cautious – more interested in keeping things smooth than pushing for answers. If Daniella White was the killer they were hunting, any delay could cost them. 'Alright, but can we get her in today?'

'No need,' Maya said, glancing at her phone as it buzzed. 'She's already here. Waiting in reception.'

In the light of day, Daniella White was even more striking than Liam had thought last night. He wasn't one to focus too much on appearances – a childhood as the only bald kid in school had taught him the futility of such judgements – but there was something magnetic about her presence. She wore a sharp business suit, the long red hair he'd noted last night now neatly tied into a bun. Perhaps it was the flawless symmetry of her jawline, or the slight curve of her lips, but there was an almost unnerving perfection to her features. And then there were her eyes, which were a piercing green so vivid that Liam wondered if they were enhanced by contact lenses. Whatever the case, they were difficult to look away from, and he was beginning to understand where her confidence came from.

'DS Kilshaw, DI Trent,' she said. 'I fear I may have been rather brusque with you last night. It had been a long day, and your late-night visit caught me off guard.' Her polished tone faltered only slightly, her Cornish roots slipping through on certain syllables.

'I completely understand. Can I get you a tea or coffee?' Maya asked.

'I'm fine. I'm sure this won't take very long,' Daniella replied, a pleasant smile softening her otherwise formal demeanour.

Liam and Maya led her to a spare interview room. Once seated, Maya ran through the preliminaries before returning to the question they'd posed the night before. She asked about her movements on Saturday evening and early Sunday morning, mentioning the footage they had of her vehicle.

Daniella listened with a calm, wry expression. 'Let me get this straight. You want to know why I was driving on the A3071? One of the busiest roads in Cornwall?'

'At that specific time, yes,' Liam replied.

'I was driving from one place to another, DS Kilshaw,' she said, avoiding the question with an edge of amusement. 'Just like hundreds of other people, I presume.'

'Not many of them were driving a twenty-year-old, two-tone Land Rover Defender at that time,' Liam said, leaning forward.

Daniella smiled, which lit up her face. 'I'm a classic girl, what can I say? And it's wonderful off-road. But let's be honest, DS Kilshaw, this is a stretch. Why are you so interested in my car?'

Liam explained the sightings of the Defender near the crime scenes. 'On at least two occasions, a woman wearing a baseball cap was seen driving the vehicle,' he added.

Daniella leant back, her eyes narrowing slightly as she considered his words. 'I've been reading about your investigation,' she said at last. 'It sounds very challenging. But this? This is absurd. I won't even bother asking if you've definitively identified my vehicle because I know I wasn't at those locations.'

Liam glanced at Maya. Daniella was sharp and confident, fully aware that they had little to hold her on. The interview was slipping through their fingers.

'We're simply trying to eliminate options from our investigation,' Maya said.

Daniella frowned, a faint line marring her otherwise flawless forehead. 'Is that so? That doesn't explain why you felt the need to show up at my house last night.' The frown vanished as quickly as it had appeared, replaced by her disarming smile. 'I respect the work you're doing. Truly. If you send me the specific dates and times when your mystery vehicle was spotted, I'll check my diary and let you know where I was.'

Liam resisted the urge to push harder. Daniella was there voluntarily, and she was offering to provide alibis. Pressing further without concrete evidence could alienate her, and risk compromising the case. Instead, he decided to test her composure. 'Have you ever been to Jesters nightclub?' he asked.

Daniella's smile didn't waver as she rose gracefully to her feet. 'Do I look like someone who would frequent a tawdry nightclub in Truro?' she said. 'Now, if there's nothing else, I really do need to get back to work.'

Liam stood, feeling a mix of frustration and admiration as she exited the room with the same unshakable poise she'd carried throughout the conversation. Maya sighed, folding her arms. 'We've got nothing on her,' she said.

'Not yet,' Liam replied, his mind already racing as he tried to formulate a plausible scenario where Daniella could be the suspect at the centre of the hessian bag killings.

◆ ◆ ◆

‘She’s definitely an interesting one,’ said Maya, a few minutes later, leaning against a desk in the incident room as Liam pinned a photograph of Daniella White on to the crime board. Despite their lack of concrete evidence, she was the closest they had to a suspect at present.

‘She certainly played us well.’

Maya grinned. ‘Us? Your mouth was so wide open I was worried it’d hit the floor.’

‘I’m not sure what you’re insinuating, DI Trent, but I would never act so unprofessionally. The fact that you’re discussing a potential suspect’s attractiveness, though, concerns me,’ said Liam, teasing his colleague.

‘Yeah, right. She did have that femme fatale thing going for her. Not hard to imagine her luring men to their doom.’

‘Like a siren,’ Liam said, a vivid image of Daniella standing waist-deep in the sea, her voice bewitching unsuspecting men, flickering in his mind.

Maya smirked. ‘Maybe she’s working in collaboration with your sea monster, Bucca.’

‘The thought had crossed my mind. What do we do now?’

‘Take her at her word. Get her to confirm her movements on the dates we’ve got.’

‘I was thinking, though . . .’ Liam trailed off, hesitating.

Maya gave an exaggerated sigh. ‘Here we go. What?’

‘If Daniella’s at work today, I could pay her house another visit. A closer look at her Land Rover in daylight might turn up something.’

Maya folded her arms. ‘You’re looking for trouble. We don’t have enough on her, Liam, and if she finds out, she’ll have every reason to file a harassment complaint.’

‘What if I just happen to be in the area? I could stop by to double-check her availability for an interview, clarify the dates.’

'That's even worse. If you do this and she catches wind, it's going to backfire spectacularly.'

Liam nodded, though he hadn't dismissed the idea. 'Just a thought.'

'Stick to the shipping company meeting for now,' said Maya. 'You're leaving in ten, right?'

'Yeah. You coming along?'

'Tempting, but I think I'll stay put. It's looking pretty cold out there,' she said.

◆ ◆ ◆

Now that the idea had taken root, Liam was struggling to shake the image of Daniella White as the siren that lured two men to their deaths.

As Maya had suggested, it wasn't hard to see how Frank Oakley or Robin Wakefield could be drawn to her, their judgement clouded by whatever allure she held over them. He thought of Bucca Dhu, and although it seemed unlikely that someone as educated and sophisticated as Daniella could hold such beliefs, he couldn't completely dismiss it out of hand; although what she would get out of sacrificing men to the mythical creature was less clear.

Liam laughed under his breath. He was getting way ahead of himself. Before anything, they needed something tangible to link Daniella to the victims, and as he arrived at S&D Shipping, he didn't have high hopes that he would find it there.

Terry Caines was unable, or unwilling, to hide his displeasure as Liam arrived. The grey stubble on his face was thicker than before, his eyes bloodshot and drawn. 'What now?' he said, meeting Liam in the warehouse.

'How are things, Mr Caines?'

'Not great. Overworked and underpaid.'

'My condolences about Jordan,' said Liam, studying Caines for any flicker of emotion.

Caines shook his head. 'Silly bugger,' he said, not unkindly.

'Did Jordan ever show any signs of depression when he worked for you?'

'I'm no psychologist. He could be moody sometimes, but that was usually when he was hungover. Never thought he'd do . . . that,' said Caines, averting his gaze.

'Do you know a gentleman by the name of Robin Wakefield?'

Caines froze for a moment, his shoulders stiffening as his gaze met Liam's again. For a brief second, he looked as if the weight of the world was pressing down on him. 'I didn't know the lad very well, but I've obviously heard about what happened. Everyone's a bit shook up, especially after Jordan.'

'What can you tell me about Robin?'

'He was a temp worker. I met him, but didn't know him, if you know what I mean. Kept himself to himself, but these young guys mostly do nowadays.'

'Would he have known Jordan?'

'Their paths would've crossed on the floor, but they weren't in the same team. Robin just did all the grunt work that didn't need any safety clearance.'

'So he wouldn't have worked with the containers?'

Caines shook his head. 'No. I understand now why you asked about the hessian bags. Who the hell would do such a thing?'

'That's what we're trying to find out. Can you think of anyone who'd want to hurt Robin?'

'Like I said, he was a quiet lad. Never heard him say a bad word about anyone. That said . . .' Caines hesitated, glancing at the far end of the warehouse. He raised his voice. 'John, who was that girl Robin was seeing from the office?'

'Heather,' came the shouted reply from a burly colleague.

'Oh yeah, Heather from the office,' Caines echoed, turning back to Liam. 'I think she's another temp. We had a social evening not long ago, and from what I heard, they hooked up. But I don't think Robin was that into her. There was a bit of a thing a few days later. She came down to the floor, words were exchanged, mostly from her, and there were more than a few tears.'

'Can I speak to her?'

'Is that Heather in?' Caines asked his colleague.

'Nah, she's off on the sick.'

'Sorry,' said Caines, pointing to a set of offices surrounding the factory floor. 'If you pop up there, you'll be able to get her address.'

Liam nodded. 'Thanks for all your help,' he said, walking towards the staircase to get Heather's details.

Chapter Twenty-Three

Alex didn't know why Adelaide was crying. Her tearful assurances offered him no comfort. The darkening sky only added to his dread, and he couldn't stop shaking. He almost missed the solitude of the cave with its constant, unchanging temperature. Out here, the cold seeped through the dowdy clothes she'd dressed him in: trousers, a shirt, a woollen waistcoat, and a pullover. They were all various shades of brown.

How the two women could stand the chill in their thin white dresses was beyond him. The cold felt alive. It got under his skin, gnawing at him from the inside.

'It's time, Alex,' Adelaide said, her tears shimmering in the dim light.

A thick mist clung to the grasslands as they led him up the other side of the gulley. At the top, Alex caught sight of the sea, its waves black and restless in the distance. He scanned the area desperately, hoping to see someone out walking, but the area was desolate and nothing seemed familiar. Behind him, he could make out the silhouette of a solitary house, but he couldn't determine where the cave system that had been his prison was hidden.

They walked on until they reached a small lake, its still surface broken by a narrow stream.

'Where are we?' he said.

'Through here, Alex,' Adelaide said, leading him to the water's edge. His heart sank at the sight of a large brown hessian bag resting there, a chain leading from the bag to an iron anchor in the frozen ground.

'You're going to need to take your clothes off now, Alex,' Adelaide said.

His mind reeled. The bag was big enough to hold a person, and the sight of it brought back the memory of Adelaide placing the dying mouse into a smaller version of it back in the cave.

Now, with chilling clarity, Alex understood: the bag was his coffin.

He didn't understand the purpose of this ritual – why he'd been chosen or what these women wanted – but it didn't matter. He knew he wouldn't climb willingly into that grave. He turned to face Adelaide and her mother, his fear turning to defiance. His wrists were bound, but he would charge at them, kick, bite, do whatever he could to resist. He refused to go quietly.

But as he moved towards them, he felt something prick at his neck.

The realisation hit too late. The mother had slipped behind and injected him with something.

'It'll make this easier for you, Alex,' said Adelaide, her smile serene, her eyes dark and soulless.

Alex fell to his knees, the world tilting around him. He fought to stay upright, before deliberately collapsing by the bag and its opening. If he could just move his hands . . .

His body felt heavy, sluggish, but in his mind, he was fighting, saving himself. Even as the poison dragged him into unconsciousness, he held on to the hope that his last motion had given himself a chance.

◆ ◆ ◆

The icy bite of the wind brought Alex back to consciousness. He opened his eyes to a sky full of winking stars, but his body was frozen, encased in the cold. He didn't need to look to know he was naked.

Adelaide's voice floated above him. 'You need to climb in, Alex.' She was standing over him, her white dress almost luminous in the starlight, her mother by her side holding something sharp.

Alex tried to move, but his limbs refused to cooperate.

'Here,' Adelaide said, crouching beside him. 'You can do this, Alex. Do this, and you'll be fine.'

His teeth chattered as he whispered, 'You're going to kill me.'

'Not you, Alex. You're going to live forever,' she said.

Despite his efforts, his body betrayed him. He felt his knees and elbows dragging him to the bag. He thought he was resisting, but every movement only carried him closer to his fate. His limbs moved of their own accord until he was inside, the rough hessian fabric closing around him like a shroud.

He tried to push against the bag, but his hands were weak, the weave impenetrable. Hyperventilating, he listened as the bag was sealed at his feet.

Was this it? Was he going to be buried alive, left to rot in the ground?

He forced himself to breathe slowly, trying to stave off the panic. His hands scrambled against the inside of the bag, searching for anything, but his movements did little to help.

Then, the bag shifted.

He felt himself being dragged across the ground, rough terrain scraping against his back through the fabric. Outside, the women's voices rose in unison, their words a frenzied chant, alien to his ears.

For a brief, wondrous moment, he was weightless. The chanting stopped, and Alex wondered if this was death, before he landed with a splash.

Alex thrashed, panic exploding through him as the freezing water began seeping into the bag, and he realised his final resting place was going to be a watery grave.

Chapter Twenty-Four

Heather Fowley had been off work since Robin Wakefield's death had become public knowledge. The office manager at S&D had given Liam her address, which, fortunately, was on his way back to Bodmin.

As he drove, Liam kept an eye out for a payphone. The note from Grace rested in his jacket pocket, and he wanted to reach out to her but couldn't risk using his police-issued phone. There was obviously a reason for her secrecy, but he wasn't ready to go to the trouble of buying a burner phone just yet.

Unsurprisingly, the only phone box he came across had been repurposed as a community library, its shelves filled with books for locals to exchange. Liam couldn't recall the last time he'd seen a functional phone box and wondered if any still existed.

Heather's address was in a quiet cul-de-sac on the outskirts of Truro. Liam pulled up outside the house, which had three cars in the driveway. The cold snap showed no sign of easing as he sprinted the short distance from his car to the door, arriving with a light drizzle soaking his jacket.

'DS Kilshaw,' he said to the woman who answered the door. 'I'd like to speak to Heather, if she's in.'

'I'm Heather's mum. What's this about?' the woman asked, standing firm in the doorway despite the wind-blown rain.

'It's to do with Robin Wakefield's death.'

'Simone Fowley,' she said, stepping aside to let Liam in. The house was immaculately tidy, and Liam rested himself by a white radiator as Simone called up the stairs for her daughter. 'Heather's been in her room. She's not coping well with Robin's death, as you can imagine.'

'Were they close?' Liam asked.

'I'm not too sure. I know she was very keen on him.'

A young woman in navy blue pyjamas appeared at the top of the stairs, and began to descend hesitantly. 'Hi, honey,' Simone said, speaking directly to Heather. 'This is DS Kilshaw. He wants to talk to you about Robin.'

Heather looked startled. She was far younger than Liam had expected. 'Nice to meet you, Heather,' he said.

'Mum?' Heather murmured, glancing at her mother as if for protection.

'It's OK, love. You go through to the living room with DS Kilshaw, and I'll make you some tea.'

Heather offered Liam a weak smile and led him through the house.

'You're a temp at S&D?' he asked, taking a seat.

'Yes,' she replied, sitting on the seat furthest away from him.

'How old are you, if you don't mind me asking?'

'Nineteen.'

'From what I understand, you were good friends with Robin?'

'Sort of.' Heather glanced nervously at the doorway to ensure her mother wasn't listening. She lowered her voice. 'We, you know, hooked up. Once.'

Liam thought about the argument Terry Caines had described. 'Just the once?'

Taking a deep breath, Heather glanced at the door again. 'It was at a work function. I'd had a bit too much to drink. I thought it was something more, certainly more than Robin thought it was.'

'You confronted him about it?' asked Liam.

'I guess those morons on the floor have been talking. I'm sure they're having a great laugh about it.' Heather sighed. 'I shouldn't have gone down there that day. Robin had been ignoring me, and I just wanted . . . I don't know what I wanted, really. I knew there wasn't anything between us. Someone even told me he had a girlfriend. Maybe I just wanted to hear it from him directly, that it was all over. Though I guess it never really started.'

Heather's mother returned with the teas, setting them down before perching on the arm of a chair. Liam turned to the necessity of establishing Heather's whereabouts on Saturday night. He doubted she was the woman seen leaving the nightclub with Robin, but he couldn't rule it out.

'She was here at home with us, weren't you, dear?' her mother said.

Liam shifted his gaze to Heather, who stared down at her lap. He wondered how much of her life had been spent with others speaking for her.

'It's true,' Heather said, managing a weak smile. 'An exciting Saturday night in with my parents watching *Strictly*.'

'When did you find out what had happened to Robin?' Liam asked.

'When everyone else did, obviously,' her mother replied.

'Please, let Heather speak for herself.'

Heather glanced up. 'A friend from work was told, and she let me know.'

'It must have come as something of a shock?'

Heather looked away, her eyes shimmering. 'I couldn't believe it. Still can't.'

Liam sipped his tea, noting the raw sadness in Heather's youthful features, as he wondered how many hearts Robin

Wakefield had left shattered in his wake and what role that had to play in his death.

◆ ◆ ◆

On his way back to Bodmin, Liam stopped at an independent phone shop and bought a prepaid mobile phone with cash. He wasn't sure it was necessary, but Grace had gone to the trouble of coming to Cornwall and slipping a note through his door so there had to be some kind of reason for her precaution.

The phone was pre-charged, and Liam returned to his car to call the number on the note.

'Hello?' Grace's voice on the other end jolted him from his thoughts.

'Grace, is that you?'

'You took your time,' she replied.

'Burner phones are in short supply around here.'

Grace laughed, the sound strangely comforting. 'Sorry for all that. With this investigation you're working on, I didn't want my number popping up on your records. You know how the professional standards lot are, putting two and two together and coming up with corruption.'

'Is everything OK?' Liam asked. 'I heard about your suspension, but is there more to it? Something I should know?'

Grace paused for a moment. 'You probably know more than I do at this point. I'm sorry to bring this to you, especially with everything you've been through, everything your girlfriend went through.'

She hesitated, as though waiting for him to say something about Millie. When he didn't, she added, 'And I've heard about the case you're working on.'

'It's OK. It's good to hear from you. Though why are you down in Cornwall?'

The line went quiet, and Liam glanced at the phone, wondering if the signal had dropped or if he'd asked the wrong thing.

'When this all went down, it gave me a good chance to look at my life. I took stock of everything and everyone in it. It made me realise that I don't have anyone I can trust.'

Liam thought about his own situation, how he'd hoped for something meaningful with Millie, only to sabotage it. 'So, you thought you'd come and see me?'

'Don't get so sure of yourself, sonny Jim. I just needed a break. Though, the thing is, Liam, when I thought about who I wanted to speak to, your name did pop up in my mind. Sorry, I'm being out of line.'

It was Liam's turn to fall silent. For the second time that year, Grace had re-emerged in his life, unbidden and unexpected. When they'd first split years ago, during their training days, he'd assumed that was it. When she'd returned earlier this year, he'd just started seeing Millie, but he couldn't deny that Grace had lingered in his thoughts. That lingering thought now made him uncomfortable, made him wonder if he was more like Robin Wakefield than he cared to admit.

'You're not being out of line. Let's meet up tonight. We can talk more, then.'

'OK, sounds great,' said Grace.

Liam lingered in his car after the call ended, staring at the prepaid phone on the passenger seat. He told himself Grace's arrival was a distraction, but wasn't sure if it was a welcome one or not.

He tried to refocus on the investigation, starting the car and setting off towards headquarters. His thoughts churned through the web of connections. Frank Oakley's mutilated body in Sennen,

Robin Wakefield's in Porth Nanven, the unsettling replica dolls, and the possible thread tying it all to Jordan Hayes and S&D Shipping.

No matter how he approached it, his mind kept circling back to Daniella White. There was still no match between her and the grainy images of the woman leaving Jesters nightclub with Robin, but Liam couldn't shake the sense she was involved. His imagination betrayed him, conjuring her once more as a siren on a rocky shore, enticing her victims to the water's edge while Bucca Dhu stormed behind her.

'I think I need some rest,' he said, laughing at himself for the bizarre images his mind had conjured.

But instead of heading to headquarters, he found himself taking a different turn, ignoring his better judgement as he set off for Daniella's house in Hendra.

Chapter Twenty-Five

Liam called Jack as he drove to Hendra, avoiding the potential fallout of explaining to Maya what he planned to do. Jack updated him on the morning's work, which focused on identifying and interviewing as many people as possible who had been at Jesters on Saturday night.

'Some of the staff are coming into the station this afternoon,' Jack said.

'Make sure everyone sees a photo of Daniella White,' Liam replied, as the turning to Daniella's house appeared on his satnav.

Hanging up, he took the narrow lane that led to her property, his mind working on what he would say if she happened to have returned from work early. He parked up, fighting the unease telling him he shouldn't be there. Maya had been right. Daniella needed to be handled carefully. Someone in her position could cause serious complications if the investigation wasn't above board. However, he still felt justified in his actions, especially every time he thought of the brutalised remains of Frank Oakley and Robin Wakefield.

Stepping out of the car, he opened the gate and walked towards the house. The two-tone Land Rover Defender sat exactly where it had been the night before, parked outside the property. Liam resisted the urge to investigate it, wary of potential security cameras.

Instead, he rang the doorbell, running through plausible excuses in his head for why he might be here.

When no one answered, Liam turned his attention to the vehicle. It had been too dark the previous night to get a proper look, and they'd been rushed. He recalled the CCTV footage of the petrol station, imagining Daniella behind the wheel. Was she the woman the teenagers had seen leaving Porth Nanven? Could she have been the one to dump the hessian bag, and, if so, why?

In the crisp daylight, it was obvious the Defender had recently been cleaned. The vehicle was immaculate – inside and out – which was unusual for something that old. Liam crouched to examine the tyres. They were almost completely free of dirt, an oddity given the muddy terrain surrounding the property. Combined with the spotless exterior, it was clear the vehicle had been cleaned at home, and Daniella didn't strike him as someone who would scrub down her own car.

◆ ◆ ◆

'Busy day?' asked Maya, when Liam returned to the incident room later that afternoon.

Though it was less a question and more an invitation to confess, Liam relayed his day's movements, although he left out his conversation with Grace. 'I happened to be in the Hendra area at one point,' he said, teeth clenched.

'Oh, you didn't?' Maya asked, not hiding her incredulity that he would do something so rash as questioning Daniella again.

'It's fine. I wanted to ask her a question, but she wasn't at home.'

Maya raised an eyebrow. 'Is that so? And what did you learn?'

'She doesn't drive the Defender to work.'

'Why would she, when she has a Jaguar for everyday errands?'

'The Defender's been recently cleaned. It's spotless, no dirt, inside or out.'

'You looked inside?'

'From what I could see, obviously.'

'Right, it's hardly a crime.'

'Maybe not, but it's suspicious.'

Maya frowned. 'This isn't like you.'

Liam held his hand up. 'What?'

'The car being cleaned isn't going to lead to a search warrant. There are more pressing things you could be doing.'

Liam nodded. 'I hear you.'

They sat before the crime board, the white screen scrolling through the investigation timeline. Maya liked working this way, and so did Liam. The images often sparked new ideas for lines of enquiry, and kept his mind focused.

'Any luck with the patrons at Jesters?' Liam asked, as two smiling images – one of Frank Oakley, the other of Robin Wakefield – appeared consecutively on the screen.

'No one we've spoken to has identified Daniella White, if that's what you mean. And no one is volunteering anything about the woman who left the club with Robin.'

'What about the video footage?'

'We've got a second team combing through it again. From what we've seen so far, the woman bypassed the main entrance. The first time she appears on camera is with Robin.'

Liam pictured Robin struggling to stay upright, leaning on the woman for support. 'Is that even possible?'

'Apparently, people sometimes sneak in through the fire escape.'

'Which means someone let her in. An accomplice?' Liam asked.

'Or someone earning a few extra quid.'

Liam scratched his head, running his fingers along the jagged scar on his skull. 'Disappointing no one's identified Daniella White,' he said.

'Not someone you'd likely forget either,' Maya replied.

Liam glanced up at the white screen, this time showing Frank and Robin's remains. 'Objectively speaking, we're saying both these men were good-looking or very good-looking?'

'Objectively speaking. You know I'm gay, right?' said Maya.

'Yes, but I still think you have a better eye for these things. How good-looking are we talking?'

'Definitely nines, at least.'

'And Jordan Hayes?'

'Not in their league.'

'And me?' said Liam, tapping his fingers on the desk.

'I can't answer that, especially with PSD in the building.'

'Great, but we could argue these two men were targeted for their looks?'

Maya paused the scrolling images, rewinding to the photos of Frank and Robin. 'They could be brothers,' she said. 'The resemblance is uncanny.'

Liam studied the two images, noting the shared qualities: mousey dark hair, large brown eyes, full lips, and prominent jawlines. 'It would take some planning to find and then target them separately,' he said. 'Although their noses are different shapes.'

'There's hope for you yet,' Maya teased, zooming in on the two noses.

'So why target two men who look so similar?'

'They must remind the killer of someone,' Maya said. 'Maybe someone who did them harm.'

'Or someone who broke their heart?'

'We could look at Daniella White's past boyfriends,' said Liam.

'And the others. Julie Patterson, that young woman from the shipping company. Maybe somewhere out there, there's another doppelgänger of Frank and Robin who has something to answer for.'

'Or worse, there's someone out there who looks like them and is potentially the next target.'

◆ ◆ ◆

Liam spent the rest of the afternoon combing through the police national computer for mispers, starting with reports of missing men between the ages of twenty and thirty. His initial focus was on those who'd gone missing in the south-west, but as Frank Oakley's case had proven, the scope needed to be broader. Any of the missing men could have visited or currently be in Cornwall, making the task feel almost impossible. Young adults were the largest demographic for missing persons in the UK, and without narrowing the parameters, the results numbered in the thousands.

What Liam needed was a way to match missing men to the physical appearance of Frank and Robin, but no such search criteria existed. Hair colour, height, and weight weren't precise enough, and the alternative – reviewing each case manually – was simply unfeasible.

He broadened his approach, looking for connections between the victims' families and the slim list of potential suspects. It was a shot in the dark at best.

It was difficult to shake the conclusion that they were, for now, at the mercy of the killer. Aside from the similarity in the victims' appearances, the only discernible patterns were the method of murder and the disposal of the bodies. Both victims had been mutilated beyond recognition, left in hessian bags, and seemingly positioned so their remains would be found.

Were these gruesome displays an act of pride, a demonstration of power, or a targeted warning? Perhaps they were intended to send a message to someone specific.

Or was the killer crying out for help? Could these acts be driven by regret, leaving clues in the hope that someone would stop them before they struck again?

Whatever the motive, the case felt like a waiting game. Unless a breakthrough came soon, it seemed the only way forward would be the unimaginable tragedy of another victim being uncovered.

◆ ◆ ◆

He left work at seven, exhausted, and drove back to St Ives, where he'd agreed to meet Grace. After showering and changing, he set off. His body ached, a dull pain stretching from the base of his neck to his lower back.

As he walked the streets of St Ives, he glanced around him. It was unlikely, but he wanted to make sure he wasn't being followed and he kept his eye out for any sign of the PSD officers.

Grace was waiting for him in a small, tucked-away restaurant near the beach. She stood as he approached, her smile warm and familiar. They embraced, and the faint scent of her perfume stirred memories he'd thought long buried. She kissed his cheek lightly before they sat down.

'I presume you've already mapped out all the exits in case Professional Standards spot us together,' said Liam, with a wry smile.

'Very funny. My career is already wrecked. Excuse me for wanting to protect yours.'

They ordered their food and exchanged small talk. After the intensity of the last few weeks, it was the closest Liam had come to relaxing in a long time. Grace, too, seemed at ease, far happier than she'd been during her time leading the Godrevy investigation.

'You're looking well,' Liam said, as Grace sipped her wine.

Grace's brow furrowed, a flicker of surprise crossing her face. 'Thank you.'

'It's just, with all this cloak-and-dagger stuff, I thought you'd be more on edge.'

'What were you expecting? A prematurely aged madwoman?'

'Maybe not quite that. But you seem happy. What's the latest on your suspension?'

'My rep thinks it'll be lifted, that it was just precautionary after my boss got the boot.'

'That's positive, then?'

'Yeah, maybe. It's given me time to think about what I really want to do.'

'I thought you were in line to be the next chief constable?'

Grace gave a rueful laugh. 'Probably not now. The thing is, I had no idea that woman was a rogue UCO. In fact, you knew before I did. And they know that. There'd be no advantage in me knowing, or managing her that way.'

'I know that.'

'They all do,' she repeated. 'I shouldn't be in this position, and it's made me wonder if it's even worth going back.'

Liam leant back in his chair. 'You can't let a bit of bureaucracy ruin your career, Grace. You're one of the best coppers I've ever met.'

Grace waved the compliment away. 'To be good in this job, you've got to care, and I'm not sure I do any more.'

'Come on, that's not true.'

She shrugged. 'Maybe I care, but not enough to put up with all the bullshit that comes with it.'

Their food arrived, and they ate in comfortable silence for a few minutes. Liam thought about his own relentless dedication to his investigations, acknowledging the truth in Grace's words about focus and desire. Yet he couldn't shake the feeling that she wasn't telling him everything. He decided to wait for her to open up in her own time.

It was surprising how at ease he felt being in Grace's company, especially so soon after his break with Millie. He wondered again what might have happened if they had not split up all those years ago, cutting the thought short as he decided it was not ideal to be thinking along those lines once more.

'What will you do if you leave the police?' he asked, as rain began to pelt the window behind her.

'That is to be determined.'

Liam nodded. 'Why are you here, Grace?' he asked. 'It's great to see you, but it's a bit of a surprise.'

'You can relax,' she said, with a narrow smile. 'I got the message loud and clear last time I was here. I know you're with Millie, and I know what she went through. I'd never try to come between you. But . . . it's hard to explain. London can be so cloying sometimes. I like being here in the summer, so I thought I'd try it out in the winter.'

'How's that working out for you?' Liam asked, glancing at the rain falling off the glass outside.

'It's like a different place, but you're a good constant, Liam. It's just nice to see a friendly face.' She leant back in her chair as the waiter collected their plates. 'One for the road?'

'Just a coffee for me,' said Liam, thinking he could be one drink away from making a wrong decision, as outside the rain finally began to ease.

Chapter Twenty-Six

The cloying atmosphere of the mortuary, with its distinctive smell, was not where Liam wanted to be first thing in the morning. Sitting in the viewing area, he stared at, but didn't touch, the coffee he'd brought with him as his mind drifted back to last night's dinner with Grace.

He still wasn't convinced she'd told him everything. On the drive back to her hotel, he'd tried pressing her for more details about her suspension, but she'd deftly changed the subject. As they reached the hotel reception, she'd pecked him on the cheek, leaving him with a lingering sense of unease. She insisted they communicate only via burner phones for his sake, though she hadn't explained why.

Why he hadn't told Grace he was single now eluded him. As Maya arrived, Liam wondered if it was a form of self-preservation, a way to avoid further complications in his already tangled life.

'You're early,' Maya said.

'You're late,' Liam replied, as Dr Wetzel entered the mortuary with his assistant, and both started to prepare for the post-mortem, washing their hands and donning protective scrubs.

'Another doozy,' Wetzel said, pulling the covering off the disfigured corpse. Despite knowing the delay in the autopsy wasn't intentional, it felt jarring compared to the same-day examination for Frank Oakley. The identity of the victim was already confirmed, but it was still hard to reconcile the mutilated remains on the steel slab as belonging to Robin Wakefield.

As with Frank Oakley, Wetzel determined that Robin had bled out from the wounds to his face and neck and hadn't drowned. Again, it appeared he had been sealed in the hessian bag before the attacks were made, with the lacerations on the bag matching the wounds on Robin's face.

'This could be interesting,' Wetzel said, holding up a tiny fragment of a bright green plant. 'If I'm not mistaken, this is what we call green string lettuce – *Ulva linza*, if my Latin is correct. It's a type of green sea algae. Usually found in brackish water, estuarine or freshwater-saltwater mix zones. Cornwall's hardly short of those. You'll need further analysis, but I hope it's helpful.'

'Could be something,' Maya said. 'We should look at areas near Sennen and Porth Nanven where salt and freshwater mix.'

'I'll get on to it,' Liam replied, though the prospect felt daunting as they endured the final, painstaking minutes of the autopsy.

The primary challenge was determining the killer's process precisely. From what they could gather, neither of the locations where the bodies were found – Sennen and Porth Nanven – were likely locations for where the murders occurred. It could be that the victims were killed in an area where green string lettuce was prevalent. Unfortunately, as Wetzel had pointed out, there were numerous estuarine and brackish water zones across Cornwall. Even narrowing the search to four or five areas near Sennen and Porth Nanven felt like hunting for the proverbial needle in a haystack.

Back at headquarters, Liam attempted to formulate a search on the PND to match missing men with those living close to brackish water zones. Unsurprisingly, no such criteria existed. The closest he could manage was filtering for missing men within a certain distance of the coast, a search he'd already run the day before.

What he *really* wanted to do was search Daniella White's Land Rover Defender for traces of the algae found on Robin's body. But judging by the newly scrubbed state of the vehicle, any such evidence had likely been erased.

Liam rubbed his face, feeling tired and drawn. He reminded himself that cases often went this way, stretches of apparent inactivity where progress felt stagnant, even though the investigation continued in multiple directions. Experience had taught him that sometimes all it took was one minor breakthrough to unravel everything.

It had also taught him that sometimes that breakthrough never came.

The most important thing was to stay proactive and work with what they had.

Sitting back, Liam stared at the crime board. The looping images on the white screen scrolled endlessly through photos and case materials. As he watched the before-and-after images of Frank Oakley and Robin Wakefield, he found the effect more maudlin than helpful, especially with the memory of Robin's autopsy still fresh in his mind.

To shift his focus, he downloaded happier images of the two men on to his laptop, once again noting the uncanny similarities between them. It wasn't just their youthful good looks or tousled hair; the details were even more precise. The noses may have been slightly different in size, but they shared the same oval-shaped brown eyes, large full lips, and strong jawline. Even their eyebrows and a sprinkling of freckles on their cheeks matched.

If he had been shown photos of the two men without knowing who they were, he could have easily believed they were related. He considered what kind of reconnaissance the killer must have conducted to select these two victims, and wondered how much planning had gone into their abduction and murder.

'I think we should run an appeal. This can't be a coincidence,' he said to Maya a few minutes later, gesturing to the images on his screen.

'The team's already looking into mispers who match their appearance,' Maya replied.

'I know, but we need to go public. For all we know, the killer could already have their eyes on a new target. This could be preventative.'

Maya sighed, the exhaustion in her eyes mirroring his own. They both knew a public appeal had risks, especially one like this. 'We'll get every lunatic in the country calling us. It'll probably create more work than we can handle,' she said, but Liam could tell she was relenting.

By late afternoon, they received the green light from Hargreaves. The DCI had initially wanted to wait until the morning, but with the weekend approaching, Liam convinced him to set something up for the evening.

Overtime was approved, and the PR department secured slots with local TV news channels for a hastily arranged press conference.

It was decided Maya and Hargreaves would present the appeal, and later that evening Liam took a seat in the audience among the assembled journalists.

'Is it because my head's too shiny for the cameras?' he said, as Maya walked past him towards the stage. She smirked at him as she took her place.

The press conference was one of the stranger ones Liam had witnessed. Typically, these appeals focused on a specific missing person or a wanted suspect. Here, Hargreaves had the unenviable task of explaining that the police were seeking information about any missing person who matched the physical characteristics of Frank Oakley and Robin Wakefield, a concept difficult to quantify and even harder to present without sounding abstract.

After showing images of the two victims to the press, Hargreaves was asked by a reporter if young men with similar physical characteristics should be worried for their safety.

Sometimes, Liam doubted whether Hargreaves was fully suited for his senior role. The man was an effective organiser and a decent manager, but he lacked the authority and gravitas the position of DCI often demanded. It reminded Liam of a young officer in the navy who'd led one of his first sections, someone who had risen to an officer role straight out of university. Despite excellent formal qualifications, the officer had lacked the hands-on experience of their subordinates, struggling to command respect. That officer had left within two years. While Hargreaves wasn't quite at that level, Liam recognised the hesitation in his face and was grateful when Maya interjected.

'We don't believe anyone is under a specific threat at present,' she said, 'but anyone matching this profile should remain vigilant. However, as DCI Hargreaves stated, our immediate concern is for individuals who fit this description and may have gone missing, or who haven't been in contact with friends or family recently. We're asking for anyone with such information to come forward.'

By the time Liam returned to the incident room, calls had already started coming in. A second room had been set up to accommodate the additional officers and civilian staff brought in to manage the influx. The appeal was already online, and Liam knew it meant he wouldn't be leaving the station until after midnight.

Still, he was glad the appeal was out there. Yes, there would be hundreds of calls to sift through, many irrelevant or from attention-seekers. But it only took one to make a difference, and that made the effort worthwhile.

In an ideal scenario, one of the calls would link back to a suspect they'd already encountered. Liam didn't hold out much hope, but Daniella's striking looks would be hard for anyone to forget. Wearing a baseball cap, as she had in the footage of her driving the Defender, wouldn't be enough to keep her hidden indefinitely. He wondered if she'd seen the press conference and whether it would alter her approach.

As the calls poured in, Liam's thoughts turned to the families and friends of missing persons affected by the night's proceedings. Many would be watching the news, forced to relive the trauma of their loved ones' disappearances. Others would feel compelled to reach out to their sons, brothers, or friends to make sure they were safe.

Liam guessed it was a small price to pay if it brought them closer to finding the killer. Of all the crimes he'd investigated during his career, it was the missing persons cases that lingered the most. The not knowing was often harder for families to bear than the finality of death. Though he had seen the despair in Robin Wakefield's mother's eyes, as well as in the eyes of Frank Oakley's relatives, he was certain that, in time, they would feel some measure of relief that they had closure, however heartbreaking that relief was.

'You should get some rest,' Maya said, sitting down next to him. 'That's why we've got everyone on overtime.'

Liam was so exhausted he didn't even want to contemplate the drive home. 'How's the new media career going?'

'What can I say? The camera loves me. Seriously, Liam, go home. You'll be much more useful after some sleep.'

'If you don't mind me saying, boss, I could say the same about you.'

'I need my beauty sleep as much as the next person. Well, maybe not as much as some,' she said, arching her brows playfully. 'But I'll probably be home before you. Now, get out of here.'

Liam smiled, grabbed his jacket, and made his way to the door. He knew Maya was right, but as he left the station, his thoughts remained on the investigation.

Despite the near-empty roads, the drive home felt longer every night. Most people were already tucked in, while Liam circled three blocks before finding a parking space. He loved this town but moving closer to Bodmin might be the sensible thing to do.

As he trudged along the frosted streets, he thought about how little he saw George. Even though that was partly his own doing, due to his relentless workload, he knew moving away wouldn't change much. He could still pick George up from school when his schedule allowed and have him stay for weekends. Perhaps he would even enjoy the break from his hometown?

The thought made him feel melancholy, a sure sign he was sleep deprived. Once inside the flat, he didn't bother turning on the light. Navigating by muscle memory, he headed straight to the bedroom, peeled off his clothes, climbed into bed, and was asleep almost instantly.

When he woke, it was after 8 a.m., which was unheard of for him. Most days, he would already be at work by now. Rolling over, he noted his phone was dead. He plugged it in and ran the shower, relieved to find no urgent messages waiting when it finally powered back on.

As he dressed, he realised that it had been over a week since he'd last visited his mother. Between Millie splitting with him and Grace's unexpected return to Cornwall, his personal life had fallen by the wayside since the day Frank Oakley's body was found in Sennen.

It wasn't a healthy way to live. In the navy, it had been different – deployment necessitated living in a bubble. But he wasn't on deployment any more. His PTSD from the near-death experience in the SBS should have been a warning that focusing solely on work wasn't sustainable. Yet here he was, leaving for another day at the station, realising he hadn't seen anyone outside of work in days.

George was in school, Kim wasn't someone he could easily pick the phone up for, and Millie was moving on with her life. That left only Grace outside of work, but the burner phone he used to contact her was safely stowed in the boot of his car.

Out of a sense of obligation, he called his mother's care home as he drove to Bodmin. The time when she might have missed his visits had long since passed, if it had ever existed at all. He realised he was barely listening as the standard response came, telling him everything was stable. He ended the call and continued his journey.

When he arrived at headquarters an hour later, the air in the car park was freezing, hovering near zero. It felt like the day they'd had their solitary snowstorm of the season, brittle and unyielding.

Inside the building, the heaters were on full blast. He sneezed at the change of temperature, and by the time he reached his seat in the incident room, sweat had formed on his forehead. He dabbed it away with his sleeve as Maya entered a few minutes later, looking refreshed and composed.

She began the morning briefing with a concise update. Calls were still coming in from the appeal, and the monitoring process had flagged several reasonable leads that warranted further investigation.

Liam shifted in his seat, his fatigue momentarily forgotten. There was still so much to do, but at least they were making progress – slow, grinding progress, but progress all the same.

Liam was assigned two leads to follow up. Within the hour, he was knocking on a door in Redruth, speaking to the parents of a young man, Ben Chertsey, who had gone missing during a gap year abroad four years ago.

The grieving parents welcomed him with a spark of hope in their eyes, showing him photographs of their son, who had been twenty-three at the time of his disappearance. Liam remembered the case. CID had been involved, liaising extensively with foreign crime agencies. It was one of those frustrating investigations that had ultimately gone cold.

He studied the pictures. Ben didn't bear much resemblance to either Frank Oakley or Robin Wakefield, and the timeline didn't align with the current case. Still, Liam was careful not to either fan the parents' optimism or extinguish their hope outright.

'I'll review the files again and see if there's anything we can connect to the current investigation,' he said, asking a few more questions before thanking them and moving on.

His next stop was a small, terraced house in St Agnes, where he met a young woman who had reported her husband missing over a year ago. She described the classic tale of a man leaving for the shops and never returning. The scenario was beloved of TV crime dramas but was far more common in reality than most people realised.

Liam examined the photos she provided. Again, the resemblance to Frank or Robin was negligible. Again, he promised to investigate further, knowing his assurances offered more comfort than substance.

Neither visit did much for Liam's spirits. The truth he couldn't voice was that sometimes people went missing and were never found. Not because of foul play, but because they didn't want to be found. It was plausible that Ben Chertsey was alive and thriving abroad, living a new life, or that the missing husband had deliberately walked away to start fresh elsewhere. But no one wanted to hear that. To these families, holding on to the possibility of answers, however slim, was better than confronting the void of the unknown.

What weighed on Liam most was the gnawing certainty that somewhere another victim was either already in trouble or about to be targeted.

He knew all too well what it was like to be trapped under water. Closing his eyes, he could still recall the unbearable weight of the water squeezing the air from his lungs.

He may have been too late to save two victims, but he still had a chance to prevent someone else suffering the same fate. And that was the person he had to put all his focus on.

Chapter Twenty-Seven

The water brought Alex a startling clarity, as if a fog had lifted from his mind. Weeks of living in a trance-like state, hypnotised by Adelaide's cryptic words and hollow reassurances, now seemed like a nightmare he could finally confront.

He wasn't fully submerged yet, and as he lay there on his back with water trickling but not covering him, he understood that something might be keeping him afloat. Was this Adelaide and her mother's watery equivalent of burying someone alive, he wondered, his mind briefly debating which of the two scenarios was worse, before the actuality of his current situation returned.

The cold gnawed at him, biting into his flesh, but adrenaline surged through his veins, pushing the numbness aside. He grasped at fragments of thought, memories of something. A chance, a desperate hope he'd planted for himself back in the cave.

The scissors.

Adelaide had trimmed his hair the last time, her movements deliberate, almost ritualistic. Half under her spell, yet somehow alert to the danger, Alex had slipped the scissors she'd left on the ground into the waistband of his trousers.

He didn't know what he'd planned to do with them. He was too enthralled to attack her, but he'd hoped they would come in handy at some point. After Adelaide's mother had injected him, he'd managed to throw them inside the bag, and had hoped neither woman had seen him.

The puddle beneath him was inching up towards his chest. He felt cold radiating through the coarse fabric, making his muscles ache. Even if he didn't drown, the cold water would soon take him in what he imagined would be a much more painful way. His breaths came in shallow bursts as he wriggled frantically, his hands fumbling for something that might not even be there, his numb fingers grasping and clawing at the slick surface of the bag.

He was almost out of time. His mind whirled with questions he couldn't afford to contemplate. *What did Adelaide mean when she said I was ready? Why the bag? Why this cruel ritual?* The answers didn't matter now. He had minutes, at best, before it was over.

Something hard and cold touched the back of his thigh. His fingers scrambled behind him, reaching out until he made contact with the scissors.

Alex's breath caught, the shock of hope cutting through the haze of fear. He twisted his body, managing to retrieve the scissors. The confined space of the bag made it almost impossible to manoeuvre, and his wrists were still bound, but he forced his trembling fingers into the scissor holes. His body was shaking violently now, his strength waning with every passing second. The water crept higher, splashing against his lips, forcing him to choke and splutter.

He jabbed at the weave, his movements wild and frantic. The thick fabric resisted, the blades barely making a dent. Tears stung his eyes, not from emotion but from the sting of the icy water as it reached his face. He imagined his tear ducts frozen, incapable of even granting him that release.

Panic clawed at him, urging him to move faster. He managed to separate the scissor blades, ramming them into the fabric above his chest. This time, something gave, a small tear opening in the bag. Another way for water to leak into the bag.

Alex kept the scissors in place, too terrified to pull them away in case he lost the spot. He ripped at the weave, the fabric resisting like tough meat under a blunt knife. He clawed at the tear with his numb hands, fighting with every ounce of strength he had left.

Water surged into the bag through the opening. Alex's head went under, the icy grip of the water clamping around his entire body. He couldn't feel the scissors any more. He was disoriented, spinning in the cold darkness, his lungs burning with the effort of holding his breath.

This is it, he thought.

He couldn't tell if he was hallucinating – his mind, starved of oxygen, trying to soothe him into death – but he thought he could feel a hole in the bag. With nothing left to lose, Alex grabbed at the hole, tearing with all his strength. The fabric gave way, splitting further as he clawed and pulled.

Faint, silvery light penetrated the water around him. Had he breached the bag?

He fought the rising panic, forcing himself to stay calm. *Which way is up?* He extended his arms, his hands brushing a rusted chain – perhaps tethering the bag to the shore? Gripping it with trembling fingers, Alex hauled himself upwards, kicking weakly as he followed the chain.

The cold was numbing, threatening to steal what little energy he had left. His lungs screamed for air, but he kept moving, inching to the surface.

With a desperate, final pull, his head broke through the water. Alex gulped in air, choking as water streamed from his nose and mouth. He clung to the chain, shivering violently but for now, alive.

Chapter Twenty-Eight

Back at headquarters, Liam was logging his visits into the system when a call came through from reception.

'Liam, I've got someone here asking for Maya, but she's out. Says it's about the hessian bag investigation.'

Glad for a break from the cloying atmosphere of the incident room, Liam shut his laptop and headed down to reception.

'Over there. David Hudson,' said the officer at the front desk, nodding at a burly man in jeans and a grey trench coat in reception. Hudson sat stiffly, his hands resting in his lap, his gaze fixed on the floor. 'He called the phoneline last night after seeing the TV appeal. Says it's about his son.'

'Did anyone follow up with him?' Liam asked.

'He spoke to someone who logged his details and gave him this reference number,' the officer said, handing over a slip of paper.

Liam checked the number on the system. It matched a call from David Hudson the previous night about his son, Alex Hudson, who wasn't officially listed as missing. 'Why's he here?'

'Whoever he spoke to suggested he check on his son's whereabouts and report him missing if necessary.'

'And did he?'

'Not exactly. Says he came straight down from Leeds by train. His son lives out towards Penzance.'

Liam sighed and walked over to the man, introducing himself. Hudson rose to his feet, extending a firm handshake. It wasn't often Liam met someone eye to eye, but Hudson matched his height, his grip solid.

'David Hudson,' he said.

'Long way to come,' Liam said, gesturing for the man to follow him to a vacant interview room.

'After seeing that appeal last night, I tried calling my son. His phone's off. Still is.'

Liam noted a faint Cornish lilt beneath the man's Lancashire accent. 'You're from this area originally?'

'Lived here for thirty years. My wife was from Cornwall. She passed five years ago. I moved back up north for work after that and ended up staying.'

'And Alex?'

'He'd already moved out by then,' Hudson replied, sitting.

'When was the last time you spoke to him?' Liam asked, pulling out a notebook.

'About six weeks ago.'

'Is that usual? To go so long without speaking, I mean,' said Liam, thinking about how he hadn't seen his mother or his own son for over a week.

Hudson hesitated, lowering his head. 'It is. We don't . . . get on too well. Never have. Don't know how to talk to each other properly.'

'What did you talk about the last time you spoke?'

'Not much,' Hudson said. 'Weather. How work was going. It wasn't much of a conversation.'

'Aside from not answering your calls last night, what makes you think Alex might be missing?'

'I also called one of his neighbours – Joan, her name is. Alex gave me her number for emergencies. She said she hasn't seen him in over three weeks. Thought maybe he was on holiday or something. But it's not like Alex. He's a quiet lad, keeps to himself, but he wouldn't just vanish for three weeks without telling someone.'

The concern on the father's face was evident. There was more here than just a father worried about being ignored. He wasn't convinced David Hudson was telling the whole truth, especially given that he and his son hadn't spoken in six weeks. Still, he decided not to push the matter.

'Also,' David said, breaking the silence, 'he's got a dog. Loves the bloody thing. Calls it Bailey. Never explained why.'

'He could've taken it with him,' Liam said.

David shrugged. 'It's a bloody big Great Dane. He's always liked them, even as a kid. No way that dog's going on holiday without someone noticing.'

'Do you have a picture of him?' Liam asked.

'The dog?'

'Your son, Mr Hudson.'

David bristled, his brow furrowing. 'You're wondering if he looks like those poor lads?'

'Please, it would help.'

David pulled out his phone, tapping the screen with slightly shaky fingers. 'There you go,' he said, handing it over.

Liam scrolled through the photos until one image caught his eye. He zoomed in, examining it closely.

'He does look like them, doesn't he?' David asked, a tremble in his voice.

Liam studied the photo further. Alex Hudson's hair was styled differently, but the resemblance to Frank Oakley and Robin Wakefield was undeniable. There was the same symmetrical face, sharp jawline, and large eyes. 'Have you received anything unusual in the post, Mr Hudson?' Liam asked.

'Like what?'

'A bag, or a doll?'

David's expression darkened. 'No. What the hell are you talking about?'

Liam frowned, setting the phone down. 'Alright. Why don't you show me where your son lives?'

Alex Hudson lived in Madron, a quiet village near Penzance. Liam drove David from Bodmin in near silence, the older man withdrawn and pensive throughout the journey.

As they reached the roundabout at the top of Hayle, Liam broke the silence. 'When was the last time you were in Cornwall?'

'Couple of years back,' David replied, staring out the window. 'Nothing much has changed.'

'Is it just you and Alex now?'

David nodded, more to himself than Liam. 'I suppose it is. When his mother died . . .' He trailed off, then took a deep breath. 'Look, I've not been much of a father to the lad, but I'm trying to turn things around. I just need to know he's safe.'

Liam pulled off the A30, parking outside a row of stone terraced houses in Madron. Their facades were worn and weathered, the signs of salt-laden winds evident on the brickwork. Alex's address was one of the smaller homes, its white paint chipped and peeling.

'You been here before?' Liam asked as he stepped out of the car.

David shook his head, his gaze downcast. 'He moved here about ten months ago.'

'The neighbour you called?'

'Number eight, I think. Two doors down,' David said, pointing at a neat house with a freshly painted front porch and a well-kept garden.

'Do you have a key to Alex's place?'

David shook his head again, looking almost ashamed. Liam knocked on Alex's door. After waiting and knocking again, he bent to peer through the letterbox. A few envelopes were scattered on the floor, but not enough to suggest Alex had been away for a long time.

'Let's try the neighbour,' Liam said, turning towards number eight. Before they made it to the door, a woman opened it.

'You looking for Alex?' she said. She appeared to be in her sixties, petite, with long braided grey hair, a flowery dress, and purple Dr. Martens boots.

'Joan?' David asked.

'Oh, you must be David, Alex's father. Pleased to meet you,' Joan said, shaking hands with Alex's father.

'DS Liam Kilshaw.' Liam showed his warrant card. Joan's friendly smile faded at the sight of it. 'Do you have a key to Alex's house?'

Joan hesitated, as though determining whether she was being tested. 'Yes, but I haven't been inside. He left it with me for emergencies.'

'That's fine. Could we borrow it, please? I'd like to take a look.'

Joan glanced at David, who nodded his consent.

A musty smell hit them as they entered Alex's house, the air damp and cold. Liam stepped into the living room. A two-seater faux leather sofa faced a widescreen television, its surface coated in dust. The room felt lifeless.

'When did you last see Alex?' Liam asked.

'Two or three weeks ago,' Joan replied. 'He generally keeps to himself. I usually see him out walking his dog.'

Liam noticed a wicker basket filled with dog toys and peered inside. 'The dog's a Great Dane?'

'Bailey? Yes. Such a gentle giant,' Joan said, with a warm smile as she looked at David.

Liam moved into the adjoining kitchen. The space was tidy but neglected, with a thin film of grease covering the work surfaces. 'Small place for such a big dog,' he remarked.

'He works from home and spends most of his spare time walking Bailey. You couldn't ask for a more responsible dog owner,' Joan said.

Liam nodded and headed upstairs to the solitary bedroom. The space felt cold and lonely, the faint smell of dog lingering in the air. Dog hairs clung to the bedspread and carpet, the starkness reminding Liam too much of his own flat.

Returning to the draughty hallway, Liam asked Joan, 'Do you know if there's anyone significant in Alex's life?'

'As I said, he keeps to himself. If it wasn't for Bailey, I don't think I'd have ever really talked to him.'

Liam thanked her and asked if he could hold on to the key for now. Joan agreed and excused herself, heading back to her own house.

'Is it alright if I stay here?' David asked, once she'd gone.

'That might be a good idea,' Liam said.

'Do you think something's happened to him?'

Liam avoided answering directly. 'If I had to guess, I'd say Alex has taken off for a break somewhere. As he doesn't have a car, I'll check with local taxi firms to see if any have been to his house recently.'

'What about the dog? No way Bailey's getting into a taxi.'

The same thought had already crossed Liam's mind. 'I'll contact local kennels. If he left the area, he might've boarded Bailey somewhere.'

David's shoulders sagged. 'Something's definitely off here. I know it.'

Liam placed a steadying hand on his shoulder. 'See if you can go through his contacts. Friends, co-workers, anyone who might know his movements. In situations like this, the simplest explanation is usually the correct one. Alex is clearly a solitary man. The train station's a short walk away. He might've taken Bailey somewhere and just hasn't been in touch.'

David nodded, but Liam could see the doubt in his eyes. He didn't believe that was a plausible explanation.

And neither, Liam realised, did he.

Under normal circumstances, Liam would have reiterated his point, urging David to stay optimistic. But at this stage, such words felt hollow. The resemblance between Alex and the two victims gnawed at him. It wasn't just a passing similarity, and he was growing more and more concerned about the missing man.

'Let me know if you find anything or remember something that might be useful,' Liam said, handing David his card. 'You can call me anytime. Don't hesitate, even if you think it's negligible. You'd be surprised at what can help.'

David stood silently by his son's front door, the card clutched in his hand, as Liam drove away. Liam hoped he'd have some good news to share with the man soon. But as his phone rang and Jack Lawson's name flashed on the screen, he feared their next encounter might be under far less favourable circumstances.

'Jack,' Liam answered, 'I hope you've got some good news for me.'

'Not sure if it's good news or not, boss, but I think it will be of interest. A mate of mine was at Penzance hospital yesterday on a domestic abuse case. He reckons he saw Daniella White there. Apparently, she was with family members and looked pretty upset. Said she was crying.'

'Thanks, Jack.' Like the DC, Liam had no way of knowing if the information was relevant. But anything that could give him a better understanding of Daniella White was worth pursuing, so he set off for the hospital a few minutes' drive away.

Chapter Twenty-Nine

Liam had spent plenty of time at the West Cornwall Hospital in Penzance over the years as a policeman. He'd never liked hospitals, although he doubted many people did. The sharp, antiseptic smell that greeted him as he walked through the main entrance triggered an unwelcome association with his mother's care home. For a brief moment, he pictured her, frail and alone in her room, so different to the woman he remembered before his father's death. Hospitals had a way of forcing such thoughts to the surface, a stark reminder that nothing lasted forever.

Liam approached the reception desk, showing his warrant card to the harried-looking woman sitting behind it. The process of trying to trace Daniella White turned out to be a laborious one. No one under the name White was currently admitted, nor had there been a patient by that name yesterday. The hospital lacked an Accident and Emergency department but did have an urgent care section, where Liam spent more unproductive time before calling Jack Lawson.

'You managed to speak to your mate yet?' he asked.

'Just got off the phone with him, boss,' Jack replied. 'He's dealt with Daniella before, during a fraud case where she was representing the defendant. Says she's quite a looker, his words, so she stuck in his memory. He reiterated what I told you. She was there yesterday with an older woman. He thinks it was her mother.'

'What department?'

'He was at the high dependency unit, handling a stabbing case in Penzance. He saw Daniella in the waiting room.'

Liam thanked Jack and made his way to the lifts. On the first floor, outside the HDU, he approached another overworked receptionist. After showing her a picture of Daniella, he waited while she consulted colleagues who'd been on shift the previous day.

Twenty minutes later, a young woman in a tailored business suit approached him in the quiet reception area. 'DS Kilshaw?' she asked. 'I'm Dr Laura Short. I understand you've been trying to track down someone who has visited one of our patients?'

'Yes,' Liam said, standing and showing her the picture. 'Daniella White. I believe she was here yesterday around 3 p.m. Your colleague mentioned seeing her.'

'May I?' Dr Short asked, gesturing to the chair next to him. Once seated, she continued in a calm, professional manner. 'Daniella's brother, Ernest Harris, was admitted yesterday. He passed away that afternoon.'

'Harris?' Liam asked, puzzled.

'That's correct, Ernest Harris. Daniella was here with their mother, Janet Harris.'

'You're sure Daniella was related? You don't check identification?'

'Not unless it's absolutely necessary. Why do you ask?'

'It's just that Daniella has a different surname but we can check into that,' said Liam, not recalling any mention of Daniella being married. 'What did Ernest die of?'

Dr Short's expression softened. 'In the end, it was organ failure. Ernest had a long-term condition called scleroderma – or systemic sclerosis. It's a chronic autoimmune disease that affects the skin, connective tissues, and internal organs by causing excessive collagen production. He'd been under our care on and off for the past five years. Things had been worsening, and they brought him in yesterday. I wanted to transfer him to an ICU in Truro, but . . . it proved too late.'

'Where is his body now?' Liam asked.

'It's been transferred to a funeral home,' Dr Short replied. 'I can provide you with the details if needed.'

'Thank you, Doctor. And do you have an address for where Ernest Harris lived?'

'Yes, I'll retrieve that for you,' she said, standing to leave.

'The condition you mentioned earlier . . .'

'Scleroderma?'

'Yes, can you tell me more about it?'

Dr Short's expression turned solemn. 'It's a very unpleasant condition, especially in Ernest's case. He'd been suffering for over fifteen years. The full term for his condition is diffuse cutaneous systemic sclerosis. One of the side-effects for Ernest was facial disfigurement caused by extreme skin tightening. This included microstomia, which severely restricted the movement of his mouth. Alongside the physical pain, his internal organs were under severe strain.'

'How does someone develop this?'

'It's typically genetic, but certain environmental factors can act as triggers.'

'What kind of treatment did he receive?'

'We didn't see him often. He was on a regimen of painkillers and anti-inflammatory medication. We'd requested he come in for a check-up, but this was the first time he'd been admitted in five years, according to his records. It was the first time I had personally seen him.'

'And his age?'

'He was only forty-two. Though you wouldn't have thought so, given the severity of his facial disfigurement. From what I understand, he'd become quite reclusive. His mother was his primary carer, and unfortunately our resources don't stretch far enough to ensure regular visits.'

'I understand,' Liam said. 'If you could provide me with those addresses, please?'

As Dr Short left to retrieve the details, Liam pulled out his phone and began researching systemic sclerosis. His mind was already making connections. The condition didn't always result in facial disfigurement, but when it did, the impact on a person's appearance could be dramatic. Liam's thoughts circled back to the two victims – both brutally disfigured – and Daniella White. The odds of these connections being purely coincidental felt like they were diminishing.

Two disfigured bodies. A vehicle linked to both crime scenes, likely belonging to Daniella. And now, a brother who had suffered from a condition that drastically altered his facial features. To Liam, it was enough to justify pursuing a warrant to search Daniella's home, though whether the courts would agree would be another matter.

He couldn't ignore the lingering question of why Daniella didn't share the same surname as her mother or brother. It could be for any number of reasons, but the detail only deepened his conviction that he needed to speak to her again.

He dialled Daniella's mobile but got no answer. Switching to her work number, he was informed she'd requested a personal day, which was unsurprising, given the circumstances.

Back in his car, Liam called Maya to update her on the hospital visit and his earlier meeting with David Hudson. 'We should take a look at why Daniella has a different surname. I don't think she is married.'

'No, me neither. I'll get Jack on it.'

'OK. And Hudson's son is definitely a physical match for Frank Oakley and Robin Wakefield,' Liam said. 'And it seems he's been missing for weeks.'

'And you think Daniella may have taken him?'

'I know it's tenuous,' Liam admitted. 'But there's a potential motive here. Two disfigured victims. A brother with facial disfigurement that no one has seen in years. And Daniella's connection to a vehicle seen near both crime scenes. That's too much to ignore.'

'Alright,' Maya said. 'Let's take it step by step. I'll speak to Hargreaves about obtaining a warrant, and we'll proceed from there.'

'OK,' said Liam. He wanted to say more, to demonstrate the urgency he felt, but he trusted Maya and knew she felt the same way.

'You coming back to headquarters?' asked Maya.

'Not yet. I'm planning to visit Janet Harris. Her address is near Sennen, almost equidistant between there and Porth Nanven.'

'Alright, I'll concede that's something. Just be careful, especially if Daniella's there. We can't afford to jeopardise the investigation.'

Chapter Thirty

The day felt like it was just getting into gear, but it was already dark by the time Liam reached the Harris property in the Cot Valley. Remote and isolated, the house sat at the end of a narrow, winding drive, with the nearest neighbour seemingly miles away.

A solitary light glowed from a downstairs window as Liam parked. The crunch of frozen gravel underfoot was the only sound as he approached the front door. The stillness of the place reminded him of Daniella's property, and he wondered if such solitude was sought out by the family.

Standing in front of the house, another vision of Bucca Dhu appeared in his mind. This time the serpent wore a distorted version of Daniella's face, and he half expected her to answer as he knocked on the wooden door. In the distance, he thought he heard the faint sound of running water before the door creaked open.

'Hello.'

Even in the dim light spilling from the room behind her, there was no mistaking that the woman in the doorway was related to Daniella White. Though she looked to be in her early seventies, she shared Daniella's sharp bone structure, and her large, expressive eyes were unmistakable.

'Janet Harris?' Liam said, displaying his warrant card. 'DS Liam Kilshaw.'

'Kilshaw,' Janet repeated, her voice carrying a distinct Cornish lilt. 'That rings a bell. How can I help you, Officer?' She made no move to inspect his identification, her gaze steady and piercing.

Liam considered fabricating a story about interviewing local residents but decided against it. He needed to speak to her about her son and everything had to be by the book. 'I'd like to ask you some questions about Ernest. I understand he passed away yesterday. My sincerest condolences.'

Janet's arm braced against the door frame, her posture reminiscent of Daniella's during his first encounter with her. Her eyes were fixed on him with an intensity that stirred a wave of déjà vu. 'Why would you want to speak about my son?' she asked.

'It would be easier to talk inside, Mrs Harris.'

Janet smiled thinly, and Liam was struck by how much it resembled Daniella's smile, calculated and distant. 'My daughter is a solicitor, don't you know.'

'Daniella White?' Liam asked.

Her gaze didn't waver, though a slight twitch in her eye betrayed her unease at the mention of Daniella's name. 'You've met her?'

'Our paths have crossed.'

'Then you'd know she wouldn't like me inviting a strange man into my house when I'm here alone.'

'I'm a policeman, Mrs Harris, and you have seen my identification.'

Janet laughed, her stance unchanging. 'And that's supposed to make me feel safer?'

Liam suppressed a sigh. 'I understand your caution, Mrs Harris. Would Daniella happen to be here, or do you know where I might find her? I'd very much like to speak with her.'

'Busy at work, I imagine.'

'Not today,' said Liam.

'Well, her brother has just died.'

'Of course. Again, I'm sorry for your loss.' He wasn't sure what he'd hoped to achieve by coming here, but whatever it was, it wasn't going to plan. After a pause, he ventured, 'If you don't mind me asking, why doesn't Daniella share your surname? Is she married?'

Janet's expression hardened. 'Now that is a very strange question, DS Kilshaw. And I'm afraid I still don't understand why you're here.'

The cold was beginning to seep into Liam's bones. Taking a chance, he said, 'I'm here investigating the deaths of two men. Frank Oakley and Robin Wakefield.'

Janet's eyes narrowed slightly, but her expression remained otherwise impassive. 'I'm afraid I don't know anything about that business.'

'You have heard about them?' Liam pressed.

'I may be old, but I can still see. It's a remote place, but we get television here. I've watched the reports about those two poor men, but I rarely leave the house nowadays. Even the trip to the hospital was a stretch for me. Now, it's bitterly cold, as I'm sure you can tell. If there's nothing else, I'd like to get back to my fire.'

Liam, knowing he would get no further, said, 'Thank you for your time, Mrs Harris.'

He felt her eyes on him all the way back to the car.

Driving away from the Harris property, the stillness of the Cot Valley clinging to his thoughts, Liam called Grace on his burner phone. He wasn't yet sure whether his next stop would be headquarters or Hendra, where Daniella lived.

'Hi, Liam, everything alright?'

Hearing Grace's voice felt strangely grounding. Despite his suspicion that she was withholding something, he found himself glad to talk to her. 'One of those days,' he replied.

'Tell me about it. Want to meet up and vent?'

'Not likely at the moment,' said Liam, thinking the risk of meeting up with her was an extra complication, professionally and personally, he could do without at present.

'The hessian bag investigation?' Grace asked.

For a moment, Liam felt a flicker of paranoia, an irrational feeling that Grace's arrival in Cornwall was somehow connected to this case. He blinked it away, forcing himself to focus. 'Don't you know it,' he said, a hollow feeling in his stomach reminding him he couldn't even remember the last time he had eaten.

'Believe it or not, I'm envious,' she said. 'I like having some time off, but I'm already itching to get back into it.'

'Any updates on that?'

'I have a meeting next week. From what I've been told, it's just a formality.'

'That's wonderful, Grace. You'll be back on the mean streets of London before you know it.'

'Maybe sooner than that.'

Liam didn't respond immediately. He was passing the heliport in Penzance, wondering what she meant. 'You thinking of coming to work with us again?' he asked, unsure how he felt about the idea.

'Well, one way or another, the job did get done when I worked with you, complications and all. But I don't think Bodmin would be the best place for me right now. Exeter might be, though.'

'So, this is what all the secrecy's been about? You're here for an interview?'

'I am,' Grace admitted, 'but that's not the only reason I'm down here. I did want to see you again. Maybe now isn't the best time to talk about it, but I thought you should know I'm considering joining the team in Devon. I didn't want it to come as a big surprise if we ended up working together again.'

Liam didn't know what to think. The idea of Grace moving closer was undeniably appealing. He considered telling her about his split with Millie, but it didn't feel like the right moment. 'You sure you won't miss the action in London?'

'I think there's enough going on down here. And a lead detective role on Major Crimes is always going to be interesting.'

Exeter was only two hours from St Ives on a good run, a far cry from the distance between Cornwall and London. 'Why didn't you tell me about this the other day?'

'I didn't want you to think it was the only reason I was in Cornwall. Anyway, I might not get the job,' Grace continued. 'Especially after all this suspension nonsense. I was going to tell you, but it didn't come up, and you have so much on at the moment . . .'

'It sounds great, Grace. I can't promise anything, but maybe we could meet up this weekend, if I ever get a spare minute.'

'That would be wonderful, Detective,' she said with a warm laugh. 'Now go and catch the bad guys.'

As Liam drove to Daniella White's house in Hendra, his thoughts drifted to Millie. He couldn't seem to shake the image of her new haircut, how something so seemingly small could change a person's appearance so profoundly. Deep down, he thought he'd known for a while their relationship had run its natural course. Perhaps things would have been different if it weren't for the Godrevy investigation, but that was something he would never know for sure.

He tried not to dwell on what she'd endured during that case. Beyond the police interviews his colleagues had conducted, they'd never talked about the hours she'd spent trapped in the water tunnel, the water rising up to her neck before he rescued her. Though he'd reached her in time, the experience had left scars she would never fully recover from. He knew, directly or not, he bore some responsibility for that.

Parking outside the gate to Daniella's house, Liam's mind shifted to the hessian bag killer. Was there another person in jeopardy now? Someone next in line to become a victim? How responsible would he feel if he failed to stop it in time?

He thought back to his meeting with David Hudson and the man's son, Alex, whose resemblance to Frank Oakley and Robin Wakefield was unsettling. Was Alex in captivity somewhere, or had the killer already struck? Would the next call bring news that Alex's mutilated body had been found on a shore?

His phone rang, piercing the eerie quiet of the isolated area. He answered without hesitation.

'Where are you?' said Maya.

'Daniella White's house,' Liam replied.

'There's something you might want to see first,' Maya said, as a notification pinged on his phone.

Liam glanced at the screen. The photo could have been of Frank Oakley, Robin Wakefield, or Alex Hudson. 'Who is this?' he asked as he looked at the familiar features. The men really were so similar as to be almost identical.

'If what Janet Harris told you is accurate,' Maya replied, 'that's Daniella's brother, Ernest Harris.'

'When was this taken?' Liam asked.

'Before his condition took hold. Eighteen years ago, when he was twenty-four. Not long before Daniella legally changed her surname.'

Chapter Thirty-One

Alex dragged himself from the water, as if clawing his way out of an empty grave. It was hard to tell how much time had passed since he'd entered it. His body was close to convulsing, the cold wind slicing through him. If he didn't find shelter soon, he knew he'd be dead within the hour. The thought almost amused him, the bitter irony of surviving everything else only to succumb to hypothermia.

He hugged himself tightly, but standing still only worsened the chill. Exhausted both physically and mentally, he forced himself to keep moving, jogging on the spot. He coaxed his mind to send signals to his unresponsive limbs, every motion a battle against inertia, cold, and – though he tried not to think about it – death.

The full moon hung low in the sky, casting a silvery light over the landscape. As he picked up the pace to generate warmth, something caught his eye. On the frozen ground near the water's edge, his clothes were arranged neatly inside a circle of stones, as though waiting for him.

He hesitated, unsure of the meaning behind what he was seeing. Was it a trap? A cruel taunt? The thought gnawed at him, but for now it was a godsend. Shivering violently, he stepped over the stone threshold and pulled on the trousers, followed by the shirt and pullover. The fabric was damp from lying on the ground and offered scant relief, but it was better than the alternative and provided some shelter for his skin. His feet, however, remained exposed.

Had the clothes been left for him in case he escaped the bag? The question lingered, but Alex wasn't about to stick around to find out. The thought of Adelaide and her mother made his heart beat so fast that it gave him chest pains. He pictured them in their farmhouse, sitting by a roaring fire, sipping hot chocolate as if the horrors they'd inflicted on him were inconsequential. He knew one thing: he'd rather risk dying out here in the wilderness than go anywhere near them again.

Needing a plan, he decided to follow the water. The small lake fed into a tributary stream, which might lead to a larger body of water. If he was still in Cornwall, and he thought he might be, reaching the coast could improve his odds of finding civilisation and rescue.

He moved as fast as his frozen limbs allowed, pushing himself to increase his heart rate. His clothes provided a faint shield against the cold, but it wasn't enough to drive the chill from his bones. He had to keep moving, had to generate heat, and above all, had to escape.

The journey was treacherous. Despite the moonlight, the frozen terrain was cloaked in shadows. He slowed as he reached a rocky path, sharp stones cutting into the soles of his feet. Pain radiated upward with every step, but he pressed on, gritting his teeth against the agony.

At times, the riverbank became impassable, forcing him inland. He paused occasionally to stuff his clothes with frozen leaves and moss for insulation. His breathing was heavy, clouds of vapor escaping his lips, but he welcomed the exertion. It meant his body was fighting, generating precious heat. The pain, the cold, and the darkness didn't matter. All that mattered was moving forward. Moving away from the nightmare.

Perhaps daylight would bring some relief, but for all he knew it could still be hours away. Even if he could bear the cold long enough to wait, staying in one place was too dangerous. He didn't fully understand why Adelaide had placed him in the hessian bag and left him in the water, but the chain attached to the bag was no accident. If they hadn't already, they'd soon discover his absence.

A wave of panic surged through him, as the memory of earlier gripped him. He was back in the bag, the suffocating darkness crushing him, the hessian scraping his skin. Claustrophobia took hold, and he had to slap a hand over his mouth to stifle the scream. He couldn't go back. He wouldn't survive it a second time.

Fear propelled him into motion. He started to run, every nerve alight with the terror of being caught. Adelaide's face loomed in his mind, her cold eyes and unnatural strength haunting him. He ignored the agony in his feet as jagged rocks tore into his soles, the desperation to escape stronger than the pain.

Reaching the stream again, an absurd thought flickered. He could jump in, let the current carry him away. The icy water would be merciless, but it felt preferable to being caught and returned to the bag. Without slowing, he veered towards the edge, the cold numbing his feet into frozen blocks as they touched the shallows. The frigid shock of the water jolted him, dispelling the fleeting idea. No escape lay in the river. He had to keep running.

His body begged for rest, exhaustion clawing at his muscles, but fear kept him going. He imagined Adelaide behind him, relentless, her inhuman strength closing the gap. He didn't dare look back. Instead, he surged forward, hurdling obstacles that appeared at the last second in the moonlit gloom.

Then his luck ran out. A jagged outcrop of rocks materialised in front of him too late to avoid. He slammed into the formation with brutal force, the impact slicing into his shins. He stumbled, falling hard, his body twisting as he hit the ground near the stream's edge.

A sharp snap echoed in his ears, followed by a searing pain in his leg. He lay there, gasping for breath, the icy water lapping at his side, and realised this could be his final resting place.

Chapter Thirty-Two

Liam wiped moisture from his forehead, the freezing air stinging his skin as he stood at the entrance to Daniella White's house. 'I think it's snowing,' he said, half to himself. 'What's this about a name change?' he asked Maya, who was on the other end of the line.

'Daniella White, formerly known as Daniella Harris,' Maya replied. 'Jack ran the check as you suggested.'

'Do we know why she changed it?'

'No, but it happened not long after she turned eighteen.'

Name changes were more common than people realised and could happen for many reasons. The process was straightforward. Some people simply disliked their names, while others wanted a clean slate or to start over. While there were systems in place to flag fraud, name changes weren't routinely scrutinised by the police.

'Maybe she was ashamed of her family. Maybe they were involved in something shady,' Liam said.

'Either way, be careful if she's there. I think we have enough to bring her in for questioning. Do you want me to send backup?'

The snow was falling harder now, thick flakes swirling through the night. If it kept on, avoiding getting stranded might become a bigger concern than backup. 'I'll be fine for now,' Liam said.

'Leave your tracker on,' Maya instructed.

'You got it, boss,' he replied, ending the call. He made sure the tracking feature on his phone was active before pushing open the gate and walking down the narrow, snow-covered path towards Daniella White's house.

Two images played through his mind as he walked. The photograph of Ernest Harris at the hospital and the younger man from eighteen years ago. It was hard to reconcile them as the same person. Ernest's condition had stripped him of his identity, and Liam could only imagine the toll it had taken on him and the family. Liam had endured teasing as a kid because of his alopecia, but his struggles paled in comparison to what Ernest must have faced.

Dr Short had hinted at the trauma Ernest's condition had inflicted on the family. Most of his recent life had been spent hidden away, and Liam wondered how that isolation had affected the man's psyche, and his family's as well.

Daniella's sports car wasn't parked outside, but the old Land Rover Defender was still there. As Liam approached, he tripped the sensor lights on the outer wall, which illuminated the snowfall. Clusters of snow already clung to the Defender's roof, as if it had been abandoned.

Liam knocked on the door, then tried calling Daniella's phone again. The interior of the house was dark and, with her car missing, it was likely she wasn't home. Frustrated, he called Maya.

'Can I enter?' he asked.

'You know we can't.'

'She's a person of interest.'

'Maybe, but everything we have is circumstantial. There's no evidence she's done anything criminal.'

The rules for entering private property were necessarily strict. Unless Liam had reason to believe there was an immediate risk to life, or if Daniella were an active suspect posing a clear danger, he couldn't justify forcing his way inside. And as Maya had pointed out, their current evidence was too tenuous to take such a step. Ignoring the rules now could end his career.

Liam hung up and muttered a string of curses into the silence. He'd been in situations like this before, but that didn't make them any less infuriating. If the killer's behaviour was anything to go by, another man's life could be at risk right now – more than likely, Alex Hudson's. It wasn't hard to believe that the answers he needed might be locked behind Daniella's door.

Although he wasn't permitted to enter the house, nothing prevented him from searching the surrounding land. And it was something he'd neglected to do on his previous visits, so arguably it would only be due diligence. Moving around the side of the property, Liam switched on his torch, its beam cutting through the darkness to reveal a flat expanse stretching into the distance.

In daylight, he imagined the view might be beautiful, especially with the fresh snowfall. But in the dark, even the torchlight couldn't dispel the foreboding atmosphere. The isolation was tangible, and he couldn't help but wonder if somewhere nearby Alex Hudson was feeling just as alone.

He stepped cautiously on to the frozen ground, his breath clouding in the frigid air. The beam of his torch landed on a cluster of outbuildings in the distance. Presuming they belonged to Daniella, he made his way towards them, his hand brushing the extendable baton tucked inside his coat pocket.

Wiping snow from his face, Liam couldn't shake the sensation of being underwater. The darkness and silence felt like another world. Even though he could make out faint lights from nearby properties on the horizon, the solitude was suffocating.

Once, he'd relished the underwater world. The weightlessness had been a kind of sanctuary, a way of life. Even during active service, he'd loved the escape it provided, the world above shrinking into insignificance. But that peace had been shattered when the water had nearly claimed his life. Now, as he approached the outbuildings, that same sense of lurking danger returned. Only the searing cold and the pull of gravity reassured him that he was still above ground.

Up close, the buildings revealed themselves as stables. Liam shone his torch into the first stall and saw that it was no longer in use. The stalls had been scrubbed clean, the cold air swirling through the open pens.

He moved cautiously down the row, checking each one. Part of him half-expected to find a bloodied hessian bag in the corner of a stall, but the place was empty. Relieved but unsettled, he took photographs of the area, running his torch beam along the stone walls. He was about to head back to the house when a faint sound like a whimper caught his attention.

He froze, straining to listen, but the only sound was the soft rustle of snow settling on the ground. Had he imagined it? If not, where had it come from?

Behind the stalls, a narrow strip of ground led to a boundary fence. Liam's mind conjured a vivid image of Alex Hudson trapped in a hessian bag. But when he squeezed through a gap in the fence, that wasn't what greeted him.

In a small space between two fences, chained and shivering, he saw a Great Dane dog. Its eyes were downcast, but its tail wagged tentatively when it saw him.

'Bailey?' Liam said softly.

The dog lifted its head at the sound of its name, the wagging tail speeding up as it stepped gingerly towards him.

Chapter Thirty-Three

Liam loved dogs, but knew he had to proceed with caution. Bailey might have appeared friendly, but the dog was scared and hungry, and that made him unpredictable. Keeping his voice calm, Liam repeated the dog's name, offering quiet reassurance as he called Maya and explained his discovery.

'I went to Alex Hudson's place this morning, as you know,' he said as Maya answered. 'He has to be the next target.'

'OK, hold tight. We'll get a full search team to you now,' Maya replied.

'Shall I enter the house?' Liam asked, glancing down as Bailey let out a soft whimper. The dog had crept closer, and was now sniffing him cautiously.

'Wait until we get there.'

'What if Alex is inside?'

Maya hesitated. 'You have a bodycam with you?'

'In the car.'

'Put it on before you go in. And be careful, Liam.'

The dog had edged close enough for Liam to stroke under its chin, its tail wagging. 'Let's get you out of here, shall we?' said Liam. He ruffled the dog's collar and shone his torch on the metal name tag, confirming Bailey's name.

Fortunately, the chain wasn't locked. Liam unhooked it from the wall, fashioning it into a makeshift lead. Bailey moved easily, staying close to Liam's side as they left the enclosed area. Snow was settling in thick layers, and the dog bent his head to sniff at the powder before plodding alongside.

'You're a big guy, aren't you?'

Bailey, who was as tall as Liam's waist, continued wagging his tail as they reached the car. 'You want to go in there?' asked Liam, opening the back door. The dog gazed up at him with large, doleful eyes before clambering into the seat with surprising grace.

'You're safe now, Bailey,' Liam said, closing the door behind him.

From the boot, Liam retrieved his bodycam, attaching it to the front of his coat. Searching the car for anything to offer the dog, he found only a bottle of water. Opening the back door again, he poured the water into his cupped hand, holding it out. Bailey lapped it up, his warm tongue splashing more water on to the seat than he managed to drink.

'Not the tidiest method, but it'll do,' Liam said. When the bottle was empty, he gave the dog a reassuring pat. 'OK, you wait here now. I won't be long,' he said, as the dog made himself comfortable, taking up the majority of the back seat.

Switching on the bodycam, Liam called Maya again. The device streamed live, and she confirmed the feed was working.

'I'm going in,' Liam said.

'We're ten to fifteen minutes away. Call Jack first and make sure he can see you,' Maya advised.

Liam ended the call and contacted Jack, confirming the footage was being streamed at headquarters. Satisfied, Liam approached the house.

Any reservations about entering were gone. The evidence pointing to Daniella's involvement in the murders was mounting, and with Alex Hudson an active missing person, time was critical.

He tried the doorbell once more, waiting for any sound from within. Testing the door with his shoulder, Liam assessed its strength. It was old, and appeared to be secured by a single lock. Waiting for backup might be the safer option, but the possibility that Alex was inside was enough to warrant the risk of entering alone.

'Trying the door,' he said, for the benefit of the bodycam. Drawing back, he delivered a solid kick just beside the lock. Pain shot through his leg, but the doorframe creaked in response. Three more kicks followed, each one harder than the last, until the lock gave way. One final shoulder ram splintered the door, forcing it open.

'I'm in.' Liam stepped over the threshold. He reached for the light switch, flooding the entryway with a dim, flickering glow.

'Hello? Daniella? Alex?' he called, his voice echoing in the stillness.

The house wasn't what Liam had expected. Given Daniella's background, he'd imagined sleek, modern luxury. Instead, the interior leant heavily towards traditional decor. If he hadn't known she lived here, he would have guessed the owner to be someone much older.

A small hallway led into a living area furnished with flower-patterned sofas and wooden floors. Exposed stone walls gave the room a rustic feel, and wooden sideboards crowded the space, each one cluttered with trinkets.

Liam picked up a china figurine, a mermaid that oddly reminded him of Daniella. He thought of the replica dolls and their mini prisons, his mind taunting him with images of the two victims brutalised in their hessian bags.

A voice called his name from behind, startling him.

'You trying to give me a heart attack?' he said, spinning around, to see Maya standing there.

A wry smile tugged at her lips. 'Sorry. Where's the dog?'

'In my car.'

'Animal services are here.'

'Good. Let me finish searching before you take him, just in case,' Liam replied.

With the potential for evidence scattered throughout the house, Liam and Maya continued searching the property. Each room was the same, cluttered with trinkets, decorated in an old-fashioned style that seemed out of sync with what Liam imagined Daniella's tastes might be.

The main bedroom was cramped, a double bed positioned beneath a window where a draught seeped into the room. Liam opened the wardrobe, finding it packed with hangers full of designer clothes, the first real sign that Daniella actually lived there.

As he sifted through the shoes at the bottom of the wardrobe, his hand brushed against something at the back. 'I've got something,' he called out. Maya appeared in the doorway as he wrestled a wooden box free with a grunt.

The ornate box reminded him of his mother's old jewellery box, the kind with a spring-loaded ballerina that twirled to tinny music when opened. He wasn't sure what he expected to find as he prised it open – passports, documents, jewellery, perhaps even a ballerina like the one from his childhood – but not this. 'Jesus,' he said, showing the contents to Maya.

Inside was a miniature burial site of sorts with tightly packed hessian bags of various shapes. Liam retrieved one and sliced it open with his penknife.

From within, he pulled out an old china figurine, similar to the one he'd seen in the living room. This one, however, was chipped, the side of its face missing, leaving behind a smooth, white surface.

Chapter Thirty-Four

CSI arrived shortly afterwards, taking over the search of the house. Liam and Maya stepped outside to help coordinate the larger investigation. Daniella was circulated as wanted, and Jack Lawson was overseeing efforts to locate her from headquarters.

Liam's thoughts were still on the box they'd found, the contents of which were being analysed by the CSIs. The figurine with the side of its face missing was another sign, if now needed, of Daniella's involvement in the recent murders. Liam was desperate to know what was inside the other bags, and wondered if and how they related to actual people.

Bailey wagged his tail, shuffling towards Liam as he opened the car door, pleased to see him again. 'Maybe we should keep him with us. If Alex is somewhere on-site, he might help us track him.'

The handler crouched to take the chain from Liam. 'We'll get him fed first,' he said. 'My guess is he won't be much use to us right now. He's disoriented, and all this commotion is probably stressing him out.'

'All right.' Liam gave Bailey a final pat. 'Speak to you soon, Bailey. I'll do my best to find your owner.'

The handler nodded, leading the Great Dane away as Bailey glanced back sadly.

At the house, DCI Hargreaves had arrived. He was accompanied by Sergeant Caleb Francis, the appointed police search advisor. Francis greeted both Liam and Maya with a firm handshake.

'I've read through the investigation notes,' the PolSA said. 'Do we have anything concrete linking Alex Hudson to this location?'

'Just his dog. We've also uncovered a set of miniature hessian bags, replicas of the ones used in the murders of our two victims. I'd be shocked if Daniella White isn't involved, but we don't have direct evidence yet to place Alex here.'

'What's the latest on finding Daniella White?'

Hargreaves answered. 'We have a full team working from headquarters. She didn't show up for work today, so we've put a wanted marker on her, and alerted airports and shipping ports.'

'Can you show me where the dog was found?' Francis asked.

Liam nodded, leading the PolSA across the frozen ground, Maya remaining with Hargreaves at the house.

As Liam pointed out the desolate piece of land where Bailey had been chained, the sight stirred a wave of unease. If he hadn't checked the property when he did, the dog might not have survived the night, and Alex Hudson's situation might have gone unnoticed.

Francis ran his gloved fingers over the wall where the chain had been secured. 'Do you think Hudson is here?'

Liam exhaled, his breath visible in the frigid air as the snowfall thickened. 'Daniella's old SUV was spotted at the scenes of the other two crimes, but it's still here. It's possible she's fled and that Alex was being held prisoner either here or somewhere else before she left. Unfortunately, there's also the chance that we'll find a hessian bag washed up on the beach with his remains. For now, I'm going with the former. We have to believe he's alive.'

'But is he here?' Francis pressed.

Liam shrugged, reluctant to commit. 'The dog was here. The only other likely place we could find anything is the mother's house in Sennen.'

'That's near where the other two bodies were found?'

'Yes. Sennen Beach and Porth Nanven.'

'Let's finish up here and work on getting permissions for the mother's place,' Francis said as they returned to the house.

By the time the search was in full swing, the snow was the heaviest it had been. Floodlights illuminated the rear of Daniella's house, their beams cutting through the swirling snowflakes as a dog team scoured the grounds. Drones buzzed overhead, scanning the surrounding land.

The Land Rover was open, its interior being examined by the CSIs. As Liam had suspected, it seemed to have been recently cleaned. Still, the team weren't ruling out the possibility of finding something that might link the vehicle to the two murders.

DCI Hargreaves remained on-site, glued to his phone as he worked to secure a warrant to search the Harris house in Cot Valley. Meanwhile, Liam called Jack for an update on Daniella's whereabouts.

'Her Jaguar's on the national list,' Jack said. 'We're hoping the number plate detection cameras will pick it up, but so far, nothing. The last anyone heard from her was last night at work, when she requested compassionate leave.'

Had she known then that everything was about to fall apart? Liam wondered. Maybe she'd spotted the officer at the hospital and realised it was only a matter of time before her brother's death unravelled the threads, leading to Bailey and the replica hessian bags being found upstairs.

'Keep me posted, Jack.'

'Will do, boss. One more thing. I've been going through the family details. Turns out Janet Harris has another daughter.

Adelaide Harris, aged twenty-one. I can't find anything on her beyond school records.'

'Last known address?'

'Same as Janet's.'

'See if you can find a photo of her,' Liam said, thinking of the grainy nightclub footage.

'I'll keep digging.'

Liam paced the icy ground to keep from freezing, his frustration mounting. Discovering Daniella's involvement should have been a breakthrough but, for now, it only deepened the uncertainty. With Daniella missing, her state of mind was impossible to gauge. If she had killed the other two men, it was hard to avoid the conclusion that Alex Hudson's life was in severe danger, assuming he was still alive.

One of the CSIs walked over, pulling down her white mask. Liam recognised her instantly. Tina Madeley, someone he'd kissed at a Christmas party.

'Hi, Tina.'

'Liam,' replied Tina, with a wry smile. 'You always pick the best weather for these things, don't you?'

'What have you got for me?'

'We've finished analysing the bags you found in the house. Quite a mixture. Some of the contents are unidentifiable, possible animal remains. We also found more figurines, some china, some cloth.'

'Were they all damaged, like the mermaid figurine?'

'No, that's the strange part. About half the items were pristine. Nothing obviously wrong with them. The unidentifiable stuff aside, every item was a representation of a living creature. Mostly human, but there was also a dog, a cat, even a hedgehog. I'll email you the full list.'

Snowflakes caught on her nose, and she blew them away with a smile. She lingered a moment too long, the air between them growing awkward as Maya approached.

'Thanks, Tina,' said Liam.

As the CSI walked off, Maya grinned at him. 'You've only just broken up with Millie, and you're already charming your old conquests?'

'"Conquests" isn't an appropriate term,' Liam replied with a frown. Before Maya could retort, their phones buzzed in unison. Liam answered first.

'Jack?'

'Boss, it's Daniella White. We've just picked her up at Bristol Airport.'

Chapter Thirty-Five

Daniella White had been caught just before boarding a private jet to mainland Europe. Though private flights had their own security protocols, the authorities had intercepted her in time and she was currently in custody at the airport.

With the search of the property ongoing, Liam joined Maya and Hargreaves inside the house. They huddled in the narrow hallway while the CSIs worked methodically around them.

'We're still trying to reach a magistrate for the search warrant on Janet Harris's place,' said Hargreaves, before either Liam or Maya could speak.

'We need to arrange a conference call with Daniella White,' Maya said.

'Can we fly her down?' Liam glanced at Maya, hoping for her support.

Hargreaves hesitated. The standard procedure would involve questioning Daniella locally before transferring her to Bodmin for follow-up. 'Let's hold fire on that for now. See what we can get from her via video link.'

'We'll be wasting our time,' Liam said, not hiding his frustration. 'She's at an airport. Can't we arrange a helicopter transfer?'

Hargreaves frowned, seemingly weighing the logistical and cost implications. Daniella might be a murder suspect, but such requests weren't straightforward. Still, Liam wanted to plant the idea in his superior's mind.

'I think that's unlikely with the current weather situation. I'm sure we can manage a video-link session from the airport,' Hargreaves replied, avoiding further discussion as his phone rang. He answered, walking off down the hallway before Liam could argue any more.

Maya moved to the front door, staring out at the snow being caught in the floodlights as Liam called the officer in charge at Bristol Airport, DS Sandra Bunker, introducing himself.

'We have her in the customs custody suite at the moment,' Sandra informed him. 'What are your next steps?'

'We'd like to set up a video-link call with her. Are the facilities there sufficient?'

'They are, but that might not be your main challenge,' Sandra replied.

'She's not talking?'

'You could say that, and then some. She hasn't said a single word. Just handed me a card for her solicitor, Miles Benchley, from a firm in London. According to your colleague, DC Lawson, it's not the same firm she works for.'

'Have you contacted Benchley yet?'

'Not yet. I wasn't sure if you wanted her moved first.'

Liam sighed, pressing a gloved hand to his temple. As he'd suspected, Daniella wasn't going to make things easy. 'Ask her if she'll speak to me via video link without the solicitor present. In the meantime, send me the solicitor's number. I'll handle him myself.'

Moments after the call ended, a message arrived with Miles Benchley's mobile number. Liam tapped the link, and the solicitor answered on the first ring.

'What, specifically, has Daniella been charged with?' Benchley asked, after Liam outlined the situation.

'She will be charged with two counts of murder, among other charges,' Liam said.

'And she is currently in detention at Bristol Airport?' Benchley asked.

'That is correct. In addition to two murders, we are investigating a missing person, Alex Hudson. His dog was found on Daniella's property.'

'I need to speak to her,' the solicitor said, brushing off Liam's last statement.

'And we need to find Alex Hudson, Mr Benchley,' Liam said. 'A man's life is at stake. We will, of course, respect—'

'Let me stop you there, DS Kilshaw,' Benchley interrupted. 'I am making no suggestion as to my client's guilt. Arrange for me to speak to her, and I will get back to you.'

Liam clenched his fists. He was fighting a losing battle. The solicitor's duty was to his client, but the urgency of the situation made Benchley's indifference infuriating. 'Please, try to make her see sense,' he said, before hanging up and relaying the request to the team in Bristol.

Outside, the weather had turned brutal. Snow fell in blinding gusts, the wind howling as a blizzard descended. Liam could only see a few metres ahead, the hum of drones above and the distant barking of search dogs the only sounds cutting through the deadened night air.

He caught up with Maya, who had just finished speaking to one of the CSIs examining the Land Rover Defender.

'I don't think Daniella's going to talk anytime soon,' Liam admitted, hating the defeat he could hear in his voice.

'If she doesn't, we can push harder for the helicopter to bring her here,' Maya offered.

'It's going to be too late.' Part of him wished he'd forced entry into the house when he'd first returned here alone. It would've been illegal, and he'd have lost his job, but if he'd found the hessian bags earlier, maybe Alex would already be safe and reunited with Bailey.

'She kept the dog alive,' Maya pointed out. 'If she's capable of that, maybe she's kept Alex alive too. There's no water here, so maybe she didn't have time to complete whatever twisted ritual she was planning.'

Liam was only half listening, his mind spinning through worst-case scenarios. 'I wish Hargreaves would hurry up with that warrant. Janet's house is the perfect place to hide a body, and that is close to the water.'

'He'll get it done,' said Maya, as Sandra called again from the airport.

'She's spoken to her brief, as have I,' Sandra said. 'She's refusing to talk without him present. He's willing to travel to either Bristol or Cornwall tomorrow morning.'

'You explained the urgency of the situation?' Liam asked, unable to hide his irritation.

'What do you think?' Sandra replied.

Liam sighed. 'Apologies. OK, leave it with us.' He hung up and muttered, 'Bastard,' under his breath. 'She won't speak to us without her brief, and he can't get anywhere until tomorrow,' he told Maya. 'I should call him again, but I doubt it'll change anything.'

Maya shook her head. 'Let me talk to Hargreaves. See if we can get her here by helicopter. She might not want to talk, but we can at least confront her in person.'

Liam nodded and headed to his car to grab another layer of clothing against the worsening storm. Though it was still early evening, the darkness, weather, and lack of progress made everything seem that little bit worse. It was hard not to feel like the investigation was slipping through their fingers.

Finding Bailey on Daniella's property had been a significant step forward. Intercepting Daniella as she seemingly attempted to flee the country had been another. But without talking to her, they were no closer to finding Alex.

Liam clung to the hope that DNA tests and forensics would soon make the truth undeniable, and that Daniella would be forced to talk.

'Hargreaves has managed to get a chopper,' said Maya, now wearing an extra fleece beneath her coat. Snow dusted her shoulders, and Liam couldn't help but hope that wherever Alex was, he wasn't exposed to the same brutal elements. 'It should be up in the air in the next thirty minutes, weather willing. Plan is to land in Penzance.'

Liam was mildly impressed that Hargreaves had managed to pull it off, but it would still be over two hours before he'd have the chance to question Daniella. 'Where's Hargreaves now?'

'Back in Bodmin. The magistrate insisted on a face to face.'

'You're joking,' Liam said, rubbing a gloved hand over his head, his winter hat now coated in snow.

'No joke,' Maya replied. 'We won't get the warrant to the Harris house without it. Even then, it might still be a stretch.'

'Her daughter was found keeping a missing man's dog captive and has been spotted leaving two crime scenes,' Liam argued, though he already knew the evidence wasn't ironclad enough to justify a search of private property without consent.

With the PolSA in charge of the search at the property, Liam decided to head to Penzance so that he'd be ready when Daniella arrived.

'I'll come with you,' Maya said, stamping her feet to fight off the cold. 'I've had enough of this weather anyway.'

'What about your car?'

'I came in the van. What is this, you don't want me with you?' she teased, feigning offence.

'How could I ever say that about you? Though I can't help but wonder if you're coming along to stop me from doing something reckless.'

'If that's on your mind, then I'm definitely making the right choice,' she said, climbing into the passenger seat.

Liam started the car, letting the engine idle as he waited for the heater to warm up. Snowflakes continued to fall thick and fast. 'Can't remember a November like this,' he said, easing the car away from the property.

Snow and ice had transformed the surface of the road into a slip-and-slide, and Liam felt the car lose grip more than once. Each skid brought unwanted images of Alex Hudson to his mind, trapped in a snow-covered hessian bag, dropped into the freezing sea. He tried to push the thoughts away as he navigated the quiet backstreets, the houses quaint and picturesque, like something out of a Christmas card with their overcoats of snow.

It felt like an age until they reached the main road. Switching to hands-free, Liam called Jack as they headed towards Penzance. 'Any luck finding the sister?'

'Managed to dig up some old school photos of her when she was fourteen. Sending them over now. Nothing more recent, though.'

Jack stayed on the line as the images came through. 'Well?' Liam asked, trying to sneak a look at the screen.

'Keep your eyes on the road,' Maya chided, grabbing his phone before he could glance at the screen. 'Thanks, Jack. Keep digging.'

'Let me see,' Liam protested.

'From what I can tell, she'd be as striking as her sister now,' Maya said, scrolling through the photos. 'She looks a bit awkward in these, though.'

‘Could it be her in the nightclub?’ Liam asked, picturing the grainy footage of the young woman supporting an unsteady Robin Wakefield.

‘Maybe. She’d fit the build, and the age lines up but seven years can change a lot,’ Maya said.

‘We could drive to the house in Sennen,’ Liam said. ‘No harm in asking Janet Harris if her other daughter is in.’

Maya didn’t answer right away, and Liam knew that meant she was mulling it over. Sometimes he forgot she was his immediate superior. Their working relationship was built on mutual trust, and they often bounced ideas off each other without hesitation. But as DI, Maya was naturally more by the book than he was, something he both admired and occasionally found frustrating.

‘Let’s wait for the warrant.’

Liam sighed but didn’t argue. He slowed the car to a near stop as they reached the tail end of a traffic jam, the snow reducing visibility to only a few metres ahead.

Chapter Thirty-Six

Alex had thought things couldn't get worse. Until the snow began to fall.

The relentless flakes settled in clumps, coating his clothes and sapping what little warmth he had left. He still wasn't sure if the cracking sound he'd heard earlier was part of his body breaking or just a twig snapping underfoot. What he did know was that his left ankle had swollen to an unnatural size. He'd tried to put pressure on it after the fall, which had sent a jolt of pain so sharp through his body that he'd almost passed out.

A dry, humourless sound escaped his lips. The absurdity of his situation was almost laughable. Maybe the cold had finally claimed his sanity. Hands numb, he scoured the undergrowth for anything he could use. He stuffed his trousers and jumper with more dry leaves for insulation and, mercifully, came across a sturdy stick large enough to use as a crutch.

He couldn't last much longer. Pain aside, he could barely feel his body any more. He had a vague understanding of how hypothermia worked and was sure it was only a matter of time before he succumbed to it. Stumbling forward like some grotesque scarecrow, he left a trail of dead leaves falling from his makeshift padding. Absurd as it seemed, part of him missed the sanctuary of the cave and at that precise moment he would have rather taken his chances with Adelaide's madness than endure this unforgiving wilderness.

If only he could see where he was going. He imagined that in different circumstances the scene might even appear beautiful. He imagined rolling water flanked by snow-covered land. This made him think of Bailey. The dog had never seen snow before, and Alex could picture him galloping through it, tail wagging, doing his silly little skip-and-dance routine. For a moment, fleeting warmth ran through his blood at the memory, before dread crept in. He shook his head, praying that out of all the things Adelaide and her family had done to him, killing Bailey wasn't one of them.

A sharp pain shot up his leg, and Alex bit back a scream. The useless limb felt like it was no longer part of his body, just a deadweight he had to drag along, its only purpose to torment him.

He stood still, leaning on the stick, letting the pain ebb away. Shivering, he felt as though the cold had frozen him to the spot. In his mind's eye, he saw Adelaide behind him, imagined her watching him stumble all this time, toying with him, waiting until she was ready to strike.

Even if she was following him, one thing was for sure: he wouldn't go back in the bag. He would rather freeze to death out here or throw himself off a cliff than let her take him again.

Gritting his teeth, he forced himself onward. Every step was agony, the frozen ground unforgiving beneath his unprotected feet. His body trembled, the falling snow obscuring his vision.

In the distance, he could hear the faint roar of the sea. He tried to convince himself that the sound meant he was close to civilisation, that there was still hope of rescue. But he couldn't quite fool himself.

He was utterly alone, trudging through what was likely the last hour of his life.

Chapter Thirty-Seven

'We might need that helicopter ourselves if this keeps up,' said Liam, rapping his knuckles on the steering wheel. They'd barely covered two miles in the last forty minutes, the unprecedented November snowfall wreaking its typical havoc on British roads.

The delay gave Liam time to study the images of Adelaide Harris that Jack had sent over. As Maya had pointed out, there wasn't much to glean from them. Adelaide looked like the self-conscious fourteen-year-old she'd been at the time, but the resemblance to Daniella was clear. Maya uploaded the blurry images from Jesters nightclub, and they scrutinised them together, neither able to definitively match the mystery woman to either sister.

Traffic finally began to thin near Camborne, though the snow continued to fall. Tension knotted in Liam's body, concentrated in a persistent twinge in his right calf muscle.

'Let's stop for a coffee,' said Maya, pointing to a petrol station ahead.

Liam welcomed the break, relieved to escape the confines of the car and stretch his limbs. He ordered a coffee and a toasted sandwich filled with something congealed and unidentifiable.

Waiting was something he'd mastered during his navy days, particularly in the SBS. Most of his time back then had been spent in stasis, waiting for high-adrenaline moments of action. The trick was to relax while staying ready. Everything could change in an instant, and if he hadn't been prepared, the consequences could have been dire, especially when switching from dry land to underwater in seconds.

But boredom had been the real enemy, something he faced less often in the police force. There was always something to do. A suspect to question, a witness to interview, or a lead to follow. Yet now, as they resumed their journey to the heliport in Penzance, Liam felt like he was right back in that liminal state. Waiting for Daniella's helicopter to arrive, for the search warrant to be granted, for a recent image of Adelaide Harris to surface. And, if he was brutally honest with himself, a dark part of him was waiting for the inevitable call telling him Alex Hudson's body had been discovered.

He shook the thought away as they pulled into the heliport. The snow had settled in deep clumps, and Maya called headquarters to check on the helicopter's status.

'Not the best news, I'm afraid,' said Jack. 'Take-off was delayed due to icy conditions, and the pilot's complaining about poor visibility.'

Liam groaned as a spasm gripped his back. He opened the car door, letting a flurry of snow swirl in as he stepped out to stretch.

'They're still on their way, though?' Maya asked, watching Liam with a bemused expression.

'For now, guv. I'll keep you posted,' Jack replied.

'You need to do some yoga, big lump like you,' Maya said, as Liam climbed back into the driver's seat.

'Charming,' he replied, arching his back. 'When exactly do you think I'd have time for yoga?'

'You shouldn't cut corners with your health, Liam. You know that.'

'I'll do some stretches, I promise,' Liam said, raising his hands in mock surrender, though he heard the grouchiness in his own voice.

Silence settled over them as they watched snow drift down on to the helipad. The events of the past weeks churned in Liam's mind. Grace's arrival in St Ives had dredged up memories he'd rather forget, reminders of the trauma caused by the Godrevy Island investigation. Too many lives had been lost then, and now it felt like history was repeating itself.

This time, at least, they knew who was in danger. But sitting here, cold and bored, wasn't helping anyone. 'We should go to Janet Harris's house,' Liam said. The car engine hummed, its meagre heat struggling against the cold.

'We don't have the warrant.'

As a DI, Maya was closer to the management line than Liam, and she had a knack for reining in his impulsive tendencies, but she didn't sound convincing, as if she wanted Liam to push the matter.

'Daniella had Alex Hudson's dog,' Liam pressed. 'It's more than conceivable she isn't working alone. We've already been to her house, so she may have decided that wasn't the best place to keep Alex.'

'We should wait for Hargreaves to get the warrant.'

'Let's go to the house, tell Janet Harris what we know, ask her about Adelaide, see if we can get her to talk. We don't need a warrant for that.'

'From what I remember, she wasn't exactly forthcoming last time.'

'Things are different now,' Liam countered. 'Her daughter's been arrested. We're not demanding to search the property, we're just asking questions. Who knows, the warrant might even be granted by the time we get there.'

Maya lowered her gaze, and Liam took that as agreement. He eased the car out of the heliport and pointed it towards Sennen.

The snow continued its unyielding assault. Though it was nearing 11 p.m., the traffic out of Penzance was still heavy, moving slowly on roads clogged by the weather. Everywhere was dusted with snowfall, and despite the circumstances, Liam couldn't help but notice how picturesque it all looked under the moonlight.

As they left the main roads behind, conditions worsened. Patches of black ice lurked beneath the powdery snow, making the smaller roads treacherous. Twice, Liam had to stop as the car drifted out of his control.

Maya called Jack as they approached the outskirts of Sennen.

'We're heading to question Janet Harris,' she said.

Jack fell silent for a moment before acknowledging her. It was clear he didn't agree with their decision, but he wasn't in a position to suggest they turn back.

The farmhouse eventually loomed ahead, more desolate than Liam remembered. The track leading to it was buried under two or three inches of snow, the untouched surface glistening under the car's headlights. The snowfall was already heavier than it had been the previous week, and if the temperatures held, it would likely be days before the area was cleared.

'You still have your bodycam?' Maya asked, as they parked up.

'It's in the boot,' Liam replied.

'I think you should wear it. We're still waiting on the warrant, so she could argue we're overstepping by being here. Better to have a record.'

Liam nodded and retrieved the device from the boot, along with his coat. Both wrapped up as if preparing for a ski expedition, they trudged the last fifty metres to the house. A floodlight illuminated the front of the building, casting long shadows across the snowy ground.

Liam stamped his feet to shake off the snow as he rang the doorbell. A clump of snow settled on Maya's face, and he nodded to it with a smirk.

Maya wiped it away as the door creaked open. Janet Harris stood there, wearing a white dress unsuitable for the outdoor conditions.

'Back so soon?' she said.

'May we come in?' Liam asked.

Janet's eyes flicked to Maya, giving her a slow, deliberate once-over. 'Who's this?' she asked. 'Pretty little thing.'

Unsmiling, Maya produced her warrant card. 'DI Maya Trent.'

'I believe I told you last time, don't come back without a warrant,' Janet said, ignoring Maya, and staring at Liam.

'This is about your daughter, Daniella,' replied Maya.

For a fleeting moment, Liam caught a flicker of indecision on Janet's face before it hardened again. 'What about her?'

'She's been arrested, Janet. We know about Alex Hudson,' Liam said, wanting to see how Janet would react to the name.

He'd seen that look before. The dawning realisation when a suspect knows their plans have unravelled. Janet's gaze darted between them, as though trying to assess who posed the greater threat.

'I don't know anything about any Alex Hudson,' she said, after a beat. 'But if my daughter's been arrested, you'd better come in.'

The interior of the house was a larger replica of Daniella's, with bare stone walls adorned with paintings and sideboards cluttered with trinkets. Janet led them into a snug, heated by a roaring open fire.

'May I get you something to drink?' Janet asked, as she gestured to two creaking armchairs.

'No, thank you,' Liam said, taking a seat as Maya settled into the identical chair beside him.

Janet poured herself a generous glass of wine from a crystal decanter. She took her seat opposite on a matching sofa, sweat visible on her bare shoulders. 'Are you recording me?' she asked, pointing to the bodycam on Liam's coat.

To the side was an antique mahogany sideboard, with an array of small drawers. Liam wondered if each was filled with hessian bags like the ones he'd found at Daniella's. 'For your protection,' Liam replied. 'So you'll have a record of our conversation. Is that all right?'

'You don't have a warrant, do you?' Janet said, her eyes narrowing. 'Now, what is this about Daniella?'

'Do you live here alone, Mrs Harris?' Liam asked, ignoring her question.

Janet turned to Maya, her eyebrows furrowed. 'What has happened to Daniella?'

'Your daughter has been arrested, Janet,' Maya said.

'For what?'

'Suspicion of murder,' Maya said.

'Oh, don't be ridiculous,' Janet said, her expression shifting between indignation and disbelief.

'We're just talking, Janet,' Liam said. 'But I'd advise you to think about your position here. If Daniella has dragged you into something, now is the time to tell us. Do you know where Alex Hudson is?'

Janet's lip curled as if tasting something bitter. A shadow seemed to darken her face. 'Stop saying that name. I don't know what you're talking about.'

'And Adelaide?' Liam asked.

Janet's face froze. 'What about her?' she said.

'Is she here?'

'That's none of your business.'

'Come on, Janet, you're not doing yourself any favours,' Liam said, leaning forward. 'Daniella was arrested because we found Alex Hudson's dog on her property. When we searched her house, we uncovered numerous hessian bags very similar to the ones used in the murders of Frank Oakley and Robin Wakefield.'

Indecision flickered again across Janet's face before being replaced with scorn. 'I don't know what the hell you think is happening here, but I can assure you, you're on the wrong track,' she said, her voice dripping with defiance, the same defiance Daniella had displayed during her interview at the house and police station.

'Janet, it's only a matter of time before we get the warrant,' Liam said. 'Cooperate now, and you'll save yourself a lot of trouble.'

'Tell us where Alex Hudson is,' Maya added.

Janet's jaw tightened, her lips pursed together as if she were physically holding back words. The tension in the room was palpable, the sound of the fire crackling the only break in the silence.

Janet's eyes darted between Liam and Maya as if she were calculating her next move. Her breaths came quick and shallow, her fingers twitching at her sides. 'Where is Daniella now?' she demanded.

'Daniella was arrested at Bristol Airport, Janet,' Liam said. 'She was about to board a flight for Europe. She knew things were about to get a lot worse for all of you.'

Janet shot up from the sofa with a speed and agility that belied her age. 'No!' she screamed, her face flushing scarlet as she loomed before them.

'Please take a seat, Janet,' Maya said, as she and Liam rose from their chairs, Liam's hand going to the extendable baton in his coat pocket.

But Janet didn't sit. Her voice rose into a shrill, almost primal cry. 'Adelaide, I need you!'

Liam and Maya exchanged a glance, both scanning the room, as from the shadows of the back door, a second figure emerged in silence. Liam blinked. For a moment he thought Daniella White had somehow appeared before them wearing the same white dress as her mother. But as the figure stepped closer, he realised it wasn't Daniella, but an almost identical younger version of her.

'You must be Adelaide,' Liam said.

Adelaide tilted her head slightly, her eyes glinting with cold amusement. She raised a shotgun, holding it steady as she trained it on them. 'And you,' she said, 'are in trouble.'

Chapter Thirty-Eight

Liam had been on the wrong end of firearms numerous times throughout his career, both in the navy and more recently in the police. Experience didn't make it any easier. Adrenaline surged through his body as he instinctively stepped between Adelaide and Maya. But experience did give him the ability not to panic. If Adelaide had intended to shoot them, she likely would have done so already, though that didn't mean she wouldn't at some point soon.

Adelaide held the gun with a steady hand. It was clear she was no stranger to pointing firearms at people. Liam had no doubt she was prepared to use the weapon.

'Think about what you're doing,' he said. 'Both of you.'

'Our colleagues know where we are,' Maya added, moving alongside Liam, so she was also in the line of fire. 'You won't get away with harming us.'

'And none of this would have had to happen if you'd stayed out of our business,' Janet said, her eyes flicking to the clock on the wall. She was close enough that Liam could have reached out and grabbed her, but the situation was too volatile. He couldn't predict how Adelaide would react, and the last thing they needed was her letting off a stray bullet.

'Sit down, both of you,' Janet ordered.

'On your hands,' Adelaide added, stepping closer, the gun unwavering in her grip.

'Do you mind putting that down?' Liam said. 'All it takes is for you to slip and . . .' He let that hang in the air.

Adelaide tilted her head again, her expression so eerily reminiscent of Daniella's that for a moment Liam wondered if they were the same person. After a pause, she lowered the gun slightly, though her finger remained near the trigger.

'Where is Alex Hudson?' Maya asked.

Liam caught the briefest glance exchanged between mother and daughter.

'Is he still alive?' Liam pressed. 'It's not too late to turn this around. Whatever hold Daniella has over you, you can break it. Show us where Alex is, and this will end far better for you.'

Adelaide smirked, a faint trace of amusement flickering in her eyes. 'You're very confident for someone in your position. Daniella told me about you. It's a shame you don't look more . . .' She trailed off, silenced by a sharp look from Janet.

'Is he here, Janet?' Maya asked.

The older woman ignored the question, instead pulling on a long coat over her white dress.

Liam's mind raced as he tried to piece the situation together. His recent focus had been on Daniella, but now he wasn't so sure of the extent she was involved. 'This is about Ernest, isn't it?' he said, taking a calculated risk.

Janet froze, her eyes narrowing.

Adelaide, triggered by the mention of her brother, lifted the gun once more and began walking towards Liam.

'Stop!' Maya shouted, but Adelaide didn't falter, her steps measured and deliberate.

Within seconds, she was beside the sofa, and before Liam could react, she jammed the barrel of the shotgun against his forehead.

The cold metal pressed hard against his skull, forcing his head back. Even this wasn't new to him. He'd been captured twice during conflict, both times with a gun at his head. But what was different now was the absolute absence of humanity in the aggressor's eyes. For the first time, Liam couldn't tell if the person holding the weapon would pull the trigger or not.

'Don't you ever mention my brother again,' Adelaide hissed, her voice sharp and venomous.

'We're sorry,' Maya said, her breath heavy beside him.

Liam closed his eyes, retreating to a memory of the beach. George riding waves on his boogie board in the summer heat. He clung to the image like a lifeline. 'I spoke out of turn,' he said.

Adelaide's response was swift and brutal. She drove the handle of the shotgun into his chest.

With his hands under him, Liam lost balance and fell on Maya. The pain was dizzying; Maya helped him to sit upright. He leant forward, wheezing. His upper body was convulsing, and he suspected at least one of his ribs might be cracked. But right now, that was the least of his worries.

'Come on,' Janet said. 'Let's show them what they're so desperate to see.'

'Are we doing it now, Mummy?' Adelaide asked, her voice childlike, at odds with her composed appearance, the gun held steady in her hands.

'It's time, dear. Daniella has made her choice.'

Adelaide turned the shotgun back on Liam, levelling it squarely at his chest. She tossed a length of rope to Maya. 'Tie him up. Wrists behind his back.'

Maya hesitated, but Adelaide's finger hovered too close to the trigger for defiance. With deliberate care, Maya looped the rope around Liam's wrists, pulling it tight. Once finished, Janet moved in to cinch the knots tighter before repeating the process on Maya.

'Our colleagues will be here any second,' Liam said, through strained breath. He was stalling for time as Janet took their phones. 'We're supposed to collect Daniella from the heliport in Penzance. When we don't show up, they'll know we're still here.'

Janet smiled, a hollow, mirthless expression. 'What have we to lose now?' she said, grabbing Maya by the wrists and leading her outside. Liam followed, Adelaide prodding him in the back with the shotgun.

The blast of icy air sent shivers through Liam's body despite his layered clothing. Janet lit their way across the snow-covered land with a torch, its beam slicing through the dark.

Liam glanced skyward. Snowflakes landed gently on his face. What he'd told Janet was true. They would be expected at the heliport. Whether or not Daniella's helicopter had made it, Jack would have tried to contact them again by now. Once he realised they weren't responding, backup would undoubtedly be sent. But how long that would take was anyone's guess.

For now, the priority was to delay things but that wasn't going to be easy with Janet and Adelaide's erratic behaviour. It was likely they had killed two men and kidnapped another without detection until now, showing cunning and forethought. So why this recklessness? They had to know Daniella's arrest would lead to their discovery. Why weren't they trying to escape?

They didn't seem to care, and if they didn't care about what happened to themselves, they certainly wouldn't care about what happened to him or Maya.

Maya dragged him from his concerns, slipping as they descended a snow-covered incline. Janet let go of her, and she slid several metres down the slope before coming to a halt.

'You OK?' Liam called, as Janet hauled Maya back to her feet with surprising ease.

'I'm fine,' Maya said, her jaw tightening as they continued to walk.

The sound of rushing water reached their ears as they descended further.

'Shall I get the bags?' Adelaide asked.

'You two, sit,' Janet ordered, waiting for Liam to hit the frozen ground before taking the gun from Adelaide.

The cold seeped through Liam's jeans as he sat, the hard-packed snow biting into his skin. His fingers, half-frozen, searched the ground for a stone or anything he could use against the binds around his wrists, as he listened to his own laboured breathing. 'You don't have to do this. Whatever you've done, we can sort it out. But there's no need to hurt anyone else.'

Adelaide disappeared into the shadows, leaving Liam and Maya alone with Janet, the older woman looming over them, the gun still trained on Liam's chest.

'You sound like you're from here,' Janet said, her torchlight glaring into Liam's face.

'Cornwall? All my life,' Liam replied, squinting against the beam. 'What is this all about, Janet?'

'And your parents?' Janet pressed.

'Both from Cornwall,' Liam said. 'And their parents before them.'

From the corner of his eye, he caught a glimpse of Maya subtly working at her bindings, her fingers moving methodically. He kept his voice even, buying time.

Janet seemed oddly pleased by his response, her expression softening briefly before a shadow passed over her face. 'So much has been lost,' she said, shaking her head.

Adelaide reappeared, her footsteps crunching on the frozen ground.

She was carrying two large hessian bags.

Chapter Thirty-Nine

Liam managed to grab hold of a loose stone from the ground before they were told to get back to their feet. It was short and sharp, but his numb hands made it impossible to get any real leverage on the rope binding his wrists. It felt like a Hail Mary. If he couldn't get purchase – if he couldn't even begin to fray the ropes – then . . .

They continued walking along the water's edge, the frozen ground crunching beneath their feet. Adelaide carried the two hessian bags over her shoulder while Janet held the gun. The glow from Adelaide's torch danced ahead of them, a swirling light making kaleidoscope-like patterns in the air.

'If you're going to do this, you might as well tell us why,' Liam said, still trying to work the rope. His fingers were numb, but every time he gripped the stone and tried to create any kind of friction, waves of pain shot up his arm.

Neither woman answered. The only sounds were the water lapping nearby and their footsteps breaking the snow.

'What did you mean earlier,' Liam asked, finally catching the thread on the rope, 'when you said Daniella has made her choice? Did she leave you? Is that what this is all about?'

Janet grunted. 'She was always a wild spirit, that one. She understood the old ways, but . . .'

'Mummy, don't,' Adelaide said.

'It's OK, dear. What does it matter now?' Janet said. 'Daniella will have to explain herself soon, but that won't matter to us. Tradition binds families, DS Kilshaw. Maybe you understand that, maybe you don't. Our family has lived here for centuries. We are as much a part of this land as the frozen ground you're walking on or the water beside you. And we continue to live on, and always will.'

Liam slowed his pace as much as he could without drawing attention to the fact he was trying to cut into his rope. 'But what does this have to do with the men you killed? And why the bags? We have nothing to do with any of this.'

'Give me the gun!' Adelaide screamed from behind him.

Liam didn't have time to turn before the butt of the rifle slammed into his shoulder. The force almost toppled him to the ground. He stumbled but managed to stay upright. However, his body convulsed from the blow, causing him to drop the stone.

'You think the bags are for you? You think you deserve to live forever?' Adelaide shrieked, trembling with fury, as she moved in front of him.

The snow blurred Liam's vision, and for a second he pictured Adelaide morphing into something inhuman, a distant part of him wondering if he was looking at Bucca Dhu.

'So who are the bags for?' Maya asked, breaking the tension.

'They're for us, of course,' said Adelaide, moving behind Liam again and pushing him forward.

Liam's mind raced to make sense of her words. It sounded as if she was talking about a suicide pact. He wondered how that connected to Ernest Harris, the two victims, and Alex Hudson. Were their deaths a precursor, or simply part of the chaos this family had unleashed?

'Why are we here, then?' Liam asked, his breath laboured as the stream began to widen into a larger body of water.

'Don't ask stupid questions,' Adelaide said.

'Why kill those men?'

'Mistakes,' Janet said, her voice like the squawk of a bird.

Liam shook his head, incredulous. 'Mistakes?'

'We had to find a replacement for Ernest. They were wrong.'

The word 'replacement' hung heavy in the air. Liam wasn't sure what she meant, but he knew he had to keep her talking.

'Is that why you mutilated them? Because they didn't look like Ernest?' he asked.

'That was . . . unfortunate.'

'Why dump the bodies on the beach?' Liam asked, desperate to keep the mother talking.

Janet's breathing quickened behind him. 'That was Daniella's doing. Unfortunately, she's caught between two worlds.'

'What do you mean "two worlds"?' asked Liam, wondering if Janet was referring to the old ways and Bucca Dhu.

'Her brother was dying, and we couldn't help him. She was doing her best,' Janet said.

Was this what Daniella had wanted all along? Had she been trying to alert them to what her mother and sister were doing?

'And Alex Hudson? Is he the replacement?' Liam asked, dreading the answer.

'We finally found one, didn't we, Mummy?' Adelaide said, her voice rising to a fever pitch before she saw something in the distance – and ran towards it screaming.

Chapter Forty

'I still have the gun, in case you're thinking of doing something stupid,' Janet said, pressing the shotgun into the same shoulder Adelaide had struck earlier. Liam winced but kept his focus ahead, watching the erratic beam of Adelaide's torch bouncing in the distance as she ran, before the torchlight disappeared.

'Move,' Janet said.

Liam complied, walking faster towards the area where Adelaide had run. Although the darkness around him made it almost impossible to navigate, he could hear Adelaide screeching incoherently, her voice distant but unsettling.

'Slow down,' Janet said, as Maya hurried to catch up, walking alongside Liam.

The shotgun jabbed at his back now and again, the pressure light but menacing. Liam tried to up his pace, though the snow and uneven ground made anything faster than a stagger impossible. Janet struggled to keep up, the darkness clearly making her footing just as uncertain.

'Slow down,' she said, her voice more brittle than before.

Seizing the moment, Liam dropped abruptly to the ground, rolling backward. Janet, unable to stop herself in time, stumbled and fell over him with a grunt, the shotgun slipping from her grasp as she hit the snow. Liam wasted no time. He pinned her to the ground, pressing her knees on to her chest to keep her in place.

Janet bucked furiously, snarling and thrashing beneath him. Despite her age, her strength was formidable, and Liam had to lean forward, using every ounce of his weight to hold her down.

'Can you get free?' he asked Maya, who had also fallen in the scuffle.

'No,' Maya replied, struggling against her bindings.

'There's a penknife in my inside left pocket. Can you reach it?' Liam said, straining to keep Janet under control.

Maya crawled towards him as Janet continued hissing and spitting, baring her teeth like a cornered animal. Maya's trembling hands fumbled at his side, her numb fingers struggling to work the zipper.

'You can do it,' Liam said, shifting his weight forward to press Janet more firmly into the ground.

The snow continued to fall, adding to the bitter cold that seeped into their clothes. Time was against them, and Liam knew they couldn't survive for many hours in these conditions. His breath clouded in front of him, his strength waning as Janet's resistance persisted.

Finally, he felt the zipper give way. Maya reached into the pocket and withdrew the penknife, her movements frantic.

'Shit,' Maya said, as the knife slipped from her grasp, her voice strained as she scrambled in the snow to retrieve it.

'We have other things we can do to you,' Janet said, snarling as she continued to struggle.

'Hold still,' Maya said.

Liam's legs trembled from the strain of keeping Janet subdued. Pain radiated through his body, a sharp line of fire running down his left side where Janet had struck him earlier.

At last, he felt the ropes around his wrists loosen. 'I've got it,' he said, his voice tight with exertion. He shrugged the bindings free, crying out as his arms came forward, the pain in his shoulder sharp and immediate.

'You OK?' Maya asked, pushing herself up from the ground, her hands still tied behind her back.

Liam nodded, though the pain was excruciating. He bore down further on Janet. 'If you struggle, I will use whatever force is necessary to subdue you. Do I make myself clear?'

Janet's chest heaved as she caught her breath, her expression defiant despite her position. 'So masterly,' she said, sneering at him before spitting at his face.

Liam took a steadying breath, rubbing his hands together before grabbing Janet's arms and flipping her on to her back.

'You're hurting me,' she protested, as Liam picked up what remained of the rope Maya had cut from his wrists and wrapped it securely around Janet's gnarled hands.

Liam ignored her protests, securing her wrists with a simple slip knot. He pushed himself up, leaving Janet restrained on the ground.

'You OK?' he asked Maya, crouching to untie her hands.

Maya stretched her arms, wincing as circulation returned. She wriggled her fingers to ease the stiffness. 'Nothing a few hours in front of a fire won't cure.'

Without thinking, Liam pulled her into a brief embrace. It wasn't a gesture they often shared, but it felt appropriate in the bitter cold and the relief of freedom. As they parted, he said, 'We need to get our phones.'

'One of us could go back to the house.' She turned her attention to Janet. 'Where has Adelaide gone? And where are you keeping Alex Hudson?'

Janet lay in the snow, seemingly indifferent to the freezing conditions. Liam hauled her to her feet. 'You might as well tell us where Alex is,' he said. 'Whatever macabre plan you had for those hessian bags is over now.'

Janet smiled, an eerie expression that didn't reach her eyes, as snow tumbled down her cheeks. 'I wouldn't be so sure about that,' she said.

With no torch, their visibility was limited to a few metres. Liam's training in the navy had prepared him for navigating in such conditions, but their resources were sparse, and time was against them. The house wasn't that far away. Going there to call for backup was an option, but every minute wasted could mean the difference between life and death for Alex Hudson.

Maya seemed to share his thoughts. 'Let's see what spooked Adelaide so much,' she said. 'Gun or suspect?'

Liam picked up the shotgun, inspecting the chamber. It was fully loaded. He nodded, and Maya pushed Janet forward as they began descending to the area Adelaide had sprinted towards.

'What did she see?' Liam asked.

'I don't know,' Janet replied.

They stayed close to the water's edge, Liam twisting his torso from side to side as he walked to help keep warm. The cold bit at their exposed skin, and while their layers provided some insulation, Liam knew the weather could have dire consequences if they didn't find shelter soon.

Progress was slow, the lack of light and the rough terrain making each step dangerous. After about ten minutes, they reached a broader section of stream that had widened into a small lake.

'What is this?' Maya asked, turning Janet to face her. For the first time, the older woman appeared on the verge of tears.

On the ground lay the remnants of a hessian bag, similar to the ones Adelaide had been carrying and the ones used to stow Frank

Oakley and Robin Wakefield. The bag was attached to a chain that linked it to a heavy iron anchor partially buried in the snow.

'There's some kind of circle here,' Liam said, walking around a collection of stones and pebbles arranged in a crude perimeter. 'Is this where you were keeping Alex? Is that why Adelaide screamed, because she realised he escaped?'

The tears vanished from Janet's face, replaced by a look of determination. 'He won't get far,' she said. 'I imagine she'll find his body close by. It isn't too late. And when she returns,' her lips curled into a sneer, 'you'll regret you were ever born.'

Chapter Forty-One

Liam pulled Maya to one side, lowering his voice. 'I need to go after them. Adelaide will kill him.'

'Christ, this is a right mess,' Maya said, shaking her head.

'Take Janet and head back to the house. Follow the water. It'll guide you straight there.'

'I don't like this at all. It goes against every kind of procedure.'

'Sometimes procedure doesn't account for situations like this.'

Maya hesitated. She was the senior officer and the decision would have to come from her, but Liam had to be the one to go after Adelaide, even with the pain in his ribs.

'At least take the gun,' Maya said, after a long pause.

Liam shook his head. 'I wouldn't forgive myself if something happened to you.'

'That's an order,' Maya said, pushing the gun towards him. 'I wouldn't know what to do with it anyway, and Janet is secure.'

Liam reluctantly took the shotgun, its weight unfamiliar in his hands. Watching Maya lead Janet away felt surreal. He stood in silence as they disappeared into the darkness, leaving him alone in the snow-draped landscape.

He was no stranger to such scenarios. Visibility was his biggest challenge. Without the stream as a reference, he doubted he'd have made any progress. Even with it, the trek was perilous, the snow masking loose rocks and patches of ice.

From what Liam could gather, Alex had escaped from whatever hessian bag prison he'd been held in and was now on the run with Adelaide in pursuit. When and how the women had planned to kill Alex was still unknown, as was the significance of the stone circle.

Janet's cryptic talk of 'living forever' lingered in his mind, as did the implication that the bags Adelaide had carried had been intended for the mother and daughter as part of some bizarre suicide pact. He thought of the old ways, his mind this time conjuring the image of Bucca Dhu as a three-headed monstrosity – the heads belonging to Janet Harris and her two daughters.

Whatever the family's beliefs, none of it explained why Frank Oakley and Robin Wakefield had been murdered. Those answers would have to wait. Right now, all that mattered was stopping the same fate from befalling Alex Hudson.

Alex was certain now that he was being followed. He couldn't explain how he knew. It felt like some deep, primal instinct. He imagined Adelaide discovering his escape after the snow had started falling, realising he'd slipped free from the bag, and deciding she would come after him.

He didn't dare look behind him. It took all his strength to keep moving forward. His right arm felt fused to the stick he was using as a crutch, and even with its support, staying upright in the snow was a near-impossible task.

Now and again, he found himself glancing at the water, estimating the depth of the drop along the stream's edge. The thought of ending his own life was foreign and horrifying. He loved his solitary life with Bailey, and at twenty-five, his future still seemed wide open.

But meeting Adelaide had changed everything. Even if he somehow escaped her, he doubted his life would ever be the same. The cave, the bag, and the days of torment had transformed him into something unrecognisable. He felt separated from his own body, a stranger in his weakened, failing frame.

He slipped, his frail and frozen limbs unable to stop the fall. He hit the ground hard, the snow soaking into his already sodden clothes. The pain in his ankle was unbearable, and he lay for a few seconds in agony, waiting for the worst of it to subside.

Desperate, he scrambled to the side of the track, his body falling once more, this time into a small gulley. The hollow felt like a custom-made grave, just big enough for his body, but at least it was sheltered.

With the last reserves of his strength, Alex pulled at the foliage and leaves around him, covering himself as best he could. He knew it wouldn't be enough to keep him alive for long, but he was done fighting. The thought of going back outside, back into the icy, relentless wilderness, was unthinkable.

This was where he would stay. All he could do now was hope that the right people found him before it was too late.

More than once, Liam had to fight the nagging feeling that what he was doing was absurd. Visibility was nearly non-existent, and he had no guarantee Adelaide had even gone in the direction he was travelling. He did his best to follow the stream, but it kept disappearing from sight, leaving him guided only by the faint trickling sound of the water that rose and fell with the wind.

The cold was an inconvenience, but now that his hands were free, it was easier to keep himself moving and stave off the worst of it. He wondered if Alex had been as fortunate. From what Liam could tell, Alex had escaped the ripped hessian bag they'd found near the small lake. The bag had been chained to an anchor, and it seemed likely it had been submerged. Had Alex been inside when it was in the water? The thought was horrifying but consistent with the fates of the previous victims. If Alex had been in the icy water and somehow escaped, he wouldn't survive for very long in these conditions.

Liam pressed forward, moving as fast as his limited visibility and injured ribs allowed. The ground remained a hazard, with loose vines and hidden rocks tripping him up, but he endured the stumbles and lacerations.

From what he'd gathered earlier using the satnav, the lake where they had found the bag was connected to the Cot Valley stream, which eventually fed into the beach in Porth Nanven where Robin Wakefield's body had been discovered. Liam strained his ears, hoping to catch the distant roar of the sea, but it was still elusive.

He resisted the urge to run. Adelaide had a significant head start, but he couldn't afford to lose his footing or veer off course in the dark. He had to reach her before she found Alex. The discarded hessian bag they'd found indicated she intended to use one, and that thought propelled him forward with urgency.

The sound of rushing water grew louder, and Liam quickened his pace. Battling through dense bushes, he emerged on to a wider section of the stream. Parts of it were frozen, the icy surface glinting in the moonlight.

The sea had to be nearby. If Alex had made it this far, perhaps he'd reached the beach and found help. Maybe he was even en route to the hospital now, safe and warm.

The fantasy lasted mere seconds, shattered by a piercing scream that echoed through the night.

◆ ◆ ◆

Alex drifted in and out of sleep. Each time he began to slip away, the raw cold and the nerve-shredding pain in his body jolted him back into the harsh reality of the little cubbyhole he'd found.

He clung to the hope that somewhere someone was missing him. Thinking of Bailey brought tears to his eyes. If his dog was alive, he would be missing Alex, just as he always did when Alex left the house for more than two minutes. That much was a certainty. But who else would notice he was gone?

Alex's solitude had always been self-imposed. He didn't understand people, and trusting Adelaide had been the ultimate proof of his ignorance. He should have known from the start that her interest in him was a charade. People had told him he was good-looking before, but thinking someone like Adelaide would genuinely take a second glance at him had been sheer vanity.

And look where that had got him.

If his mother were alive, she would have missed him. But his dad? Alex doubted his father even knew he was missing. Their relationship was so distant, they may as well have been strangers. Alex didn't blame him, not really. They were kindred spirits in a way, both preferring solitude. He knew his mother's death had changed something fundamental in his father, drained him of whatever connection they might have shared.

It was still difficult for Alex to accept that his father had needed to take the job up north. Alex had never told him, but he'd wanted him to stay. It didn't matter that they barely saw each other; it was enough just knowing he was nearby, especially so soon after his mum had died.

Curled into himself, Alex tried to find some warmth. Part of him wanted to fight and stay alive. But another part – at that moment, a much stronger part – just wanted it all to be over. No one missed him, and no one was coming for him. He'd give anything to see Bailey again, but that wasn't going to happen. Without that hope, he couldn't see a good reason to keep going.

His body trembled, his limbs numb and unresponsive. He looked around at the makeshift grave he'd nestled into, deciding there were worse final resting places.

He closed his eyes, willing the cold to take him. His breaths grew shallow as he began to drift, slipping towards unconsciousness, as a voice, soft but distinct, called to him.

'I see you, Alex. There's still time. Let's get you out of there, shall we?'

Liam wanted to run, but progress would be faster if he paced himself, even though it felt counterintuitive. A fresh flurry of snow had descended, reducing visibility to almost nothing. He could see only one step ahead. The sound of rushing water to his right was his only guide, though he still couldn't see the stream. He was certain he was on high ground and feared that any lateral movement might send him over a drop.

It had been a couple of minutes since he'd heard the scream, and now he was doubting if he'd heard it at all. In his mind, the sound had an unsettling, guttural quality to it, almost animal-like. He tried to convince himself it was just the wind or some wild creature. But as he pressed forward, he noticed a faint glow cutting through the darkness ahead.

It had to be Adelaide's torch.

With each cautious step forward, the light grew brighter.

The illumination helped, but it didn't make his path easier. The relative silence felt oppressive, amplifying every crunch of snow underfoot. Liam tried to move faster, but the uneven terrain made every step precarious. Foliage snagged at his legs, and loose stones threatened to send him sprawling, yet somehow he kept his balance.

The shotgun, slung uselessly at his side, felt more like deadweight than a weapon. Its barrel hung open, the bullets removed. He wasn't even sure why he'd brought it – it wasn't like he planned to use it – but guessed it might serve as a deterrent if needed.

He pressed on, the torch's beam now casting light on the snow-covered path ahead. It seemed to be pointing to him, improving his visibility. Liam slowed his pace, wary that it could be a trap.

He clicked the shotgun barrel into place and held it in front of him, but didn't speak, not wanting to give away his position too soon.

The torchlight grew closer, but still there was no sound beyond the faint trickle of the stream. Numerous scenarios raced through Liam's mind. Adelaide could be waiting in ambush, torch in hand, ready to pounce. Or she might have dropped it in a rush, having heard him approaching. Worst of all, she might have found Alex already. The thought of her forcing him into the hessian bag sent a fresh wave of urgency through Liam.

In his desperation, Liam quickened his pace and tripped. His knee hit the frozen ground hard, the impact reverberating through his body.

Breathless, he lay where he fell, unable to move as the snow continued to fall.

◆ ◆ ◆

Alex had never felt more helpless. Even during his time in the cave, chained to the wall, there had been a sliver of hope that he might escape. But now, he felt transformed. He was no longer Alex Hudson, a solitary but capable young man. He was a hollowed-out version of himself, aged and broken, physically weak and mentally drained.

Adelaide's voice echoed in his mind, sharp and commanding. He had no fight left in him, no option but to succumb to whatever she demanded as she dragged him from his resting place. Her actions were a bizarre mixture of inhuman strength and unsettling tenderness.

'You feel so cold, Alex,' she said, her voice almost maternal. 'Why did you leave the bag?'

The question was absurd, but Alex's broken mind tried to respond. He wanted to scream, *Why the hell do you think?* but no words escaped his frozen lips.

The world around him seemed to vibrate, or perhaps it was just his body shivering. Snow fell in thick, otherworldly clumps, illuminated by the beam of Adelaide's torch, which she had planted in the ground like a grim sentinel.

She knelt over him, stroking his face as though he were a child. Her voice softened. 'It'll be OK. We can try again. You're not going to be alone, Alex. You're going to be my new brother, and I'll be with you, too. Forever.'

The words were madness, and Alex could have laughed at their absurdity if he'd had the strength. How had he not seen it before? The insanity must have been there from the beginning, in her eyes, in her smile. He'd been too blinded by her beauty to notice, too distracted by her charm to sense the storm beneath the surface.

'Will you climb in, Alex?' she cooed, her voice soothing and sickening all at once.

Alex turned his head and saw the bag lying in the snow beside him. *At least it'll be warmer,* he thought, shuffling towards it with what little strength he had left.

As he moved, his hand brushed against the stick he'd carried with him. The rough wood felt fused to his frozen fingers, his grip vice-like. He was about to ask Adelaide to help him unclench his hand when his body acted on its own volition.

As if in a dream, Alex watched himself summon the last reserves of his strength. He twisted his body, swinging his shoulder towards Adelaide. The large stick, an extension of his failing body, came with him, and the solid wood struck her squarely across the head.

Through the blur of snow, he saw her stagger. Her lips curled into an enigmatic smile, a fleeting expression of both surprise and amusement, before she hit the ground and stopped moving.

◆ ◆ ◆

Liam's time in the SBS had taught him pain-control techniques – part state of mind, part breathing exercises – but right now, they weren't helping.

He lay motionless, his breathing shallow, snow pressing into his face. The ribs on his left side felt like splintered glass cutting into him with every breath and he worried about the pressure on his lungs.

Waves of pain radiated through him, each pulse hitting every nerve. He fought to stay conscious, focusing on his breathing, waiting for his body to find its equilibrium.

Gradually, the pain subsided to a dull throb. It was still agonising, but bearable. Liam forced himself into a seated position, each movement a battle against the screaming protests of his body.

The torch lay within reach. He stretched out a trembling hand, finally grasping it and bringing it to his chest. For a moment, he just sat there, catching his breath and willing himself to continue.

He swept the torch around the area, moving the beam in a slow, circular motion through the darkness until it alighted on the body he had tripped over.

Even from a distance, Liam knew there was no need to check for a pulse.

Adelaide Harris lay on her back, blood-tinged snow falling from her mouth.

◆ ◆ ◆

Alex hadn't meant to kill her, but he was certain that was what he'd done. The heavy stick had struck Adelaide with tremendous force as Alex swivelled all his weight into the blow, screaming into the night, as he hit her squarely on the side of the head.

Why had this happened to him? Meeting Adelaide had changed him irrevocably, carving scars into his psyche that he knew he would never escape. Even now, with her lifeless body lying in the distance, he was still terrified of her. His life would forever be plagued by the memories of his imprisonment, of the godforsaken bag filling with water, of the cold and suffocating darkness.

And now he would have to live with the knowledge that he had taken another human life.

Even after all she'd done to him, it was this final act that felt impossible to bear. And while the weather would soon strip him of the choice to live or die, Alex wanted it over now.

Still using the stick as a crutch, he hobbled through the snow towards the sound of rushing water. He left the torch behind, no longer needing its light to guide him. The ground rose, as his frozen body moved on autopilot until at last he reached the water.

It was a small waterfall, the drop below obscured by snow and shadows. He didn't need to see it to know it would serve its purpose.

Dropping the stick, Alex stood at the lip of the fall, his mind battling his instincts. It whispered excuses, reasons to stop, to reconsider. But what would be the point? Even if he wanted to live, that choice was slipping from his grasp. It was either this, a quick release, or a drawn-out, painful death. And even if he had survived, what was left for him to return to?

He stepped forward, his foot hovering at the edge of the drop. Snow swirled around him as a blazing light broke through the darkness, illuminating the sheer drop below and momentarily blinding him.

◆ ◆ ◆

'Stop!' Liam shouted, his voice cutting through the icy night air.

He caught sight of Alex, who had left a trail of blood through the snow to the waterfall. The man stood on the edge of the drop, his balance uneven, as if the next gust of wind might take him over.

'You must be Alex,' Liam said, gasping for breath as he stopped a short distance away. 'My name is Liam Kilshaw, I'm with the police. It might not look like it but I'm here to rescue you.'

The man, balancing on one leg, turned his wide-eyed gaze to Liam. He looked dazed, like he didn't believe what he was seeing. His lips moved, forming words Liam couldn't quite hear.

'It's all OK now,' Liam said, inching closer. 'You're safe. You *are* Alex, aren't you?'

Alex nodded, his mouth still hanging open.

'I met your dad today,' Liam said, though it felt like a memory from another lifetime.

'My dad?' Alex said.

'He was worried about you, Alex. He's the reason we found you. He came down from Leeds to speak to us.'

Alex shook his head, the motion small and uncertain. 'I'm tired. I can't,' he said, stepping closer to the edge.

Liam's heart pounded, the pain in his ribs hurting with every breath. The uphill trek to the waterfall had drained him, and he wasn't sure he had the strength to cover the last ten metres in time if Alex decided to jump. 'I know it doesn't feel like it now, Alex, but you'll get through this. I'm living proof. I've been in captivity. I've come close to drowning. I know how this feels, but you're in shock. There are people who love you. People who will help you.'

Alex shook his head again. 'I can't,' he murmured, turning his back on Liam.

Liam's breath caught as he saw Alex's foot shift, his weight leaning towards the drop. Desperate, pain rushing the side of his body at the effort, he shouted, 'Bailey!'

Alex froze, almost toppling forward. 'Bailey?'

'Bailey, your dog,' Liam said. 'I found him.'

'He's alive?'

'He sure is. Big lad, but a big softy. A real sweetheart.'

Alex staggered towards Liam. 'He's alive?' he repeated, with a hint of desperation.

Liam hobbled forward and managed to put his arms around Alex, pulling him away from the edge. 'He sure is. Now let's get you back to him,' he said, his strength giving out as both of them crumpled to the ground.

◆ ◆ ◆

Liam lay breathless in the snow, his back flat against the frozen ground as clumps of it fell on to his head. He closed his eyes and for a moment he wasn't there any more. He was back under the water, back in the ocean where he'd almost lost his life.

He blinked, trying to push the memory away, but reality wasn't much better. The sharp pain in his ribs anchored him in the present, each breath sending another surge of agony through his body. He thought he'd talked Alex out of jumping, but he couldn't be sure. The pain was so intense that unconsciousness seemed almost preferable.

'Here,' Alex said, shifting and lifting Liam's shoulders. 'What have you done?'

'I think I've cracked my ribs,' Liam managed to say, each word an effort.

Alex shifted behind him, struggling to lift Liam into a semi-upright position. 'Is that better?'

'Yeah,' Liam said, his breathing easing slightly. 'Though I'm supposed to be here to rescue you.'

'I think someone needs to rescue us both,' Alex replied. 'My leg's useless now.'

'Someone will be here soon,' Liam assured him, his words more hopeful than certain. He imagined how they must look. Two battered, frostbitten men huddled together in the snow. 'Tell me about Bailey,' he said, trying to keep them both conscious.

Alex didn't answer at first, and Liam couldn't turn to look at him. 'Come on, Alex. You've come so far. Just a few minutes longer.'

Liam felt Alex shivering violently behind him. 'You're right,' Alex said. 'He's a big dog. I probably should've thought that through.'

Liam knew they both needed to keep talking to fend off the encroaching hypothermia. 'His paw was about the size of my arm,' Liam said.

'Tell me about it. He knocks me over every time I come home. Easier just never to leave him.'

Each word seemed like a monumental effort for Alex, and Liam struggled to find the energy to respond. 'I can imagine. We'll have to make sure he's on a lead next time you see him.'

Alex didn't reply this time, though Liam could feel him shaking harder. 'Stay with me, Alex,' Liam said, his own voice growing weaker. 'Keep talking. Don't stop.'

But silence fell between them. Liam's body was frozen, but the sharp pain in his chest still flared with every attempted movement. He tried to shift and face Alex, but the searing pain locked him in place. 'Alex,' he whispered, his eyes fluttering shut as the faint sound of approaching footsteps reached his ears.

A bark pierced the quiet, snapping Liam back from the brink of unconsciousness. He forced his eyes open to see a German Shepherd bounding through the snow towards them.

'Alex,' he said, relief flooding his voice as the dog reached him. Its snout nuzzled into his neck, sniffing him.

The dog barked and turned back to the sound of crunching boots as, in the distance, the rescue team arrived.

Chapter Forty-Two

Driving to Bodmin, Liam found it hard to believe that less than a week ago the hills and valleys had been buried in snow. Now, a cold rain pelted his windscreen as he turned off the main road towards headquarters.

It was his first day back at work since the rescue in Cot Valley. If he moved too fast or strained, he could still feel the pain in his side. Eight cracked ribs, one of which had caused a minor lung contusion, and had impaired his breathing on the night he'd rescued Alex. Combined with the brutal conditions of that night, it had landed him in Treliske Hospital for two days before his release.

During his stay, Maya, Jack, and a few other team members had visited, their concern thinly veiled by casual banter. George had visited too, telling Liam repeatedly that he was a hero for what he'd done. Even Grace had made an unexpected evening appearance when he'd been alone. She'd told him about her interview for the role in Exeter, and he'd finally shared with her that he'd split from Millie.

Alex Hudson hadn't been so lucky. He'd suffered from hypothermia and frostbite in three places but was due to be released later that week. His father had visited every day and was now taking care of Bailey, awaiting Alex's return home. No charges had been brought against Alex for his role in Adelaide Harris's death.

As Liam parked up at headquarters, his mind wandered to those final moments in Cot Valley. The breathlessness and cold had pulled him back to his near-death experience in the ocean, and he wondered if he'd ever be free of that haunting memory.

There was no fanfare for his return as he entered CID a few minutes later. Today wasn't about him.

After being brought in by helicopter, Daniella White had been arrested for the murders of Frank Oakley and Robin Wakefield, as well as the abduction of Alex Hudson. She was currently on remand awaiting trial. Janet Harris, meanwhile, was under psychiatric observation to determine her fitness to plead.

Liam hadn't been there when Janet was informed of Adelaide's death, but Maya had recounted how the woman had broken down, screaming and cursing, blaming everyone but herself. Daniella, in contrast, had shown no visible reaction, taking the news with unsettling calm.

Despite the strong case against her, Daniella had refused to speak to anyone about the crimes until today, when she had requested to speak to Liam.

Hoping for a confession, the team spent the morning preparing. Liam, Maya and Hargreaves had gone through mock interviews, considering every possible angle Daniella might take.

At 11.30 a.m., a notification came through. Daniella had arrived with her prison escort and was meeting with her solicitor in one of the interview suites.

'Let's go,' Liam said, pausing to glance at the crime board. The images of Frank Oakley and Robin Wakefield stared back at him. He didn't need any more reminders of why they were here.

◆ ◆ ◆

The transformation in Daniella White was staggering. Liam had prepared himself for some change in her demeanour – there always was when a suspect found themselves in custody, no longer in control – but this was more profound than anything he'd seen before. The confident, exuberant woman he remembered was gone, replaced by someone who seemed to have physically and mentally collapsed into herself.

She sat in the interview chair, arms wrapped around her torso, her shoulders drawn in as if trying to shrink away from the world. Her hair hung limp, and her face was devoid of make-up or the sharp expressions that had once defined her.

Liam and Maya greeted her solicitor, exchanging the usual formalities, Maya walking them through the legalities of the interview.

'Thank you for speaking with us, Daniella. I know this last week must have been difficult for you,' Liam said.

For the first time since the interview began, Daniella looked at him. Her large eyes, once disarming and powerful, now seemed vulnerable, almost pleading.

Her solicitor cleared his throat. 'Miss White is prepared to provide the information you require. In exchange, she would like her assistance to be noted.'

'Are you admitting that you killed Frank Oakley and Robin Wakefield?' Maya asked.

Daniella shifted in her chair, her movements slow and deliberate. 'No. But I will explain what happened.'

'We have your DNA on both victims and inside your vehicle,' Maya said, referencing the evidence that had come through since Daniella's arrest.

'I transported the bodies,' Daniella said, her focus fixed on Liam. 'But I didn't kill either of them.'

Liam sighed, exchanging a brief look with Maya before addressing Daniella again. 'Tell us everything you want to share, Daniella. I can't make any promises, but if your evidence is helpful, we can discuss your charges.'

Daniella glanced at her solicitor, who nodded. A flush of colour rose to her pale cheeks, and she began to speak.

'Preservation has been part of our family's lives for centuries. We've lived on the same land for generations.'

Liam and Maya stayed silent, allowing her to continue.

'Since I was a little girl, my mother instilled in me the importance of preservation. The idea is simple. Take things and encase them before they deteriorate. That's why you found the bags in my house, and no doubt have found similar ones at my family home.'

Liam resisted the urge to interrupt, sensing that now was a time for listening. He wanted to ask how this concept of preservation had extended to humans, but forced himself to stay quiet.

'I realised not long after starting school that this wasn't considered a normal pastime,' Daniella continued, a faint smile tugging at her lips. 'My parents were called in once because I wrote in a school diary about preserving our family dog before he died. That was the last time I made *that* mistake.'

She laughed, a sharp, unsettling sound that echoed around the room, making Liam wonder if she should be under psychiatric observation alongside her mother.

'It's impossible to explain to someone who doesn't understand,' Daniella said, her tone softening. 'Imagine something you love so much, or a perfect memory you don't want to tarnish. By preserving it, you get to keep it that way forever. Do you understand?'

Liam nodded, not in agreement, but to encourage her to continue. He understood the concept but the reality of what

Daniella was describing was as alien to him as her actions had been. 'How does this relate to the murder victims?' he asked.

Daniella turned to her solicitor, raising her eyebrows. 'Maybe I shouldn't have mentioned the dog,' she said, half to herself, before returning her gaze to Liam. 'Anyway, as a family, we didn't preserve the dead *that* much. When we preserved that dog, I'm pretty sure he was dead already. My dad put him in a bag. We cleansed him in the water, then buried him.'

Liam's stomach churned as he thought of Alex Hudson's testimony. That morning, he had reviewed the interviews conducted in his absence. Alex had described being forced into a hessian bag while still alive, and left in the water for dead.

He studied Daniella as her demeanour shifted. The mocking smile was still there, and her previous confidence seemed to be creeping back.

'Go on, Daniella,' Liam said.

'Fifteen years ago, my father died,' Daniella said, her voice devoid of emotion. 'I'm afraid my mother didn't take it well. He had a heart attack at home, and we never told the authorities. Mum decided we were going to preserve Dad, just like we had with everything else. She put him in a bag, we cleansed him, and we buried him.'

Liam shifted in his seat. 'This was on your land?'

'Yes. I can show you where.' Daniella's expression didn't change. 'I was young, but old enough to cope. Adelaide was too young, and Ernest was too susceptible. I saw it that day, as we buried Dad. Mum was indoctrinating them. She made us promise – made us *all* promise – that none of us would end up that way.'

'What way?' Liam asked, though he wasn't sure he wanted to hear the answer.

'She didn't like the way Dad looked when he died, and certainly not by the time we buried him. She couldn't handle the thought that her lasting memory of him would be that . . . shrivelled version she saw after the heart attack.'

Liam suppressed a shudder. 'So?'

'So, she set about making amends—'

'Please note,' Daniella's solicitor said, interrupting, 'that what my client is about to tell you is voluntary and that she had no part in what occurred.'

'How did she make amends, Daniella?'

Daniella tilted her head slightly, as though the answer should have been obvious. 'She tried to find a replacement.'

Liam's stomach tightened. As he listened, he wondered if Daniella's story was an elaborate fabrication, a desperate attempt to divert blame to her mother. But the details were too specific, too surreal to dismiss outright.

'I didn't understand at the time,' Daniella continued. 'Mum was seducing men who looked like Dad.'

'To what end?' Maya asked.

'At first, I thought she was trying to find a new father for us,' Daniella said. 'But then she killed one of them.'

Liam felt the air shift in the room. 'When was this?'

'Don't worry,' Daniella said, flashing a small, unsettling smile. 'I know where all the bodies are buried. Literally and figuratively. You see, that first body wasn't the last. At the time, I didn't realise it, but she was trying to find the perfect replica of Dad. So that he could live forever.'

Liam exchanged a brief glance with Maya. 'And did she?'

'Yes,' Daniella said.

Liam already knew what she was going to say, but he asked anyway. 'And what happened to him?'

Daniella tilted her head again, the same semi-smile forming on her lips. 'She wrapped him in a hessian bag, cleansed him, and buried him.'

Liam's stomach churned, the pain in his side radiating upward to his cracked ribs. He forced himself to ask, 'And was he alive at the time?'

Daniella's smile widened, and she nodded.

At any other time, Liam would have paused the interview, tried to locate evidence to verify her claims, but they couldn't risk losing the momentum.

'Is that what happened to your brother?' he asked.

Daniella's smile faded. 'It was me who insisted on bringing Ernest to the hospital. If Mum had her way, he would have died on the land and been buried there.'

'But Ernest hadn't died before you killed Frank Oakley and Robin Wakefield,' Liam said.

Daniella's solicitor moved to intervene, but she raised a hand to silence him. 'Good try, Detective, but I didn't kill those men. Mum had been planning a surrogate for Ernest ever since his illness began taking his looks from him.'

Liam wondered if she understood how utterly psychotic her story sounded. 'So Frank and Robin were meant to be replacements for Ernest?'

'From what I understand, yes,' Daniella replied. 'Adelaide found them and brought them to Mum for approval.'

'And they failed the approval process?' Liam asked, incredulous.

Daniella shrugged. 'Apparently so.'

'And the facial injuries?'

Her expression darkened, and she cast her eyes downward. 'Adelaide had a temper. When it didn't work out . . . she did that.'

'And you witnessed this?'

'No,' Daniella said. 'They told me about it afterwards.'

Liam exchanged a glance with Maya, who was trying to hide her disbelief. 'Right. So, what about Alex Hudson? From what we can tell, he was abducted before Frank and Robin, and held in captivity for some time before he was intended to be . . . preserved.'

'That I didn't know about,' Daniella said. 'My guess is Adelaide had a soft spot for him.'

Liam shook his head. 'Is that what your family does to someone they have a soft spot for?'

'It's the only reason I can think of.'

'And they decided Alex was a good replacement? Then what?'

'Mum would know more about that,' Daniella said. 'But he would have been cleansed in the water before being buried.'

Liam thought back to Alex's testimony earlier in the week. How he had been placed in a hessian bag and sent on to the lake, and how it had felt like being buried alive.

'OK,' Liam said. 'Let's say I buy this for now. What was your involvement?'

Daniella didn't even glance at her solicitor. 'I told them it was too risky to keep the bodies on-site, so I said I would deal with them.'

'Very gracious of you. And by "deal with them" you mean . . . ?'

'They thought I was going to bury them on my land,' Daniella said matter-of-factly.

'But instead, you left them on the beach. Why?'

Daniella hesitated before answering. 'I wanted you to stop them.'

'Right,' Liam said, his patience wearing thin. 'Because there's no easier way to get our attention than dumping mutilated bodies on a public beach.'

'It's the truth, I swear,' Daniella said.

Her solicitor interjected. 'My client is cooperating fully, DS Kilshaw. She was under significant duress at the time of the murders.'

Liam stared at the man before turning his attention back to Daniella. 'There are much simpler ways of getting our attention. You could have called us.'

'I couldn't bring myself to do that,' Daniella said. 'But I promise you, I wanted them to stop.'

Chapter Forty-Three

Two days later, Liam was back on the Harris farm. The last time he'd been there, it had been dark and blanketed in snow. The trepidation he'd felt then was somewhat nullified by the daylight, but after everything Daniella had told them, the place still exuded an unsettling air.

The area had been thoroughly searched after Alex Hudson's rescue, including a cave structure where Alex had been imprisoned. While numerous hessian bags similar to those found at Daniella's home had been recovered, no other bodies were found.

Today, Daniella was with them under police escort, as they trudged across the uneven terrain towards the stream that cut through the land.

Before she was returned to prison after questioning, Liam had asked Daniella if she thought the two hessian bags Adelaide had carried during the night of the snowfall had been intended for him and Maya. Daniella had answered that they were meant for Adelaide and her mother, though she conceded that had things gone according to plan, she doubted if either Liam or Maya would have made it out alive.

She'd also confessed that her mother had been the one who had sent the miniature dolls to the families of their victims, claiming she'd thought it was the honourable thing to do.

'How far now?' Liam asked.

Daniella was bundled in her prison-issue overalls and a three-quarter-length coat. Though some of her earlier confidence had returned, Daniella was still a shadow of her former self. Liam wasn't sure what to make of her claims from earlier in the week. It would take time for the team, and ultimately the CPS, to decide what charges she would face. But one thing was certain: Daniella would be spending a significant portion of her life behind bars – a reality she seemed to fully grasp.

It was hard now for Liam to think of Daniella as Bucca Dhu. Like her mother and sister, she had lost the power she'd once exercised. Liam was still coming to terms with the fact that someone in Daniella's former position – well educated, a successful solicitor – could ever entertain such thoughts about preservation. He recalled Janet saying that her daughter had been caught between two worlds, as he remembered the hessian bags they had found on Daniella's property and wondered what other secrets were yet to be revealed. 'The bodies are buried throughout the land,' Daniella said. 'I can show you the first one. Follow me.'

She led the group across rough terrain that Liam vaguely recognised from his last visit. After half a mile, Daniella stopped by the small lake where Alex Hudson had made his escape. She pointed to the opposite end. 'It's around there.'

The pathway around the lake was narrow and uneven. One of Daniella's prison escorts led the way, followed by Daniella and a second guard, with Liam and Maya bringing up the rear.

'Good to be back?' Maya asked, her dry humour cutting through the tense atmosphere.

'It's lost its original charm without the snow,' Liam replied.

'Through here,' Daniella said, pushing through an overgrown hedgerow. 'Seven rocks.'

Liam stepped forward and examined a circle of loose stones. He counted seven. 'What does this signify?'

'Seven stones for the dead,' Daniella said, as if it were the most obvious thing in the world. 'We weren't going to put up little crosses, now, were we? A circle of seven stones means a body is buried beneath.'

'Who's buried here?' Liam asked, scepticism creeping into his voice.

'My father.'

◆ ◆ ◆

Though they had started early in the morning, it was dusk by the time the necessary machinery arrived to begin excavating.

Daniella remained on-site, standing under police watch in case she was needed for further assistance. Floodlights were erected around the area, casting stark, artificial light on to the small lake as the specialist teams began their work.

Liam stood a short distance away, hands buried in his coat pockets, watching as the dig started.

The sound of machinery broke the stillness of the evening. If a body was discovered beneath the circle of seven stones, it would add a new dimension to the investigation and complicate the case against the Harris family.

With Janet Harris still under psychiatric care, it was increasingly likely she would never be tried for any of the deaths. And with Daniella's cooperation making her version of events seem more plausible, the possibility loomed that she might avoid a murder charge altogether.

The call came in after forty minutes. A hessian bag had been unearthed beneath the seven stones. CSI specialists on-site confirmed that the bag contained human remains.

'It looks like she was telling the truth,' Maya said.

Liam rubbed the back of his head, his fingers brushing over the scar tissue on his skull. 'I don't even want to think about what that means.'

Earlier in the day, as they had waited for the machinery to arrive, the team had coordinated a broader search of the property. With Daniella's revelations in mind, the land was being combed for additional burial sites.

By dusk, they had uncovered twenty-seven locations marked with circles of seven stones.

Epilogue

The snow had long melted, but with the crisp cold air and the abundance of Christmas lights, Liam felt a stab of seasonal nostalgia as he strolled along Fore Street with George. The boy had just broken up for the holidays, and Liam had arranged to take him out for dinner.

'You're sure you want pizza? It's hardly the most festive of meals,' said Liam, as they walked down to the wharf, passing the lifeboat station.

'I've already had two turkey dinners this week,' said George, as they climbed the steps to the restaurant with its views of the harbour.

'I hear that,' said Liam, deciding to join his son in the non-seasonal choice.

They sat by the window, both facing the water. The tide was out, leaving the boats in the harbour lopsided on the sand, waiting for the sea to return.

Christmas songs played over the speakers as their pizzas arrived. Liam watched George's face light up as he devoured his food. The expression was so reminiscent of the way he'd been as a toddler, and it made Liam wonder how long his son would stay this carefree.

'Why are you smiling at me?' asked George, wiping his mouth.

'No reason,' said Liam, still smiling as he took another bite of his own pizza.

Moments like this made him feel normal, which was something he'd needed more than ever lately. Since the recovery of Daniella White's father's remains from the land in Sennen, much of the past few weeks had been spent excavating the sites marked by circles of seven stones.

The work had been slow and painstaking. With so many locations to cover, they'd had to prioritise the most accessible. The lack of daylight and unpredictable weather made every dig a struggle.

So far, they'd excavated four sites, each revealing a body wrapped in a hessian bag.

'Ice cream?' asked Liam after they'd finished eating.

'That's why we have two stomachs,' said George, grinning as he referenced the family myth that everyone had one stomach for savoury food and another for sweets, meaning dessert was always an option.

They returned to the wharf, where Liam glanced at the lifeboat station before heading to the ice-cream parlour. He was back on the roster now, but there hadn't been a callout. Part of him was looking forward to the next one. He missed the adrenaline and wanted to test his regained confidence in open water.

'Oh no,' said George, under his breath.

Liam looked up to see Millie walking towards them along the wharf. She wore a full-length wool coat with a festive scarf wrapped around her neck. The wind tugged at her short bob, ruffling it as she approached. Liam's eyes followed the line of her arm to her hand, which was clasped with someone else's.

'Liam, George, how are you?' she said, stopping to greet them.

George mumbled something inaudible as Liam caught the eye of the man holding Millie's hand.

'Very well, just out for an early Christmas dinner with George,' said Liam.

'This is Richard,' said Millie, letting go of the man's hand.

'Pleased to meet you.'

'You must be the famous policeman,' said Richard, shaking hands with him.

Liam nodded slightly. 'I wouldn't say famous.'

'Well, you're doing an amazing job. I've been reading all about those bodies in Sennen.'

'Come on, Richard, no one wants to talk about that,' said Millie, glancing at George, who looked like he wanted to be anywhere else at that precise moment.

'Enjoy your evening,' said Liam, holding Millie's gaze for a second before moving on down the wharf.

'Awks,' said George, as they arrived at the ice-cream parlour.

'Certainly was,' said Liam, holding the door open for him as a blast of heat and more Christmas tunes greeted them.

Liam was still thinking about his encounter with Millie when he dropped George off later that evening. She had looked happy, and it would be churlish for him not to be pleased for her. Still, it had been a bit of a surprise to see her move on so quickly, and he wasn't sure he would ever get used to seeing her with short hair.

It felt harder than usual to say goodbye to George, even though he would see him again before Christmas. He gave him a hug outside his mum's place, noting how much stronger the boy felt as he hugged him back.

'Good night?' asked Kim, opening the front door.

'Usual Christmas delights of pizza and ice cream,' said Liam.

Behind Kim, Liam noticed a line of Christmas decorations and lights on the walls and decided he would have to decorate his flat before George came to visit next.

'Glad you had a good time,' said Kim, kissing George and nodding goodbye to Liam.

◆ ◆ ◆

The four additional bodies at the Harris farm had yet to be identified. Although still cooperating, Daniella was biding her time, using her insight for leverage. Liam remained concerned she was going to pin everything on her mother and sister, but the CPS lawyers had assured him that even with her cooperation, she would be going away for a long time.

Liam parked up, for once finding a spot near his flat. He didn't know if his continued melancholy was due to being overworked and the daily trauma of finding new bodies at the Harris farm but, opening the door to a cold blast of air from his bare flat, he felt as if everything was changing, and he was being left behind.

He made some hot chocolate, turned on the radiator in the living area, and switched on the television. In many ways, he should have been enjoying the success of this year. He'd been integral in two major investigations, with more unsolved murder cases soon to be added to his name. If anything, he should have been celebrating, and he toasted himself just as his phone rang.

'Grace,' he said, answering. 'I thought you only called on burner phones.'

'No need for all that now,' said Grace.

Liam pictured her smiling on the other end of the line. Her suspension was over, and she'd returned to London and the Met, the last time he'd seen her being her visit to the hospital. 'How are things back in London?'

'They're all OK, but that won't matter for long. Say hello to the new DI of Major Crimes, Devon and Cornwall.'

'You got the job?'

'I start in Exeter in January.'

Liam took a deep breath. 'Amazing.'

'You sound unsure.'

'No, I'm not. I promise. It's just . . .'

'You didn't think I was serious about moving.'

Liam sat back in his chair. 'It wasn't that I didn't think you were serious, it was more that I thought once everything was settled, you would find the allure of London too much to turn down.'

'So, you're pleased for me.'

'If it's what you want, Grace, then of course I am.'

'Then you can come celebrate with me?'

'That would be great. When are you next down?'

'I'm in Exeter now. I've been looking at flats.'

Liam realised he wasn't the only one affected by the Godrevy investigation. Millie's life had been altered by those events, and now so had Grace's. When he'd seen Grace again in the summer, she'd seemed to be on a fast track through the police force. While Major Crimes in Exeter would undoubtedly be a challenging role, it was still a significant shift from her work in the Met.

He checked the time. Exeter was at least a couple of hours away. 'How about we meet halfway?' he suggested.

'Sounds good to me,' said Grace.

ABOUT THE AUTHOR

Photo © 2019 Lisa Visser

Following his law degree, where he developed an interest in criminal law, Matt Brolly completed his Masters in Creative Writing at Glasgow University. He is the *Wall Street Journal* and Amazon bestselling author of the DI Blackwell novels, the DCI Lambert crime novels, the Lynch and Rose thrillers *The Controller* and *The Railroad*, and the standalone thrillers *Zero*, *The Running Girls* and *The Alliance*. The Replacement is the second in a new series set in Cornwall, featuring DS Kilshaw. Matt lives in London with his wife and their two children. You can find out more about him at www.mattbrolly.com or by following him on X: @MattBrollyUK.

Follow the Author on Amazon

If you enjoyed this book, follow Matt Brolly on Amazon to be notified when the author releases a new book!
To do this, please follow these instructions:

Desktop:

1) Search for the author's name on Amazon or in the Amazon App.
2) Click on the author's name to arrive on their Amazon page.
3) Click the 'Follow' button.

Mobile and Tablet:

1) Search for the author's name on Amazon or in the Amazon App.
2) Click on one of the author's books.
3) Click on the author's name to arrive on their Amazon page.
4) Click the 'Follow' button.

Kindle eReader and Kindle App:

If you enjoyed this book on a Kindle eReader or in the Kindle App, you will find the author 'Follow' button after the last page.